Breakfield and Burkey

Enigma Jewels

3

Enigma Heirs
Thriller Series

Novels by Breakfield and Burkey in **The Enigma Series**

Out of Poland (novella)

The Enigma Factor

The Enigma Rising

The Enigma Ignite

The Enigma Wraith

The Enigma Stolen

The Enigma Always

The Enigma Gamers
A CATS Tale

The Enigma Broker

The Enigma Dragon
A CATS Tale

The Enigma Source

The Enigma Beyond

The Enigma Threat

Novels by Breakfield and Burkey in the **Enigma Heirs**

Enigma Tracer　　　*Enigma Forced*　　　*Enigma Jewels*

Short Stories

Remember the Future

The Jewel

Love's Enigma

Nowhere But Up

Destiny Dreamer

Riddle Codes

Hot Chocolate

Hidden Target

Caribbean Dream

Fears, Tears, or Cheers

Trusted Friends and Lovers
(a collection of short stories)

Magnolia Bluff Crime Chronicles

The Flower Enigma (Book 5)　　　*The Killer Enigma* (Book 16)

The Ransom Enigma (Book 27)

Acknowledgments

We are grateful for the support of our readers.
Thank you for providing a review.

Saturday Night in Puerto Rico

In the corner of the dimly lit San Juan drinking establishment, Julian Lafluer's eyes widened as he read the caption on the breaking news story on the giant television screen.

**AUTHORITIES SEIZE A PRIVATE PLANE
AT LUIS MUÑOZ MARÍN INTERNATIONAL AIRPORT
CONNECTED TO A POSSIBLE
HUMAN SMUGGLING OPERATION.
MORE TO FOLLOW.**

"Crap!" Julian growled tugging Ryu's sleeve. He inclined his chin so his bodyguard would read the screen. "Let's go. Now," he hissed, looking around at the bored bartender smoking at the far end of the bar and the local drunk slumped over his latest drink. He placed a few bills on the table as Ryu powered down their laptop. They quietly exited and then rushed to the car.

"You drive," Julian snarled, getting into the passenger seat. "What a mess. I've lost the girls. Head toward the hottest teens' hangout."

Ryu nodded and maneuvered the Tahoe to the side of the downtown area where kids hung out. "What are you thinking, Boss?"

"First, you'll stop when I tell you to. Then you'll find an old vehicle you can hotwire on the poor side of town. Switch its plates with another vehicle at least a block away. Tomorrow is Sunday, so folks will stay home to rest. Then come pick me up, and we'll head to the other side of the island."

"Yes. I can do that. I hate to leave you alone."

Ryu drove for a few minutes toward the newer side of town, where sounds from boom boxes permeated the vehicle. Turning right, he noted the lit porches with cushioned chairs, a couple of shiny bicycles, and people visible through open windows. He scanned the area, seeing exactly what he'd hoped to find. "There's my target. Perfect. Make a right at the corner, then head a few blocks over. I think there are some older homes two blocks east." They passed a convenience store. "Pull over. I'll meet you outside this store within the hour. I'll keep my briefcase. You take everything else."

Ryu pulled over and got out, slinging his backpack over his shoulder. "I'll find us a ride."

Julian got into the driver's seat and headed back to negotiate with young men who always had big egos. He grinned as he rehearsed his pitch to the unsuspecting punks.

CHAPTER 1

Ride Share

An hour later, flashing lights and screaming sirens pierced San Juan's Saturday night. The cop dropped his car into gear, speeding after the black SUV after it squealed past. The officer shook his head. "Jerk!" he said, realizing the chase was on when the culprit surged forward and took a radical right at the next corner. He notified headquarters and then focused on the pursuit.

Being a seasoned pro, the officer laughed, closing the distance and pulling onto the left side of the Tahoe. The driver jerked the wheel to the right to evade him and clipped the curb. He overcorrected and then braked to miss the police car. Losing control, the car careened into a commercial trash container, pushing several feet with a crumpled front end.

The officer pulled his car to a stop and jumped out with his revolver drawn. He clicked his shoulder radio with his current status as he rushed to the driver's door and tapped the gun's muzzle on the window. Carefully minimizing his body exposure, recalling his fellow officer from a few months ago shot in the gut pulling over a taillight violation.

"Get out of the car. Keep your hands up," he shouted, squinting through the tinted window.

Moments ticked by before the heavy SUV door creaked open. "Don't shoot," the young male voice cracked. "I'm hurt and can't open the door any wider. I'm not armed. Can you help, please?"

Sensing fear, not animosity, with the request, the officer kept his weapon level as he grabbed the door with his left hand and opened it. Surprised at seeing a young teen, he rolled his eyes. "Kid, who are you? This vehicle is registered to Julian Lafluer, not a punk teenager. Why didn't you stop when you realized I was behind you? The lights were flashing."

Struggling out of the SUV, the teenager moaned when the officer pulled him over and then made him face the vehicle.

"My parents are going to kill me." The teen fumbled with shaking fingers to get his wallet from his back pocket.

"I'm sure your folks will enjoy visiting you in jail. I'm locking you up unless you start answering my questions. Who are you?"

"Alan Beacon. I'm not even eighteen. You can't put me in jail."

"There, you're wrong, son. I can hold you in a cell for hours. Start talking. This vehicle is wanted in connection with a serious crime. Why are you driving it around like a bat out of hell?"

Tears streamed down his cheeks while the teen spilled his guts. "Honest, Officer, some dude pulled up to my friends and me. He flashed some cash and said there could be more if one of us volunteered to tear around the city fast. He said to meet him at noon tomorrow at the Tiki Bar by the waterfront in San Juan to get the money. I was the dumb ass who let him walk away carrying his briefcase."

The officer clicked on the handcuffs. "Didn't you think something was wrong with racing around the streets? You're lucky you didn't kill someone or yourself."

The sniveling teen winced. "He laughed, saying only a man would take his dare. I couldn't resist the hundred bucks. There's a girl I wanted to take out next Friday."

"Describe the guy, and why did you notice the briefcase?"

"He was older, with greying blonde hair and a French accent, and smelled of cigarettes. He said he made a bet he could get someone to drive it around on a dare. The briefcase was camel-colored leather, like my dad's. He put the cash inside when I agreed to the deal."

"Where was he headed?"

"He said he was meeting up with his buddy at the San Juan Bay Marina. He told me to drive around for an hour and then park the car at the bar. He'd meet me there in the morning with the bonus cash."

The officer spun the kid around by the arm and pulled him toward his patrol car. He opened the back door, helped him in, then shut the door. He tapped his radio and transmitted the facts he'd learned, annoyed at missing the expected tag.

JJ Rodreguiz ran his hand through his black hair in frustration as he glanced around his screens inside the CATS team's headquarters office in Luxemburg. He clicked the contact on his laptop to join the video call. "Gracie, I know it's late. Are you still at your office in Manhattan?"

"No, I left the World Bank a few hours ago. I've been reading some of your reports. It appears you're getting close."

Grateful, his twin sister was familiar with the current situation. The lights above her head highlighted the healthy shine of her blonde hair, reminding him they were not identical in appearance.

"We had a lead, but Julian Lafluer escaped while the targeted plane was stopped. Judith and Xiamara are safe and secure. Two of Julian's people are being questioned. We're trying to get his possible location to provide to authorities."

"JJ, my team has eyes on San Juan, looking for the cryptocurrency parasite we introduced into Mateo's organization to track him when we discovered his human trafficking and drug business. With Mateo dead, we expect to find activity directly from Lafluer since he was Mateo's accounting money man. Your group engineered the bogus hosting infrastructure that allowed us to seize and copy Mateo's records. We know Julian and Mateo had business dealings, but there could be more between them."

JJ chuckled. "I wish I'd seen the *astonished, we're screwed* look on his face when he tried to demo the system to Mateo. At least Mateo is no longer a problem, but Julian needs to be found."

As was her habit, she shook her hair back from her shoulders. "The authorities saw no trace of him at the airport," she offered. "They're trying to determine where he might have gone. According to the authorities who interviewed them, his compound was deserted except for several local groundskeepers who are devoted to Lafluer. I'm not sure how we can find him, dear brother."

"He's on the island. The authorities have the airports under guard. No one's going to airlift him out. That only leaves a charter boat service. The team is running down those leads. We didn't get his crypto when we searched the cloud data. He must have it in other wallets. If we're tracking the right ones, maybe we'll be lucky. Since we haven't analyzed the accounting records yet, we don't know how much cash he has. He appears to favor cryptocurrencies, so we hope to see the infected crypto we introduced as he tries to exit the island. It is doubtful he'd risk staying there." JJ heard her tapping her pen on the work surface. They had evidence of his lavish homes on two Caribbean islands but suspected there could be others. The guy seemed to live large.

"Whenever we think we have these jerks ready for gift-wrapping with a bow, JJ, we find an empty box. He and his lieutenant must know someone is on to them. Either that or he is innately cautious. They're changing their patterns. Did you start backtracking to Saint Kitts, where we got the first blip on the beaconing signal?"

"That's a good idea. I can do some digging there. We might locate something. His best option is to set up shop somewhere else. A smart, black-hearted rabbit always has another exit to the burrow. Gracie, can you have JW and the team hunt for other properties in the Caribbean that he owns or has access to?"

Gracie smirked. "Yep. We'd do better if we had an idea of his aliases. The man is too careful not to have other names that he works under."

JJ chuckled. "True. Don't be surprised if he used other identities to arrange safe houses to flee to at a moment's notice. After all, one of his resumé highlights is identity theft."

Gracie groaned. "It's like looking for a needle in a haystack."

"That's what our R-Group and CATS team does best, dear sister."

Gracie smiled. "How are Judith and Xiamara doing after we secured them from the plane? You sent a message that Brayson was ready to return to Luxemburg, but Marian wanted some downtime for him to recover. She was probably more scared of losing him than she let on." She sighed, understanding Marian's feelings. "Are you still in Europe, too?"

"Yes, I don't plan to return to Brazil for a week or so. Judith and Zee are under observation by the doctors until tomorrow." He frowned and let out a frustrated-sounding breath. They weren't pleased to hear Julian escaped and wanted to help search the islands. I asked them to return here. I'd rather they work from here for the time being."

"Good. They are tough ladies and good team members."

"Yep, we're lucky, Sis. I'm going to get some rest. I'll check in with Brayson in the morning."

CHAPTER 2

Short-Term Reprieve

"Ryu, how much more of this evasive action are we taking?" Julian fisted his palm with his right hand while staring intently at the bodyguard's square chin, grateful to have this tough, intelligent, devoted man beside him. "I'm glad you had us change to the black jeans and tee-shirts. It'll make us harder to spot in the shadows." Julian combed his longish blond hair with his fingertips, then insisted, "I told you we need to head to Sint Maarten." His French accent grew more pronounced when he couldn't control a situation.

"I know, sir. You also said we shouldn't get caught. I am trying to make sure we can't be tracked. This old Chevy isn't as fast as your Tahoe, but we can reach San Juan Bay to buy passage on a trawler before authorities connect the dots."

Julian frowned with tightened lips. "You're right. We must find a way off this island." He pulled his laptop from his case, powered it on, and then tried logging in. "Hey, pull into the next bank parking lot. I must secure a quick Wi-Fi connection and do a fast ATM transaction."

Moments later, Ryu located a bank without deviating from his route. He watched Julian complete his keyboard activity and input the keystrokes required for the ATM withdrawal. Reaching through the window, he secured the wad of cash and handed it to his boss.

"I need one other withdrawal, then we can go."

Ryu completed the instructions as directed and passed the additional U.S. currency to his right.

"Perfect, let's go."

Ryu shifted the Chevy into gear and sped toward the marina.

"When I phoned my buddy, he said two fishing boats were in the harbor. We should be able to buy our passage on one called *Ruby's Slipper*. This captain is known for keeping a secret for a price."

"Good, we have cash. I have access to our funds. You can protect me. Let's get off Puerto Rico as quickly as possible. I still don't understand how they found out about the transport. They must have tapped our calls. Thank goodness I have a couple of burners to use."

"I'm glad you taught me long ago, Julian, to have backup plans."

Dark settled over the area as Ryu pulled into the far side of the parking lot. The night sky crackled with lightning and thunder, promising a heavy storm was approaching the island. Julian thought it would provide cover for their escape.

They located the *Ruby's Slipper* tied to the end of the pier. Julian saw the grizzled captain chatting with the marina owner and walked toward the pair. When the marina owner returned to his shop, Julian approached the captain. He noted the dark, shaggy-haired man's baggy, stained pants and grey, full-sleeved, woven shirt. The man appeared to be over six feet, in well-worn dark boots. He inclined his head as he stated, "We'd like to purchase passage to Sint Maarten. We were told you liked fishing in those waters, Captain."

Julian felt the man's once-over appraisal with distaste. The captain grinned, picking the last chunk of dinner with the worn toothpick from his teeth. "My name's Shaughnessy, and you are?"

"I'm Jules, and this is Ryu." Julian extended his hand, which the man enveloped in his massive, rough fist to shake from a show of strength.

"Nice to meet you. What takes you to Sint Maarten, Jules? Wouldn't it be easier to fly?"

"Possibly." Julian clasped his midsection. "I get airsick but somehow have no issues on the water."

"I can take you. It'll cost you a thousand U.S. each."

Julian looked at Ryu, who shrugged.

"No problem." Julian pulled a small wad of bills from his jeans pocket and counted out twenty Franklins. Only a few were left, so he added them as well. "Here, take it all. Consider it a tip for transporting us on such short notice."

Shaughnessy grinned, showing his white teeth brightened by a streak of lightning. "Stow your stuff in the sacks in the cabin below." He gestured toward the stairway. "You can rest there, too." He looked into the sky. "Make yourselves at home while I check on the storm."

Waves slapped the fishing trawler, driving it back against the dock buntings. Winds increased, making it hard to hear. Julian yelled, "This is the best you could do?"

Ryu shouted, "We weren't safe at the airport, and if they knew your name, we would have been caught in the terminal. The only other option was a watercraft. This fishing trawler carries enough fuel to get to Sint Maarten by traveling around the storm."

"What if this tub won't go fast enough to outrun the storm?" Julian tamped down his fear with a couple of deep breaths.

Ryu fatalistically deadpanned, "We'll probably drown."

Julian laughed. "We've dodged every problem so far, thanks to you. I guess you're right. This is our best chance."

The pair stowed their gear. Julian watched Ryu cleverly block their spot by moving crates of supplies. Rain hammered the dock area, increasing with each flash of lightning and booming clap of thunder. Julian felt the warm raindrops drench his hair and head toward his toes. He shouted, "Can we tow that tied-up cigarette boat behind us as an insurance policy?"

Ryu wiped a hand across his face, clearing his eyes. "We could, but it would slow us down. We can slice through the waves faster to get around the storm, but we wouldn't have enough fuel."

"Where could it get us to?"

"The Virgin Islands, possibly."

"Damn. I don't have nearly the same connections in the British or U.S. Virgin Islands, but maybe as a waypoint to stop and refuel."

"Sir, this boat isn't elegant," Ryu quipped, "but no one can trace it to you."

Julian watched the captain approach. "Gentlemen, we aren't going anywhere. This storm is massive. The Coast Guard issued orders to secure boats for twenty-four hours or until the storm passes. We're safer here than out on those swells expected to exceed fifteen feet. It's not a hurricane-class system, but still dangerous for this boat."

"Shaughnessy, I paid you for room, board, and discretion."

"That you did, Jules. But not enough for me to risk death on a fool's errand. There are slickers in the hold if you need them. I'll fix us some grub after securing the ropes for the night."

Julian nodded.

JW rushed to join the virtual conference room, finger-combing his thick black hair, itemizing the latest details of their search efforts he planned to convey. He clicked a key to add his older cousin, JJ. "Hey, are you there?"

Half-awake, JJ fumbled to tie his bathrobe before pressing the join link to the virtual Gigazon. "Why don't bad guys sleep on my schedule?" JJ stopped long enough to retrieve the missing slipper for his left foot.

JW yawned. "I feel your pain, sir. Granger was doing some update work on ICABOD when the crypto parasite surfaced. He woke me immediately to review the data. I thought you'd want to know."

JJ strained to look awake and cleared his throat. "Is this going to be a pot of coffee discussion, or is it some sort of imaginative material that will keep my mind spinning half the night?"

Granger interjected, "We got a cryptocurrency exchange for some hard currency at an ATM outside San Juan that converts Ethereum to dollars. Our parasite code was part of the transaction. I bet it's Julian doing a quick conversion to flee the island."

JJ frowned. "I'm hearing short creative material. Rats!"

"Sorry, JJ," Granger apologized. "Minutes later, Julian also made a secondary transaction for more hard currency."

"The good news is he stopped long enough to alert us he was converting digital funds to U.S. Dollars," JW added. "We lost visibility on him as soon as the exchange was completed, though we are tapping into the bank's cameras to verify it was him."

JJ rubbed his face to wake up. "That's inconvenient. So, he's not trying to leave San Juan using conventional methods. He'll buy his transport and their silence. The switch-up escape methods are getting old," he growled.

JW cleared his throat. "I thought this was important so we could collaborate on the next steps he might take."

"I'm not angry with you or Granger, only the situation. Good trap on his activities. I'm glad you woke me. We need to review the possibilities. I need to brew some coffee and make another call. You both try to get some sleep. When I have some options, I'll let you know. Thanks again."

CHAPTER 3

A Fool's Errand

The night sky was darker because of the blanket of black storm clouds, which had spewed heavy rain for hours. Winds buffeted the fishing boat against the rubber fenders, adding periodic thuds to the booming weather concert. Little by little, it eased, the worst passing Puerto Rico on its way to soak other islands. Julian, Ryu, and Shaughnessy awoke to loud voices claiming to be harbor security. The three exchanged glances. Julian nodded to Shaughnessy to take care of it. He watched the captain race up the stairs to the deck.

"Find us an option, Ryu," he whispered through clenched teeth. "I'll listen to the exchange."

One deep voice demanded, "We need to inspect your boat. We're looking for a suspect in a high-speed chase in San Juan proper."

Shaughnessy retorted, "Why would I assist you unless you help me bail the water left by the storm? Do I look like I'm running a hotel for fugitives? Get out of here before I call the police on you two prissy rent-a-cops."

Harbor security stepped onto the trawler, ignoring the burly captain.

"Hey, you have no right to board my boat," Shaughnessy shouted.

Julian listened to the heavy feet stomp across the deck and then open and close doors, obviously tossing stuff about. After several minutes of searching, they lumbered into the sleeping area and the hold below with flashlights that awakened the shadows.

Julian heard them return to the deck and felt the shift when they stepped off. The boat bobbed slightly away from the dock, and Ryu motioned for him to follow him into the shadows.

"I guess our tip wasn't good," the deep voice complained. "Let's look at the boats on the other side. I want that reward."

Julian heard the noise as footsteps raced around the deck. He felt the rope he clung to being pulled. Moments later, he and Ryu bobbed to the surface, gasping for air. Smiling,

Shaughnessy helped them back aboard. "I wondered how you left without being seen." He laughed. "Quick thinking, lads. I was afraid I'd have to give you up. Go below before you're seen. I'll get us underway."

"Thank you," they said through clenched teeth.

"No problem. When we reach port on Sint Maarten, you'll want to increase my tip to maintain my silence."

Julian turned with narrowed eyes, then shrugged and nodded, heading toward the stairs to go below.

Shaughnessy released the ropes securing his boat to the dock. The wind snatched his maniacal laughter, casting it into the still-sharp breeze.

JJ started on his second cup of coffee before calling Brayson, his right-hand man and confidant, who answered on the first ring.

"Hey, JJ, tell me you need me back at work."

JJ chuckled. "I wanted to check on you, but Marian asked for both of you to remain in Texas for a few days."

"I'm fine. I've had enough of Texas for now. I can book a flight back to Luxemburg and bring her along."

"Does she realize you're saying this to me?"

"I'll tell her if you approve it."

Marian's voice joined the conversation with an annoyed tone as if she were near Brayson. "Tell JJ I know now."

"I heard, Brayson. Why don't you put the call on speaker?"

Brayson cleared his throat. "What can we do for you, JJ?"

JJ grinned, knowing Marian wouldn't let her husband out of sight again. "I wanted to know if you two might travel back to San Juan to search Julian's estate. We're reasonably certain he didn't return to that location. We have the man in custody who gave the camera the finger as they left out the back exit. The camera's still transmitting, but no movement has been detected in the days since their abrupt departure."

Marian sighed. "I wouldn't mind retrieving the things I stored in town. But why the estate?"

"Even if Julian shows up, he's not seen you or Brayson. You present no threat to him and can use the *I'm lost* routine. We believe he's finding a way off the island but have no idea of his destination. If you can get inside, I hope you find something to tell us where he might go. We don't have much on the man. It's possible he had an alternate home on Saint Kitts since that was the location of the original beacon signal you trapped on, Marian."

Brayson said, "You want us to break in and search the place. Is there an alarm?"

"Honey, I have Zee's gate code and door automatic sequence. She sent them to me after they learned they were staying on-site," announced Marian. "Judith told me he has an office overlooking the pool. They were in the guest house with a few local servers for Julian's required data backup."

"What do we say if anyone asks who we are or why we're there?" asked Brayson.

"Judith said there weren't many guards. A gardener drove the golf cart to pick them up from the entrance gate on their first visit there."

"According to Zee, the grounds were maintained perfectly," Marian interjected, "so there might be a permanent crew and maybe a housekeeper."

"If you gain access using the code at the gate and enter the house without setting off an alarm, tell anyone you are Mr. Lafluer's guests. If you bring in groceries and overnight duffle bags, you can say you rented it from him for a few days as a private romantic getaway. Tell the help, if they bother you, to take a few days off."

"Marian, thanks to your care, I feel better. This doesn't sound dangerous to me. Let's see if we can find some information."

"I'm in, JJ." Marian leaned into Brayson, fluttering her eyes. "When can you book us tickets from Houston?"

"You have two seats for tomorrow morning from Houston Hobby to San Juan. I reserved a car in your name, Brayson. I'll send the information to your secure email accounts."

Brayson laughed, and Marian chorused in. They caught their breath, and Brayson confirmed, "You must have been confident we'd do it."

"Not really," JJ admitted. "But I was certain Marian would go with you. I know you guys well."

CHAPTER 4

Loose Ends

The steady drone of the trawler engines and the moderate rocking of the boat should have made the two exhausted men sleep soundly. It didn't.

Julian whispered, "How much more to keep Shaughnessy happy and silent, do you think?"

Ryu calmly offered, "Nothing."

"Nothing?"

"You pay me to keep problems off your back. Shaughnessy is the needed savior until the next bidder arrives. We're going too slow to outrun radio communications from San Juan. However, he's just the opportunistic bastard to sell us out once we get to Sint Maarten. Julian, let me take care of the situation."

Julian thought a moment before he spoke. "When do we end our contract with him? As soon as we're docked or sometime earlier?"

"Earlier. Shaughnessy stated that the trip would be roughly less than two hundred nautical miles. At a little over ten knots, we have around fifteen hours to reach the coast of Sint-Maarten. My waterproof diving watch says we've been traveling for thirteen hours. We are roughly two hours from land unless he doesn't know how to navigate. Sunrise occurs in an hour, a perfect time to take advantage of his tired state."

Julian nodded. "After Shaughnessy is dispatched, we take the dingy and row ashore?"

"No," Ryu sneered, "I have something in mind with a little more finesse."

Two hours later, Julian gave one final kick that helped him reach Ryu's outstretched hand at the water's edge. Weary, Julian staggered as he struggled to his feet from the warm water, still breathing hard. Bent down, resting his hands on his knees, he tried to get as much air as possible. He was grateful to be in the Caribbean seas rather than the northern Pacific. Ryu was busy gathering the life preservers and their precious cargo items.

Finally catching his breath, Julian asked, "Tell me you got our briefcases with the cash, jewels, and my PC."

Ryu chuckled. "Everything's accounted for. I need to bury these *Ruby's Slipper* life preservers, and then we can be on our way."

"On our way with no clean clothes or cigarettes? I've only got one shoe left from that long swim. Hell, it felt like we crossed the English Channel, only warmer, I bet."

"I sank everything of ours that can be replaced. We will only be inconvenienced until we can buy more. We don't want to look like survivors from a shipwreck after. When *Ruby's Slipper* shows up in Sint Maarten, they won't find evidence of us. By then, we'll be on the other side of the island, away from the nosey Dutch."

"Good. When we get to the house, we'll have fresh clothing and food." He brushed off his outerwear. "Thank you, Ryu, for getting us to land."

Ryu announced, "Truck approaching. We must look and act like laborers heading to work who can use a lift. Let me do the talking. Avoid looking anyone in the eye or letting them see your face. Hide your bare feet, too. We'll ask to be dropped close but still walk for a bit. It's safer that way."

Brayson and Marian had an easy flight to San Juan. They took carry-ons, so they didn't have to wait at baggage claim. After picking up the rental car, Marian provided directions to the hotel. Brayson waited outside in the car while she retrieved her bags from the bellman and stored them in the trunk. Then, they plotted their course to Julian's estate.

"When we arrive," Brayson reminded her, "we need to have a running conversation like this is the best trip ever, in case someone's listening."

Marian rubbed her hands together. "I agree. I'll be the wife in love, and you can be the hunk. It'll be so much fun."

Brayson pulled up to the front and stopped. Marian entered the code on the keypad, and the heavy black gate opened. No workers were seen as he drove toward the estate to park. They got out laughing and hugging like a couple in love, looking for a delightful respite.

"I'll bring our groceries and luggage, honey," announced Brayson.

"Thank you, sweetheart. I hope this code works." Marian approached the door and fed in the numbers. Moments later, the lock released. She pressed the latch on the handle to open the front door. "You've got to see this place. It's more beautiful than Julian boasted. Oh, my goodness, the artwork is stunning. Wow. I think I'm in heaven." She pushed the door wider, holding it so Brayson could enter. She'd memorized the floor plan and led him directly to the kitchen to store their food and wine.

"Honey, you found us the perfect honeymoon place." He turned a slow circle to see everything. "Not a dish in the sink, nothing out of place."

Marian poked her head above the refrigerator's open door. "We have condiments, a dozen eggs, butter, and wine here. You're right, though; it's spotless. I will make sure to clean it when our long weekend ends." Methodically opening the cabinets, they each made comments.

"Honey, we can create anything with this array of pots and pans! It's like a chef wannabe's dream come true."

"Plates and glassware are so brightly colored. I bet our food looks way more enticing when served. I may not want to leave at the end of our long weekend."

"Let's look around the rest of the place and find our bedroom," she said with a sly smile and eyes he knew were mischief-filled.

They stayed close as they walked through the dining, sitting, and formal living rooms, peeking into nooks and crannies. Each glanced out the floor-to-ceiling windows, expecting to see staff on the property.

"If the weather stays nice, we should eat by the pool and enjoy the fresh air and beautiful flowers."

She nodded in agreement. "A swim before or after dinner may be in order as well. I'll show you my teeny bikini, which you drooled over the last time I wore it. And sunscreen. I love how you apply lotion."

He laughed. "Come on, you feisty woman. Let's find our bedroom and change into swimsuits."

The first four bedrooms were decorated in bright colors. Everything was neat. Marian mused aloud, "I wonder if there's a housekeeper. I forgot to ask Julian when I paid him. It would be great to know before we run around naked."

"I haven't seen anything that would account for anyone being here, but this estate is expansive. Look, this bathroom has an attached soaking tub with jets. The massive king-size bed is perfect. Since you weren't directed to a room, honey, let's use this one."

Marian spun around and then opened the closets. A few items of men's clothing were hung up, with a shoe tree. She nodded. "I agree. This room is perfect."

For the next hour, they methodically searched the room while making sounds of passion in case there were microphones. They doubted any were in the master suite but didn't want to take chances. Brayson launched his stud-finder application to hunt for a safe. He shook his head, sensing defeat.

Marian squealed, "No, don't stop, sweetheart; it feels so good. I am so close," she added, with heavy breathing and intermittent sighs.

He joined the breathing along with determined groans as he used the stud finder in the closet. He grinned at her, arching his eyebrows.

"Yesssssssss," she screamed.

"You are mine, honey, all mine," he announced, mocking a heavy sigh of release. He wiggled his fingers like he was typing and inclined his head.

Marian retrieved the laptop, soundlessly crossed the thick carpeted floor, and returned to his side. She connected to the bridge and typed, using her phone as a hotspot.

> We found a safe. Brayson is opening it now.

Seconds later, JJ texted.

> Good.

Brayson used his sensitive fingers to rotate the dial slowly one way and then the other. In under five minutes, the door swung open. He took photos of all the contents, then moved out one thing after another, grabbing pictures of each item. He paused to share them with Marian and continued itemizing the contents. She sent another text.

Incoming pictures.

Marian transferred the photos, stacks of U.S. currency, an ID with Julian's face but a different name, loose blue stones in various sizes, an old book in a box, and a couple of silver pendants with the same type of stones mounted. She sat the worn hardback to the side.

I think the stones might be larimar.

The Blue Jewel of the Caribbean?

The blue and white are very distinctive.

Interesting. The man likes jewels.

There are a lot here,
plus a few diamonds and maybe tanzanite.

Marian flipped open the old book's pages and blew a long whistle. Her fingers went to the keyboard.

A 1911 First Edition of *The Book of Buried Treasure:*
True Story of the Pirate Gold and Jewels.

JJ texted.

That's impressive.

Brayson put everything back into the safe and locked it. He embraced her. "We know what's there," he whispered in her ear. Then he announced. "Honey, you're so good to me. Let's change and head to the pool."

He carried a bottle of wine as they strolled toward the flickering blue water. He leaned in, running his tongue on the edge near her earrings. "I promise we will make that little show in the bedroom a reality later."

She laughed and spread towels on the loungers. He poured the wine, serving her the first glass. Getting his own, they shared a toast. She took a sharp breath and shifted her eyes, alerting him that someone was approaching.

"Excuse me," a woman's voice said. "Who are you, and why are you here? The master is out of town."

Marian piped up. "Hi, I'm Mary, and this is my husband, Bray."

Brayson turned and smiled at the woman.

Marian continued, "Julian rented us the place for the weekend for our romantic getaway. It's a lovely estate. Do you work here?"

"Yes, ma'am, I'm Emma. I wasn't told. I have no supplies."

Marian flitted her hand. "No worries, we brought groceries to do our cooking. Bray, here, promised he would clean up."

"Oh, okay. Do I need to open the guest house for you?"

"Great. That way, we could quickly shower and change clothes before entering the house. I would hate to track anything inside."

The woman appeared confused, so Brayson added, "He must have thought he'd given you the time off because he gave us all the codes to get inside."

"All right," she slowly said. "If you need anything, pick up the phone in the kitchen and dial four. I live on the far side of the estate, but I'm happy to assist you anytime."

Marian grinned. "That is so sweet. Thank you."

The woman unlocked the guest house and walked away without another word.

"Marian, did you find it strange that she gave up so easily?"

She looked around and thoughtfully replied, "Yes, but we don't know her background."

"If she is gone for twenty minutes, let's get into the guest house and take photos of what's left. Then we can clear out the safe and boogie earlier than planned."

"I agree. I would like to see if we can find anything on the servers in this room."

"Fine, but I don't want to stay longer than necessary. I feel uneasy, honey."

A half-hour later, Emma hadn't returned. Brayson agreed that Marian could enter the guest house while he kept guard by the pool. She transferred interior photos to his phone, matching the journey he tracked her with on his phone. Everything seemed normal until she approached the rear exit of the building.

His cell rang, and her number appeared on the caller ID. He slid the bar to answer and heard her say,

"RUN."

KA-BLAM

Parts of the building rose into the air before crashing into a ball of red-orange fire. Dread soared through him, then anger when he discovered it was too hot to enter. "Marian," he keened repeatedly. Alerted by sirens in the distance, he snapped into action.

Working Alone

Chief Amani guided his craft toward the out-of-control vessel, matching its speed. Jaden, his First Officer, flipped the side bumpers to protect the sides of both boats before he worked to join the boats.

The Harbor Patrol operator's frantic voice stated, "Dead air from *Ruby's Slipper*. I've tried to raise him again, sir. Shaughnessy must have fallen asleep. According to my radar, he's heading right for the dock."

"We're alongside," Chief Amani announced. "I've got a man boarding to bring the trawler under control. Stay tuned."

"Yes, sir," acknowledged the radio operator.

The echoing sounds of the fishing trawler's engines diminished as the vessel's gears shifted into neutral. It finally slowed.

First Officer Jaden waved toward the chief as he opened the radio communications near the wheel. "I've got control of the trawler, sir. You should be able to reverse the engines and toss out the anchor. No one's visible on deck. I found the wheel lashed so it would travel in a straight line. I've kicked a couple of Crown Royal bottles out of the way to stand at the wheel. The evidence suggests that someone wanted to take a break and fastened the wheel to direct it toward the port. Perhaps he had to take a leak or recover the nets."

"Why the fishing nets?" Chief Amani said, flexing his muscles as he tossed out the anchor. He took off his hat and ran his arm across his brow.

"They're still overboard. The way the trawler handles, it seems like a great catch."

They secured the trawler to a mooring post. A couple of workers at the dock boarded, moved to the aft, and assisted with pulling in the nets. The last heave-ho on the fishing net brought up what was left of the captain.

Chief Amani closed his eyes, trying not to visualize it any longer than necessary. "Poor, dumb bastard fell overboard into his fishing net, and the bowlines didn't hold, so he slid back to the stern. He slipped in and out of the prop. This is why you don't work alone." Overwhelmed at the gore, Jaden rushed to the side and barfed.

CHAPTER 6

You and Your Wingman

Terrified at the possible outcome, Brayson called for Marian as he moved farther into the burning building. He ignored the pieces of debris that peppered him.

BLAM!

A secondary explosion knocked him to the ground. Smoke, dust, and debris rapidly filled the air. Coughing, he pulled the neck of his tee-shirt over his mouth like an air filter and slowly crawled toward the guest quarters. Disoriented, he muttered, "Come on, she warned you. Now find her. She was caught in the explosion." He closed his eyes, spotting pieces of burning furniture and equipment starting to settle.

"Urgh!" he cried, feeling a piece of metal searing the top of his left shoulder. He caught the scent of burning flesh and knocked the painful piece of hot metal from his shirt.

Looking through the dense smoke, he moved to avoid the flames, searching for her. "Afghanistan was worse when the vehicle exploded from the RPG. You got two buddies to safety. You can locate her. Keep moving, soldier." Broken bits of glass with wood and metal fragments bit into his hands and knees as he crawled. "Marian. Honey, where are you?" Sounds of sirens grew. A gust of wind allowed the smoke to clear. He froze at the sight of a charred body a few feet ahead.

Seeing fragments of burnt clothing and hair on the blackened flesh of thin arms caused him to drop his head onto his arms and sob. Brayson heard responders cursing the fire and intensifying heat, likely from the electrical connections to the battery back-ups. Defeated, he stretched his fingers toward the charred hand to await the fire's worst while emitting a low keening sound, praying she had felt no pain.

Seconds later, he felt a tug on the belt of his pants and heard, "Dammit, Brayson, I don't have time to find a forklift to move your lard ass from this burning inferno. Let's move on two."

"ONE."

The sound of Marian's voice instantly registered. He grabbed her with one arm and crab-walked toward the poolside entrance. Outside, acrid smoke refused to yield to the fresh air their lungs begged for with repeated coughs. They inched toward the main house to grab their things, hoping for a clean escape. Hiding behind furniture and debris, they avoided emergency workers and focused on containing the fire while they assessed the situation.

"I don't want to explain why we're here or comment on what happened," Brayson said. "Let's see if we can get to our vehicle and leave."

Edging further away from the explosion epicenter, they headed toward where their car had been left. Emergency vehicles were parked behind their SUV.

Marian looked into his eyes. "We're both alive after sneaking into the once opulent home of a human trafficker's lair that was booby-trapped. Our clothes and support gear are inside. Emergency teams surround the house. All the evidence we found is stuck inside. They will discover we were here. We won't escape without the cooperation of the officials. I've had worse days, sweetheart, but that was when I was in combat."

"Marian, how did you escape the blast? How did you know to warn me? And why are you soaked?"

She shuffled her feet, then shot him an innocent look. "My two tours in Iraq taught me a lot about IED bombs and booby-traps, mostly how not to get killed. I was checking out the guest cottage when the gal we met entered through the other door while on her cell phone. I think she was getting instructions from someone because I heard her say, *I see it. So, I lift the cover and push the button, right?* As soon as I saw her move to it, I called you. I deadheaded through the open door and dove into the pool. The blast came from above. I dodged the burning shrapnel as it hit the water."

Brayson pulled them into the hedges to help conceal their presence. Wrapping his arms around her, he whispered, "Why did you come looking for me back into the blaze?"

"I couldn't hold my breath any longer and popped up in time to see you crouching to enter the building. I got angry that you didn't run like I said. Why did you go into danger?"

"I wasn't about to leave my wife to an unknown fate. We're far too similar to do anything less for each other."

She slipped out of her black t-shirt and wiped his hands, flicking out a couple of pieces of glass. Then, she brushed off the legs of his jeans before shaking out the shirt and sliding it back on. She finger-combed his hair and then her own.

He looked around, lamenting, "I wish I had one of our phones to ask JJ for some help getting out of here with our goods."

Marian grinned, then slipped hers from a plastic bag and handed it over. "When you talk with JJ, leave out that I need fresh underwear. He'd laugh, but I'd be humiliated beyond belief."

Brayson nodded and kissed her forehead. "What happens in San Juan…"

They chuckled.

Brayson pressed to connect and placed the phone on speaker. The call went through, but they heard nothing from JJ, head of the CATS team.

Brayson and Marian exchanged a few quizzical looks.

"JJ, are you there, or so mad at this mess in San Juan that you can't speak?" asked Brayson.

JJ finally engaged. "Sorry, I had two conversations going. I didn't want your call to roll to voicemail. Fortunately, the cameras Judith and Xiamara had installed at Julian's estate were still broadcasting. I hope you can skirt past the authorities and head east toward the small neighborhood store about a quarter of a mile down the lane. Buy groceries, then wander back onto the estate. The police want to talk to you."

Marian tried to suppress a smirk while staring at Brayson's sour look with an exaggerated eye roll. He sputtered, "I was trying to avoid walking into the hands of the authorities, JJ. I don't want to rot in another dungeon because I didn't have a clever exit strategy."

JJ interrupted, "I was on the phone with the San Juan detectives explaining our leads on Mr. Lafluer. They wanted to understand what we knew about him. I recounted the incident where he hired a teenager to drive his car around the city as fast as possible so he could escape. I told them our intelligence indicated he did the same thing by hiring you and Marian to stay in his house. You were supposed to be killed by the explosion that was initiated. The assassin blew themselves to smithereens, not realizing you were gone. You must convince the police you were hired to stay at the property to dissuade squatters. Unbeknownst to you two, Mr. Lafluer orchestrated your assassination. He wanted to be presumed dead with his lady friend. We want to let the investigators come to this conclusion when you appear with groceries. Do you think you can sell that story?"

Brayson's lips curved up. "The dead housekeeper, who could have disputed our tale of woe, is painted as the assassin. Genius."

JJ added, "The stuff in the safe is irrelevant now since the police will take it as evidence. I have the photos you took. After you confirm the details, they should send you on your way. It would be good manners to offer the cash you were paid to house-sit for Julian. However, they'll probably laugh at the mere hundred and fifty dollars you accepted for your near-fatal experience."

Brayson ground his teeth. Marian nodded in agreement with the plan while she gently stroked his hand. He released his breath. "Yes, sir. We'll call you when we're done here to discuss our next move."

"Thanks, JJ," they both said before he disconnected the call and handed her the phone for safekeeping.

Brayson grabbed her hand, looking for a clear path to the roadway toward the store. They nimbly made their way toward it.

She deadpanned, "Sorry you tripped over the log in the road, then cut your shoulder on a thick branch. At least this walk will dry my clothes."

"I kind of liked the wet tee-shirt look."

She slapped at his injured shoulder.

CHAPTER 7

After the Fox

Gracie squared her shoulders, took a breath, and spotted the familiar name on the screen of her phone. She tucked a wayward lock of her long strawberry-blonde hair behind her shoulder. "How's it going, JJ? I'm caught up on the most recent file notes, but I want to know what isn't logged yet."

"We had a close call in San Juan with Marian and Brayson. I'm certain the housekeeper called Julian about people who insisted on staying at the estate. The poor woman was following instructions to help her employer maintain his privacy. I doubt she had any idea that pushing those buttons would result in an explosion of epic proportions. She paid the ultimate price, no questions asked nor answered."

Gracie groaned as she stared across the elegant cream furnishings in her New York office with a breathtaking skyline view. "Wow. I'm glad we didn't lose any of our team. Are they in the clear yet, JJ?"

"I ran some interference with the San Juan authorities to keep Brayson and Marian out of jail. Perhaps this will give Julian a reason to surface somewhere. The island authorities agreed to report to the media the accidental death of Mr. Lafluer and his as-of-yet-unidentified female guest. They will announce, too, that all other investigations where he was considered a person of interest will be closed. I provided them a viable way to close three open cases but promised to keep them informed. I hope Julian relaxes his guard and makes a mistake."

Gracie nodded and unconsciously thrummed the pads of her fingers on the smooth desktop, keeping time to the cadence of the pendulum of the antique clock sitting on the right corner.

"Good idea. I'll get my team working on the housekeeper phone angle. If she did call Julian, maybe we can triangulate the location from the signals bouncing off the cell towers and discover other numbers to track."

"I took the liberty of teeing that up with JW on your behalf because your schedule indicated the board meeting. I felt you couldn't be disturbed." Laughing, JJ added, "JW has the wit of his dad. He said finding Julian is like an old-fashioned whack-a-mole game. The man pops up from one hole. Disappears. Then resurfaces somewhere else in random succession. JW said Granger, Satya, and Auri are catching snippets of visibility every time he converts crypto to hard currency. I'm sure they've set up a scoreboard to track who can pinpoint him the fastest."

Gracie snorted. "My money's on Satya leading in the points, even if Granger is writing the program to predict the moves in advance." She focused on the horizon without seeing any of the building shapes. She placed her elbows on the desk and rested her chin on her thumbs. "We think Julian's the last of these brothers. Each one appears as a bigger monster. Phillip, the ecological gangster with nasty side hustles, is in jail. I received notice this morning that he's in the infirmary after one of the gang members rammed a shiv into his gut in the exercise yard. Mateo, with his drugs and human trafficking, is a confirmed kill by the cartel boss Flores, whom the Mexican and U.S. agencies are working to eliminate. Talk about a whack-a-mole game; the borders are a mess.

"Julian seems more mobile than the others, with vastly different connections. His money sources aren't tied to his brothers and are spread throughout the Caribbean. I believe now that he was the youngest and perhaps more spoiled. I'm working on a few leads regarding his mother's identity, which might yield something useful. Julian's connections suggest a different level of upbringing, almost aristocratic. I want to prove there are no other siblings." She tapped her pen on the desktop for a few moments. "I'm glad we have cryptocurrency parasites on the Ethereum we got into Julian's hands."

"Agreed. But we can't wait for him to go for cash to appear on our radar screen. JW and I asked your team to hunt for other properties in the Caribbean where he may have connections. Your research on his mother could be helpful for this avenue."

Chuckling, she said, "I'd stay away from going door to door asking if the residents know a man named Julian Lafluer."

"You know, you're irritating when you try to be funny, right?"

"Sometimes I'm funny. But you're right. Other times, I miss the mark. Ah, well. I'll upload what I have so far, which isn't much. I'll keep on it while you and the rest of my team play the game. Anything else?"

"Just one." He let out a long-held breath. "Brayson and Marian took photos of the contents of the safe in Julian's house. They saw loose blue stones in various sizes, and a couple of silver pendants mounted with the same type of stones. I confirmed they are larimar, the Blue Jewel of the Caribbean. There were also loose diamonds along with some tanzanite. The other item is confusing. It was a rigid, high-end gift box containing a book. No branding is indicated on the box; it's simply high quality. The book is a 1911 first edition of *The Book of Buried Treasure: True Story of the Pirate Gold and Jewels.*"

Gracie wrinkled her nose. "That's weird. I can see him keeping stones in a safe, but a book like that? Admittedly, it's a first edition and likely valuable, but…"

"People keep valued items as secure as possible. I believe this may be a clue to how Julian thinks. We know so little about him. To a degree, he is more of a loner, a slime-ball weasel, but how did he make his money? As you noted, he entered the crime brother's party on the boat pretty well set and is almost aristocratic in his behavior. He's behind his brother's accounting and money laundering. Can Satya and Auri dig into his background to learn how he made his money? He had two estates. Maybe there are others. Now we learn he likes precious stones. The safe also contained a Martinique passport with his picture but Pierre Sainte as the name with no issue or expiration date."

She picked up her pen. "Was that P I E R R E first name and S A I N T E as the last?"

"Yes. Why does a supposedly honest businessman need a phony passport? How do, or did, these three men connect if they had different mothers?"

She flexed her fingers on the polished surface of her desk to release the tension. The name meant something. Ideas rushed into her mind in a confusing jumble. "I love it when you get me thinking. We uncovered information that Phillip's father was buried in the same town as his official residence in California. We assumed he was the oldest as he seemed to have been the mastermind behind the shipping of the plastics. We have Phillip's birth certificate, which lists his mother as Caroline Appleton. News articles indicated she died in childbirth, and his father, Gerald Pliant, raised him in Texas until Phillip moved to California. I'll work this avenue. Thanks, JJ. Talk soon."

CHAPTER 8

Maritime Forensics

The Harbor Patrol operator radioed in their preliminary report to the U.S. Coast Guard. Thirty minutes later, the cutter *Jaguar* eased into the area, docked, and two guardsmen stepped onto the dock where *Ruby's Slipper* was moored. Standard salutes were exchanged.

"Gentlemen, I'm Captain Turmerone. This is Guardsman Coffee, my assistant. We heard you intercepted a runaway vessel. What do you have so far?"

Officer Jaden stepped forward as a spokesman for the locals. "Captain, I boarded the ship to power down the engines. They were set to full speed, with the wheel lashed tight to hold a straight course. No one was on deck. Once we powered down the boat, we moored it here. Then, we located the captain, Mister Shaughnessy, in his fishing nets under the boat. He lost the fight with the boat propeller and cannot provide his side of the story. I found several empty bottles of Crown Royal about the wheelhouse. This led us to believe he had been drinking and roped the wheel steady so he could relieve himself but fell overboard. However this doesn't explain the high speed it was traveling."

Turmerone nodded and stepped onto *Ruby's Slipper* to review the situation. After a few minutes, he returned to the pier. Unconvinced, he stated, "A man drinking onboard would have thrown his bottles overboard to avoid being questioned by Harbor Patrol when he docked. At the very least, the empties should have been hidden." He stroked his chin, narrowing his eyes at Officer Jaden as he sized up his speculations. "You said the engine was set to full throttle. No one trawling for fish, sober or drunk, runs their boat at maximum speed because of the wear and tear on the engine. Especially when they have nets behind the boat, candling and not expanded enough to catch anything."

Jaden's face blossomed pink as he swallowed while considering the assessment.

"Sailor, can you tell what kind of knots are holding the fishing nets?" Turmerone gently asked.

"Sir, they are standard hitch knots for quick tying and untying," Jaden confidently replied.

"Good. What kind of knot was used to lash the steering wheel, Sailor?"

The man tilted his head and seemed to review thoughts in his mind. "It was a standard bow like my mum used to tie my shoes before I was sent to school. I didn't even think about it until you pointed that out, Sir."

"I submit," Turmerone suggested, "if Shaughnessy had lashed the wheel as an experienced sailor, he would have used a regular maritime knot. The knots used to secure the wheel were not up to that code. A second person is responsible for tying off the wheel and setting the speed to full throttle, headed straight for the pier."

He watched the men nod in silent agreement, schooling his features not to look smug but to provide a lesson they wouldn't soon forget.

"I think the whole thing was staged. Who would want to make anyone think Shaughnessy was drunk and fell overboard, a victim of his stupidity?"

"Sir, we found no evidence of any passengers."

Turmerone grinned and waggled his eyebrows. "Then where are all the life preservers?"

Both Harbor Patrol men bolted onto the boat to verify. After a thorough search, they returned to the dock. Turmerone thought Jaden appeared shaken, likely due to his poor assumptions.

"Nothing in the way of life preservers, Sir. A complete violation of maritime law."

Nodding approval, Turmerone said, "I think we better assume Mister Shaughnessy was assassinated and thrown into the fishing nets, or sent there to tangle himself into a fatal struggle. The engine engaged, steering purposefully pointed here, and empty whisky bottles set the stage, which provided a fair assumption at first blush. The orchestrated scenario was probably meant to explode and destroy all the evidence. Whoever was on board took the life preservers and swam ashore to avoid unpleasant questioning. It would be best to comb the beach for discarded *Ruby's Slipper* vests. Please keep me informed of any additional information."

They all saluted each other as Turmerone boarded his vessel.

CHAPTER 9

Getting Back to Business

Julian grinned when the red roof of the villa appeared between the branches of the wooded lot. He had chosen Pic Paradis, the highest point on Saint-Martin, to gain the beautiful panoramic view of the Caribbean atop his island paradise. "Ryu, there it is!" Julian jumped around like a kid when he first saw Christmas presents. Then, his fingers brushed his filthy shirt. "I can't wait to take a hot shower and change into clean clothing. You can use the downstairs room with an adjoining bathroom. I'll take my suite upstairs." Energized by their proximity to his creature comforts, Julian picked up his pace.

"I am grateful you decided not to rent out this villa to visitors for the season, Julian."

"This is my most prized property. It's not as elaborate as some of my other villas, but no one will ever be able to trace it to me. The housekeepers should have cleaned and provisioned it a week ago, so we should be in great shape."

"How do you manage that, Boss? How can you trust them?"

Julian chuckled and wiped his brow with the soggy square of cloth, promising not to bother washing it. He approached the Welcome Home hanging by the back door, which hid the entry keypad. He set the wall art on the ground and then pressed his hand to the screen, waiting for the scan to verify his identity.

"They get paid handsomely to tidy up twice per month. I have them replace my preferred refrigerator contents, and they take home the older products. They know me by an alias who negotiates for the legal property owner whom I said is a French woman I serve."

The two men entered. After securing the door, Julian commented, "I'll extract the new laptops and burner phones from the safe. I'll need your help downloading the backups from our private storage cloud. I'm glad I trusted my instincts and didn't share that with those two lying geeks I used to centralize Mateo's business. My wealth is still intact."

"I think the burner I used remained dry in the plastic bag, but I need to shower and change before I verify that."

"Good. I trust you." Julian turned and climbed the steps to his private quarters. He inhaled deeply the fresh scents of clean linens and opened the window to the salty ocean breeze of the Caribbean.

They met in the great room an hour or so later. Julian set the laptops on the coffee table, admiring the magnificent Douglas fir exposed beams against white ceilings. The cream-colored walls highlighted the bright colors of the rugs and furniture, superbly tied together with local artworks featuring vibrant yellow, red, blue, and green hues. A sense of peace and comfort settled over him, relaxing the tension after their trek. Ryu paused at the bar under the stairway and poured each of them a glass of bourbon over ice. He joined Julian in gazing out the window at the pulsing waves of the blue sea.

"Lovely and peaceful, isn't it, Ryu?"

"It is. May I take a minute to enjoy this success before I work on downloading our data stores?"

Nodding, Julian moved his glass to his left, offering a toast: "Santé, my friend."

"Salud."

A comfortable silence hung around them. Thirty minutes later, Ryu slipped his old burner phone from his pocket. "The phone made the trip intact, and I charged it while I showered. I'll check on things."

Ryu placed a call. Julian could tell it was about San Juan, so he held his tongue. Ryu began with the usual pleasantries and asked for a status update. Julian fidgeted. Ryu nodded at the conversation Julian wasn't hearing. Ryu finally disconnected.

"Well!" Julian demanded, "Why didn't you put it on speaker so I could hear both sides?"

"Because then they would have known someone was with me. It could put you at risk if they wanted to tell the authorities. Plus, if you had blurted anything out, our cover story would dissolve."

"Out with it. Are we okay or not?"

"I'm sorry about your loyal housekeeper. When she called me about the guests staying at your villa, I knew it was the team that had almost captured us. I told her to protect you. She threw the detonation circuit that leveled the guest house, the servers, and herself. She bought us the time we needed to escape. The two operatives were eliminated in the blast as well. The police believe it was you, Julian, and an unidentified lady friend. Depending on the forensic activity, the story may not hold up forever."

Stunned, Julian leaned back on the supple, smooth, butter-cream-colored lambskin sofa. He lit a cigarette to help steady his nerves. "And my stuff in the safe in San Juan? Can we get my first edition of *The Book of Buried Treasure*? It has all my hand-drawn maps. I want my larimar or the Atlantis Stones I've been collecting. They're valuable."

Under Julian's critical eye, Ryu appeared lost in thought.

"I can try to get my buddy to dress up as your old spinster aunt to call on the police for the contents of the safe. She'll have to forgo your phony passport and ask for the book and the stones. With the extra cash you had stashed there, sliding into his pocket, he should keep my confidence. I will go meet him when he succeeds in keeping you safe."

Julian groaned. "When you put it like that, perhaps I should wave goodbye to those items. I'm thankful that's all I lost."

Ryu's shoulders relaxed. "Don't forget I photocopied the maps and sent them to Harto, your shipwreck hunter. After you spent all that time drawing them, I figured they should be in two places. I will download the copies when I configure the laptops."

Julian yawned and grinned. "You're right." He pointed to the items on the table. "Configure one of these phones, too, so I can check in with Harto and provide a new number for him to reach me. My focus from here on is securing the treasure."

Ryu reached up his arm and stretched a bit. When he twisted his back, it sounded like kernels of exploding popcorn. His expression soured. "Can't we wait a little longer before you do that? Whenever we talk to Harto, the tone is like puppies and rainbows of how close he is to the sunken treasure. Then he requests more funding."

Julian smirked. "True, he can be tedious, but if I don't give him a pat on the head with a fatherly, well-done phrase of praise, he pouts and does nothing. I do trust him to do his job. Plus, I'm thinking about how we might adapt our line of business and re-engage with Flores. I promised to help launder his drug money after he took care of Mateo. Flores's funds will help give us operating cash until we bring in the shipwreck."

For a moment, Ryu appeared lost in thought. "How do you expect to do that?" he asked. "Our server farm at the San Juan estate is toast. Where were you—"

"Those two traitorous contractors who conned me into that hosted service taught me how to use a cloud service provider. The instructions and notes are valid, but I must research my hosting service. I can have our new service spun up in a day, and I'm ready to move crypto through the exchanges I've used. Flores will be satisfied. We get a percentage. And we get time to find the treasure. My buyers won't wait forever."

Ryu nodded. Julian was itemizing the next steps he needed to take when the silence was suddenly pierced by competing growling, rumbling, and gurgling from both men's guts.

Julian chuckled. "I'll fix something for us to eat while you configure the machine. I cook far better than you."

JW realized the Gigazon virtual space illuminated brighter as each member arrived. The interactions of high-fives and smiles enhanced the vibrations one might have at a family reunion. His hand warmed as he clapped Granger's virtual back. Satya and Auri looked adorable as they hugged their older cousin, who laughed and appeared to tussle their hair.

"ICABOD, the enhancements to this space are more realistic every time we meet. I can almost smell the bubble bath Auri and Satya washed in earlier."

"I'll do you one better, Cous," Granger stated. "I smell the eggs and bacon on those tables in the back and hope our deliveries will arrive soon."

"You should answer your door now, Master Granger," announced ICABOD.

JW smiled at everyone. "I wanted to check the status of our search for Julian Lafluer, who disappeared three days ago. Granger and I have captured brief snippets of him cashing in crypto-currency in San Juan. We got word from JJ that while his operatives were prowling Julian's San Juan estate, they had a near-fatal experience that destroyed the guest house. The authorities were summoned to investigate. We got our people out; however, the evidence is either burned or in the hands of the police. We don't have much to go on."

He faced Satya and Auri. "Have you had any luck searching for what we believe must be safe houses for Julian across the islands? I know it's a long shot, but anything of interest?"

Satya and Auri beamed with their most impish smiles and sparkling blue eyes. Satya, a cute redhead of twelve, favored her mother. Auri ran his fingers through his brown, unruly curls, saying he would celebrate his eleventh birthday next month with a surprise party for everyone in Europe during a long week of relaxation. Both youngsters were maturing in their high-tech endeavors, so they were often reminded to disengage from help-ing to solve a cyber case to finish their homeschool homework.

Their excitement was palpable. JW grinned. "Don't keep us in suspense. Share what you've discovered."

Satya couldn't wait. "Auri and I were playing a game about hiding in our safe house. We decided it would need to be main-tained continuously, rented or not. Auri suggested he might turn it over to a rental company to maintain the grounds and the interior. I said it won't work as a safe house if rented, and Julian has to move in immediately. Maybe it's a rental that never gets rented. We began hunting for rental properties that never get rented, and we found forty likely properties across the Lesser Antilles in Antigua, Saint Kitts, Guadeloupe, and Sint Maarten.

These properties are managed by three different property management companies that have a history of working to help one another. None of the property management companies will disclose who owns them."

"Great detective thinking," admitted JW. "Give us what you found. Let Granger and I investigate those locations deeper. Perhaps we will luck into a different entry point. I'll let Gracie know we have some leads to follow up regarding the properties. While we're doing that, can you dig into Julian's past? We know very little about him. He acts well-funded, and we'd like to learn how that occurred."

Satya and Auri grinned and began pounding on their keyboards on their new assignment.

Somehow Get the Evidence

Marian seemed distracted as she watched the officers digest their responses to the interrogation.

Brayson pulled her against him and whispered in her ear as he fiddled with her hair, pushing it behind one ear. "It seems they're buying the groceries tale. Let's get our stuff and clear out."

She pushed away slightly and whirled around, looking at him directly. "I want the material in the safe. I've got an idea of how to get it. The combo was left four turns to eighteen, right three turns to thirty-seven, two turns left to eighty-nine, and then a right turn to stop on zero."

Brayson slapped his head, appearing flabbergasted. "How the hell did you remember that? I was using the stethoscope and cell phone app to break in. Did you memorize it?"

"A girl must know the combination to unlock wall safes to retrieve her valuables. You keep the older officer busy while I work the other one."

"Why am I short of breath and my palms sweaty after hearing you say that?"

She laughed and chatted as she edged next to her target. The police escorted them into the master bedroom, where they split up to divide and conquer the officers. Marian edged towards the wall safe, with Brayson making as much commotion and idle talk as he could. She promptly fed in the combination to open the safe without concealing her actions.

The second officer wasn't entirely paying attention to her activities until the safe door swung open and she innocently reached in to retrieve the contents. The officer who was supposed to be watching her did a double take as she removed the stones, passport, and the first-edition book. A thick bundle of cash fell onto the floor.

Quickly spotting the cash, he said, "Hey, lady, what are you doing? That is site evidence. You can't just—"

Marian stopped abruptly and innocently stated, "These are my things. I keep my valuables in the room safe whenever I stay at a hotel. You saw me open the safe with the combination. That should be proof enough that I locked it." She extracted the cash from his hand and deposited it into her bag.

Not entirely convinced, he demanded, "I'd better see the items removed first. Do you always carry that much cash?"

Marian, a practiced study of distractions, adjusted her swimsuit top only to have it magically become unfastened. She hastily caught the garment before she could be accused of a wardrobe malfunction. She nervously giggled after almost offering a peep show. The officer focused on the hand fixing her bra while her other hand slid the passport into the book and both into her bag. The officer was focused on every move she made as she regathered her female cargo and refastened her top.

She picked up where the interruption began. "These are my semi-precious stones that I put in the safe. And yes, I always carry that much cash so I don't have to pay ATM fees when traveling. Do you want to grade or inventory anything else?"

Somewhat flustered, the officer looked at the stones, counted them, and added the information to his notepad. He lovingly caressed the brick of cash and inventoried her from head to toe, ending with a winsome sigh. "Everything looks in order, ma'am. I believe you are free to leave."

Marian moved over to Brayson's side and smiled at the officer. "I hope you weren't embarrassed by my top coming undone. Thank you for being a gentleman." She looped her arm around Brayson's elbow as they approached the exterior door.

Outside, after the door closed and Brayson was heading toward the car, he complained, "Your great idea was to show him the girls to get the contents from the safe."

Marian corrected, "I did not show him anything, Mr. Hays. He was hoping to get visuals that never occurred. Guys can't resist a peep show, but he only got a tease. I got the evidence."

"Humph, a pretty good show from where I was standing." He sighed. "Well done, sweetheart."

CHAPTER 11

Keep Looking

Jaden rotated his eyes rapidly, searching for out-of-place items like a rotary sprinkler intent on thoroughly drenching the appointed space.

Amani pulled off his beret vigorously, rubbing his head. "I don't know why I always get the crummy landlubber assignments. I can't believe we're rooting around the shoreline like a couple of feral pigs looking for something to eat."

"As a part of the Coast Guard, we are responsible for solving this mystery if we can." He eyed Amani like a patient father. "Why do you complain no matter what assignment we're given? With you, it's always too hot, too rainy, or interfering with your date night. Why don't you admit that you only want to sit in the captain's chair with your feet up and issue orders while drinking coffee?"

"Not true, Boss." He started singing a consistent tune from a Lonny Lupnerder melody. ♫ "We've been up and down this shoreline and haven't seen anything." ♫

"You got that right," Jaden guffawed. "After last night's torrential downpour, your enormous footprint is the only evidence of human presence."

Amani resumed his assigned path, tripping over something partially hidden in the sand. He recovered his balance then leaned over to investigate the buried item. "Hey, what's this? It might be a buoy or something like that. Help me get it out."

Jaden reached over and dug. After a few moments, he uncovered the item. "All right, it's a life preserver."

Amani brushed off the sand before he turned the item over. "It's from *Ruby's Slipper*. That means we're done. Let's report back so we can get our medals."

Jaden rolled his eyes. "No, we gotta keep looking for others. There have to be three, maybe four. The heavy rain did us a favor by exposing this one. The others can't be too far away."

"You're not serious?" the younger man sputtered. "We found a *Ruby's Slipper* life preserver on Sint Maarten, but you want to keep digging? I'm headed back to our boat. You can dig if you want."

"If we show up with one, they'll send us back to look for the rest after they chew us out for our lack of follow-through."

Amani's features twisted into a scowl. He groaned but dug for other missing gear in raised areas of the sand surrounding them.

At Coast Guard headquarters, the Communications Officer marched the teletype fresh output to the Duty Lieutenant. "Sir, this just in from San Juan. It answers our questions regarding Captain Shaughnessy and *Ruby's Slipper*."

The man scanned the paper and read, "The marina owner recalls two men approaching Shaughnessy the night of the big storm. The marina owner wasn't surprised to see Shaughnessy and *Ruby's Slipper* gone the next morning. He was sure they hired Shaughnessy for a charter. The two men match the description of one tall, muscular male accompanied by a smaller male with blond hair. One carried a briefcase while the muscular one had a worn duffle bag slung over his shoulder." He turned toward his officer and mused, "Perhaps three men left San Juan aboard *Ruby's Slipper*, but only one man was found. He was dead fifteen hours later. Let's ask our contacts in San Juan if anyone can verify that two men boarded the boat with the captain. It's suspicious, but there's no evidence we can use yet."

"Did anyone find cash on Shaughnessy or stuffed into a hidey-hole in his cabin? Shaughnessy wasn't known for his generosity."

"Sir, no cash was uncovered anywhere. We opened everything, including the safe in his cabin. Nothing in his logs either."

"If you're running from the law, paying upfront and retrieving it if you eliminate the vessel's captain makes sense. I realize I'm speculating that Shaughnessy saw the coin upfront but not the change in the charter once they were close to the island of Sint Maarten. Perhaps our shore walkers will locate something useful."

CHAPTER 12

How Did We Get This Wrong?

Images from Marian's phone filled the screen, making JJ tingle from head to toe at the possibilities. The anticipation and ideas were on par with when he delivered his first perfectly crafted program to prove that a video was a deepfake. He grinned as he flipped through the downloaded images and zipped them up to Dropbox to transfer to JW, along with his perspective on the value of the contents. When the enormous file finished loading, he released the breath he didn't realize he'd been holding. "Granger and JW will compete to find the answer first." He followed up with a text asking for a thorough evaluation by the team as quickly as possible. Not for the first time this week, he wished he could do more hands-on work rather than coordinating the teams.

JJ followed up with a thank-you text to Brayson, confirming receipt of the images. He requested that they return to Zürich on the next available flight. He had nearly finished assembling the updated information to share with his twin during their upcoming call when an encrypted call from JW was presented on his computer. He smiled, looking forward to adding the new data to share with Gracie. "Hi, JW. I hoped but didn't expect to hear from you so fast. Do you have a target island where we can start hunting for Lafluer? Some of the latest chatter from authorities in San Juan suggests he's escaped somehow."

"I'd like to tell you we do, but the images don't correlate to any of the twenty-six islands. Following exhaustive searches, we suspect these drawings are merely a joke or the person was practicing cartography. Granger and I fed all the images into ICABOD to map the fractal geometry to any coastline. The result is the drawings don't relate to any island in that part of the ocean."

"Huh." Disappointment settled on his back like the proverbial elephant. "That's not what I'd hoped for. Did you have ICABOD widen the—"

"Tried it, cousin," JW interrupted. "The lines don't correlate to any coastline on the planet. We're baffled trying to understand why a man like Julian, who seems organized, secures detailed maps inside a first-edition treasure-hunting book in his safe. We don't know if he drew them. I couldn't find any initials or signatures on the pages. I've asked Satya and Auri to take a look. Their perspective might shed some light."

"Good idea. Maybe our first take was too obvious. What if these drawings are only a part of the bigger picture? I still think they're valuable to Lafluer and his ultimate goals, whatever those are. He fled like a scared rabbit. We need to outline his warren for all his sleeping quarters and exits. Let's map out his history, properties, and family tree. Something may pop."

"It'll take some time, but your idea has merit. Leave it with us. I'll alert you as soon as we've assembled the data points. Research is our forte."

CHAPTER 13

We're Still Hunting

Julian heard Ryu swallow hard as he picked up the burner phone to call his salvage specialist. He tasted the faint flavor of bile, knowing it had been too long since he had touched base. Two calls went to voice mail. On the second, he demanded, "Phone me back immediately, Harto!"

Rising, Julian clenched his jaw. His face contorted into a glare while his fist banged against his leg with each determined step as he paced in front of the windows. "He better make it fast."

Ryu nodded.

Five agonizing minutes later, the phone rang. Julian answered and engaged the speaker so Ryu could hear both sides of the discussion.

"Julian," Harto breathlessly drew out the word almost like a whine. "I'm sorry. I didn't know it was you. The screen indicated a SPAM caller trying to sell male enhancement drugs for bigger and better..."

Julian saw Ryu close his eyes in distaste, and then he stated, "I've had some setbacks requiring a new phone. I have an alternate one I may have to use as well. Answer any call. No one else better have your number, per our agreement."

"Ah, no. No, sir. Yes, sir."

"I'm glad I can trust you, Harto. Get me up to date on where we are in the recovery. I've cranky customers wanting new merchandise."

The rapid, high-pitched sounds of the man's nervous giggle echoed from the speaker, causing Ryu to roll his eyes. Julian shook his head at Harto's latest lame attempt to please him. "We are still tweaking the calibrations of the new equipment. Thanks to our mapping exercise of the coastline of Little Bahama Bank, we have the final optimum navigation path for *Maravillas* after her hull was rammed."

"The details are only relevant if you've solved the problems. Where are you at in the final location of the sunken vessel?"

A loud phew came through the speaker, and he said, "I'm trying to blend the two probing tools to give us a tighter field of position. I need something smaller than eight feet in diameter to begin harvesting your stones."

Julian kept silent, sensing another request.

Harto cleared his throat. "I need the two appliances to narrow the search area so we can harvest faster and avoid detection. If we spend too much time in the target area, we get the local authorities demanding an inspection of our craft and papers, alerting other hunters of our presence. I want to avoid the mess and make a strategic harvest. Following that, we only need to worry about avoiding pirates if they think we found anything worth stealing."

Julian emitted a low guttural growl. "Gurr. You said you could do this, Harto. I provided the extensive investment in the advanced salvage gear and gave you the map to pinpoint the wreckage. You promised you could use the gear to locate and harvest the millions of dollars in lost precious stones. Buyers are ready to receive gems, but your timeline has doubled. If you don't have the stomach for this project..."

"No, please, don't be angry with my progress," Harto whined. "We're close. I feel it. Give me more time to fine-tune the calibrations needed to zero in on the stones. I'll make good. I promise. You said if I bring this one in, we could work on hunting the others. I like the Spanish Galleon *San José* ship, sunk by the British in 1708 as it was heading to Colombia's port city of Cartagena. I want a crack at the *Flor de la Mar*, the Holy Grail of shipwrecks said to be the richest vessel ever lost at sea with her gold, silver, and precious stones cargo estimated at billions today." He sighed as he took a breath. "And I can't stop thinking about the Merchant Royal, *El Dorado* of the Seas from the early 17th century, that went down with a hundred thousand pounds in gold and gems. Think of the stones, Julian. If I can perfect the hunting technology, these prizes will be ours."

The overwhelming thrill of ecstasy coursed through his body at the thought of possessing the lost jewels. "I need proof, Harto, not promises. Perhaps an extra set of hands would help. Should I send in Nohea or Ryu to keep the management burden off you?"

"Another pair of hands would be appreciated, Julian. I have my cousin's twenty-something twins, Blake and Bradley. They're both fit and good at handling the vessel and maintaining the diving equipment. They are also devoted to me. It's too bad they were born with genetic cleft lip defects. I am grateful that when we secure these gems, you will find a surgeon to treat them and provide speech therapy." Harto asked, "When can I expect the additional help?"

Julian caught Ryu's confused look and shrugged. "Give me a few days to shift some current assignments. When he's headed toward you, I'll text to coordinate boarding your vessel at your closest port. Meanwhile, send me the location and specifications of the two appliances so I can secure them. Zero in on the location as much as possible until then without raising any suspicions. I'll be in touch soon, Harto. Please give my best to the twins."

After disconnecting the call, Ryu cautiously said, "Julian, Nohea is stuck in jail. Any attempt to contact him could alert the police to your whereabouts."

Julian grinned. "Yeah. It won't be me. Fix us some lunch. I need to outline the next steps needed to secure his release. I must also alert my buyers to the delay with an optimistic outcome." He watched Ryu leave, pulled out his phone, and ran through the list of clients who had bought into this program. Mentally organizing the list into priority order, he rapidly typed into his Note app who to contact and the primary content of the exchange to keep them abreast of the project's status.

The following morning, Julian placed a call to work his way down his current task list. "Flores, it's me. How do you like your new villa? Is it suitable?"

Flores snorted. "I am happy with the location, but this is the gaudiest place I've ever possessed. Your half-brother Mateo packed the place with paintings, wood carvings, stylized furniture, and woven rugs. But I must admit that I'm comfortable with the villa's luxury. I like the peace away from the continual bustle of the city. I bet the lesser cartels are jealous of my private turf."

Rolling his eyes, Julian looked toward heaven with a sarcastic head shake. "Of course, you got a place to rest when you aren't smuggling fentanyl components and other opioids over the border. I'm glad Mateo's villa suits you. When can we iron out the money laundering and cryptocurrency details you require to move your business forward?"

"You promised me you'd handle this if I ended Mateo. Where the hell are you?" Flores's tone sounded apprehensive. "I deal only face-to-face with someone managing my money."

Julian soothed, "Flores, crypto laundering is always done remotely over secure internet data connections. We agreed. I'm not touching your hard-currency transactions. Therefore, we don't need to be neighbors."

"Let me mull this over for a couple of days. So far, everything has worked fine using hard currency, so I'm not yet—"

"The Chinese source for your fentanyl only deals in crypto. If you want your sources to dry up, then by all means, stay with hard currency. Flores, the Chinese can't launder hard currency, which is why they insist on cryptocurrency."

Flores sighed. "I said, let me think on it. I'll call you in a few days."

The abrupt disconnection irritated Julian, but he dismissed it. Flores wasn't stupid. But he needed to get Flores to pay the first installment of his debt. If Flores didn't call him, he would follow up soon.

CHAPTER 14

Need a New Angle

Seeing the name appear on the screen, JJ stopped typing and grinned as he answered the call. "Hey, Gracie. To what do I owe this unexpected call?"

"How can you sound so upbeat with your beautiful wife, Jo, away at some fabulous filming location while we struggle to get a lead on the beast Julian? We're supposed to have our hands on this jerk, but it seems we're suffering from butter fingers. I want a line on where Lafluer is or proof of his demise. We believe he whacked the captain of the boat he chartered. We don't understand his business model or next steps."

JJ rocked back in his chair, feeling a similar sentiment crawling up his spine over the stall in their investigation. He stared at the vacant space beyond his computer screens. "And I was hoping this was a social call so we could breathe for a minute. Brayson and Marian managed to extract the contents of Julian's safe into our hands after the San Juan estate guest house explosion and fire. I shared everything with JW and hoped you were calling with good news."

"We have five drawings that don't map to anything on this planet. JJ, I think he's hiding out in the Caribbean, waiting for enough time to pass so he can re-engage into his despicable human trafficking and money laundering businesses."

"Possibly. Speaking of which, how are Elena and Sophia's recoveries progressing? Have you spoken to them recently?"

"I got word they are about to be released from the hospital. Protective Services are ready to take them into custody and potentially relocate them."

JJ rubbed his face with the palms of his hands as he considered the possibilities. "It occurs to me that you might make a surprise visit to wish them well on their next adventure. It would be a great opportunity to get them to open up about their experiences. Since they initially knew you as a trusted friend, they might tell you what they heard and saw while under Julian's protection."

"Wow. When I think I'm smarter than you, dear brother, you demonstrate your genius ability to think outside the box."

JJ chuckled. "Without boring you with the details, Jo is always pleased when I think out of the box."

"She does adore you. I'll head out to San Juan on the early flight tomorrow and surprise them each with a small gift. I'll see if I can get them to open up over a nice lunch. Those girls need to be in school around other kids their age. I would like to see them get a clean start. You're right. They probably know more than anyone can imagine. Lafluer would have risked everything to reacquire them if he thought they knew anything about his business. We girls often seem to gain information without effort … at least the sly ones do."

JJ laughed aloud. "You never said anything about being a crafty female. But now that I think about it, since I'm your twin and you're a designated shrewd female, that must mean I'm the male version of that."

Gracie groaned. "I wouldn't update your resumé just yet."

Not willing to end the teasing streak, JJ brightly added, "But after we catch Julian, okay?"

"Yes, of course, my delusional brother. I'll update you on what I find out. Thanks for the talk."

JW peered across the virtual Gigazon space to monitor the current participants. "Granger, how are you coming with locating Lafluer properties?"

Granger pushed his long red ponytail over his shoulder as he turned toward JW with a frown and slightly furrowed eyebrows. "Even tracking someone who moves between islands regularly, I'm not coming up with much. The place we know of as his property in San Juan wasn't in his name. We're pretty sure he was staging his operations in Saint Kitts before moving to San Juan, but there isn't any record of ownership there either. The guy's good. Every property we suspect is his has different names for legal ownership. Each name is a dead end, with no person behind it. I can't find any places tied to him across the Caribbean region. He's a whip-smart criminal who knows how to live an undetectable life. We're not convinced that Julian Lafluer is his real name except in San Juan, where the locals speak of him fondly."

Satya and Auri lit up at the statement. They bounced in their chairs, vying to speak.

JW acknowledged them with a grin and a wave of his hand.

Satya began, "Auri and I agree with Granger's statement. We were digging through the birth certificates in the region, with the help of ICABOD, and got a hit. Here's the weird thing. We found a birth notice for Julian Lafluer, followed a few days later by a death certificate. Julian Lafluer was born and died within a week. The man we're chasing is a dead child."

Auri blurted, "Identity theft of a child only a few days old got us thinking. What about Julian's half-brothers and their identities? We hunted for Mateo Hernandez and Phillip Pliant on a hunch. Both names brought up actual babies born in a year that approximates our criminals' current ages. Each of the babies died within days of their birth. We believe this proves all three half-brothers grew up with stolen identities."

Satya and Auri suppressed smirks, likely due to the sour look Granger shot their way.

"Great," said JW. "We're supposed to be closing in on the last bad actor of the bunch only to discover we're chasing ghosts. Nice work, kids, but why can't we get good news for a change?"

Granger postulated, "They've been taught to hide their deceptions and run cloaked to evade capture for their entire lives. We don't need to know who they were so long as we know who they are now."

"I concur," said JW. "The fact that they were given new identities is irrelevant, but we still need any information on Julian to locate him. The brothers were raised to work in the criminal trade, but who would know these men would need different identities while growing up?"

Satya interjected, "Auri and I believe the people who raised them must have been connected to a crime family. They knew false identities would be useful for the brothers. We speculate that whoever sired them wanted the people working close to him to be family. Having sons was a bonus."

Auri added, "At this point, we only have conjecture, but it does map nicely to our current facts."

CHAPTER 15

There's Sunken Treasure Everywhere

Satya and Auri looked at one another and scowled at the "these don't exist" reports on their respective screens. Jumping out of her chair, she stomped her foot, her green eyes flashing as tendrils of her red hair escaped the flowered clip. "None of this makes any sense. Why would Julian painstakingly hand-draw five island maps that don't exist? The detailing is exquisite, and the photo images map to the scale of the originals found by Brayson and Marian. These were rescued from Julian's safe along with a first edition treasure hunting book."

Satya paused as Auri shuffled the images over one another, shifting the overlaps as best he could on standard paper.

He and Satya had a connected relationship as the R-Group family's youngest members. They'd played well together from the moment they met as toddlers. Trying to divine the answer to the complex puzzle, his big, blue, intent eyes met his cousin's green as he stated, "Here's another inconsistency, Satya. Each map has a different letter of the alphabet, with each in a slightly different position on each map. I'm curious. The pictures we were sent are all on solid backgrounds. Were the originals on solid paper as well?"

Satya scrunched up her face and cocked her head. "Why wouldn't they be?"

Auri removed the white background from the images, making all five maps transparent. Then he stacked them atop one another so the letters aligned in a row.

Satya gasped with astonishment. "Auri!"

"These aren't five different maps but one. With everything stacked, we can easily read – *N S de las Mara*. But I have no idea what that could mean." Auri rotated the single image several times. "If you view the image as a single, does it match any current islands?"

Excited, Satya jumped back into her chair and let her fingers fly across the keyboard. "ICABOD, does this image match any modern-day islands or coastlines?"

ICABOD replied, "My esteemed hunting pair, I'm sorry, there are no matches to any current topographical land masses."

Satya deflated like a pin-punched balloon, watching Auri slump into his chair with arms crossed and a massive frown of defeat. "Another dead-end clue. Poop!"

ICABOD continued, "However, when I added the letters assembled as overlays of the map, I found a Spanish galleon that sank on January 4, 1656, en route to Cádiz, Spain. I located a lost treasure ship. The Spanish ship was named *Nuestra Señora de las Maravillas* and was reportedly laden with treasure. The letters match its abbreviation, *N S de las Mara*."

Auri sat up straight. "Where's the island?"

Satya grinned, nodding her head in sudden understanding. "The *Maravillas* didn't sink on an island, did it, ICABOD?"

"No, it did not, Satya. The *Nuestra Señora de las Maravillas*, which means Our Lady of Wonders, sank in the shallow waters of the Little Bahama Bank of the northern Bahamas. *Maravillas* lost the six hundred and fifty souls on board when the Spanish Galleon was rammed by its flagship, then collided with a reef, suffering significant damage. At the time, it was laden with treasure—including a large quantity of contraband and objects salvaged from another sailing vessel lost off the coast of Ecuador two years earlier. Spanish salvagers stripped *Maravillas* first, followed by various expeditions led by European and American crews. The wreck was fished for treasure on at least twenty-one occasions between 1656 and 1683. The current thinking is that the wreck was picked clean of all its precious metals."

Satya intently read the flow of detailed information. "The map is of the Little Bahama Bank shallows where *Maravillas* sank."

Nodding, Auri asked, "ICABOD, you said *Maravillas* got stripped of her precious metals, but how about the precious stones?"

"That is unknown, Auri. If the diamonds and larimar found in Julian's safe are clues, Lafluer is hunting precious stones that a metal detector wouldn't locate."

Auri wrinkled his nose and furrowed his brow. "How can one possibly hunt for precious stones lost five centuries ago in the sea? And with what devices?"

Satya felt a surge of excitement at the prospect of this logic. "ICABOD, can you identify a hybrid scanning technology that combines light detection and ranging, known as LIDAR, with three-dimensional mapping and ground penetrating radar currently available to search the sea floor for objects denser than the surrounding plants, animals, and coral, using AI programming?"

Auri added, "I've seen some impressive studies using these processes together, but these have been above ground. Thermal imaging is only useful for finding buried metal objects. Julian would be hunting precious stones."

ICABOD affirmed, "LIDAR technology is easily reflected and is not designed to penetrate the soil. An enterprising treasure hunter might be able to fine-tune a mash-up for the technologies you mentioned while cruising over known sunken wrecks. They might have a workable model for locating precious stones."

Satya reasoned, "A different focus. They hunt in a known sunken treasure area, which is reported as completely salvaged. They're using advanced technology to find stuff others missed. Regular treasure hunters deride those who hunt in a fished-out area. Interesting."

ICABOD added, "Understand, my young explorers, many sunken treasures still have yet to be found or exploited. Not everything is in the Caribbean. The so-called Treasure Fleet of 1715 had eleven Spanish ships laden with treasure from the Americas set sail from Havana, Cuba, heading for home. All eleven sank. More than a thousand lives were lost at sea during a hurricane off the coast of Florida. The Portuguese ocean-going ship *Cinco Chagas* sank during the Battle of Faial Island in the Anglo-Spanish War in 1594. Faial Island is an island of the Azores in the Atlantic Ocean belonging to Portugal. When the *Cinco Chagas* went down, it was rumored to have two thousand tons of treasure, including twenty-two chests filled to the brim with diamonds, rubies, and pearls. This type of treasure seems to spark Julian's interest, but the water depth has kept the treasure hidden from those seekers."

"Then we should expect that if Julian and his treasure-hunting team are successful in the shallows of the Little Bahamas," Satya mused, "he will move to other locations looking for precious stones, not coins."

\Julian finished his cigarette and sipped the hot coffee Ryu had refilled. He was pleased with the positive discussion with his second investor. This next call was to his prime investor, who was short on patience and long on rapid rewards before penalties. He took a deep breath and dialed the number. Expecting it to connect to voice mail due to the unrecognized caller ID, he flinched when the gruff voice answered.

"You better have a good reason for calling this number. Identify yourself."

"It's Julian. I had to change cell phones. Do you have time to talk, Sir?"

"You are overdue with the promised product and late in communicating. This is the only reason I answered. Get to the point, and no lies."

Julian swallowed hard. "Mark, our recent endeavor has fallen behind its timetable. It will be at least thirty more days before I can retrieve—"

"What?" he roared. "I provided you enough upfront capital to secure your supply of high-quality stones. I don't want buyers going to the Russians for their products. Plus, the quality of the stones you promised is believed to be far better. I manage a tight hold on our supply of the precious stones we mine. They are priced high for all to enjoy. Secondary markets, including the industrial ones, are harder to manage. I need a reliable supply so the manufactured technologies don't erode our clientele. With their high-pressure equipment, those clowns are gaining market share. We are in price wars. I can compete on price better with this unexpected windfall you guaranteed. So where are they?"

"Sir, we are pioneering a new harvesting technology that will increase the yield tenfold. I've had to rethink how they will be delivered. There is also the small matter of how they will be graded and priced at this quantity. Security is another matter when you put them in the blockchain conveyor belt for traceability. I won't be handing over a modest briefcase full of stones. You'll need a pallet jack to move what I'm about to provide. I recommend we discuss the logistics of product transfer."

Mark snorted in disbelief. "Julian, you've always told a good story, but I sense confidence in your statement. If you are lying, you know the penalty. I've been a buyer of your sourced precious stones for many years. This is the first time we've suffered such an immense delay. I can afford to wait on your timetable, but I'm under pressure to deliver. I will give you thirty days. It would be best if you kept me updated weekly. I'll be exploring other sources to cover my bases. My investment in you will start adding interest on the payback as of today."

Anger and pride surged through his veins. "I won't fail."

CHAPTER 16

Re-Connecting with Friends

The seatbelt sign turned off. Gracie stood, smoothing her bluish, green flower-printed shirt over her jean-covered hips. She grabbed her rolling suitcase from the overhead compartment while smiling at her fellow passengers. Minutes later, following the signs to the designated ride pick-up area, she punched the codes into her app and received the affirmation chirp.

When a black windowed SUV slowed and pulled to a stop close to the curb, she grinned at the efficiency and gave a little wave. The powerfully built, sun-tanned man, dressed in cargo shorts and a tee-shirt, emerged from the driver's side. Seconds later, he secured her bag in the rear and opened the passenger door for her to sit.

"Thank you, Brayson," she quietly said.

"No problem," he replied before he closed her door and bolted around to the driver's side.

She spotted Marian in the front seat and wiggled her fingers to greet her. Once they moved toward town, Gracie leaned between the seats and affectionately squeezed Brayson's shoulder. "I didn't properly thank you both for your assistance on the cruise ship earlier this year when we nailed Pliant. And, Marian, thank you for ensuring we could find Sophia and Elena with the tracking sandals. Brilliant."

Brayson chuckled. "She's good, isn't she, Gracie?"

"You're both the best."

"We have a solid team," remarked Marian.

Brayson shifted the subject. "I trust you and Jeff Wood have made a full recovery."

"Jeff's still in therapy but coming along nicely," she confidently said. "I hope JJ briefed you on my objectives for this meeting?"

They nodded.

"Good. I want to do a meet and greet with the girls at a quiet venue for lunch. If I can crack open the topic, I want to feel them out about things they saw and heard while with Lafluer. Some things may be unimportant, but I suspect there is a gem somewhere we can leverage to find him or at least get a lead to chase."

Marian griped, "I wish we had found more at his villa."

Gracie's stomach churned, recalling their escape from the explosion and fire. "I'm grateful you both survived, and it was a bonus that you could gather additional clues from Julian's safe."

Gracie noticed Brayson frequently checking the mirrors as he navigated the traffic, which seemed a little heavy.

"That was all Marian," said Brayson. "Plus, she pulled my butt out of the burning building. She is the poster child for running into the fire. I'm beyond grateful to be alive. We have Judith and Xiamara standing by if needed."

Marian reached over and patted Gracie's arm. "JJ also told us to prevent you from engaging in cowboy heroics."

Gracie burst into laughter. "As if I would ever do something like that. He's so protective." She caught Brayson's eye roll in the rearview mirror and bit back her giggles.

"No disrespect intended, but sometimes you are a little headstrong."

Marian playfully swatted Brayson's arm. "All you had to say was, we're here to help. I'm sure she doesn't want to be held hostage and on a drug tap while waiting to be sold into slavery again."

Gracie stared out the front windshield, reliving the threats from the men who captured her and impacted those around her. Partially reliving hers and Bailey's abduction, Gracie absent-mindedly nodded. "I hope this is the last of the three horrific criminal brothers. We need to end their reign of terror. Thanks for the reminder, Brayson."

"We have reservations at a nice restaurant with the approval of a known contact at Child Protective Services. After lunch, we need to call to meet with them to transfer the girls into their custody. Marian and I have vetted them, so no bad guys in the mix again."

Gracie was confident the I's were dotted, and Ts crossed. "All good."

"We've arrived. Let's make certain the girls feel confident in our presence," suggested Marian. "Leave the bad juju thoughts outside. I, for one, can't wait to see them."

Gracie signed the papers, provided by the woman with Child Protective Services, for temporary custody of the girls. Moving past the awkwardness, Gracie and Marian rushed to hug each young lady. Brayson held back, but both girls moved close and asked, "May we hug you, too?"

Smiles and words in Spanish and English surrounded the foursome as they moved to be seated. Conversation flowed easily with the second round of beverages. The girls loved their Shirley Temples, giggling at the bubbles tickling their noses.

Sophia and Elena excitedly chattered in their mixture of languages as the meal progressed. Gracie asked about the girls' plans for the future.

"Think about where you want to be in five years," Gracie suggested. "Do you want to get additional education?"

Elena outlined her desire to go into fashion design and perhaps even modeling.

Sophia fell quiet and appeared thoughtful. After seemingly seeking approval to speak her mind, she asked, "Gracie, we had friends from school that Julian allowed to come over and play in the pool on Saint Kitts. They were such good friends, but they were like us, no real family who wanted them. When we were told we had to leave for San Juan, we thought they would get to go with us. Madam Chloe told us they had changed their minds about leaving the day we left. She said they were fickle teens who went back to school. It hurt not being able to see them again."

Elena had tears brimming in her eyes when she said, "We discovered while in San Juan that Lisbeth, Maria, Consuelo, and Raul never returned to school like we were told. We had gotten the information on social media from another girl who didn't like us. She said we were responsible for them being gone. I liked Raul."

Sophia complained, "Julian threatened to take our phones away since we had loaded forbidden applications without permission. At that moment, he received a call that was so important to take that he told Nohea to remove the apps."

Elena nodded. "I remember that. He told Nohea to clean the apps while he talked with Harto."

Sophia teared up. "We begged Nohea not to take them away because we needed the social media apps to invite other kids to play at our pool. Nohea took pity and said he would speak with Julian about leaving the apps on our phones. Gracie, I don't believe our friends would vanish without a goodbye. We often discussed getting modeling jobs, which could lead us to acting. We promised to send for the others if one of us made good."

Elena reminisced, "We were trying to help Julian get modeling candidates in San Juan, too. We never heard another word about the ones selected for interviews."

"I'm sure something was wrong. It never felt right," blubbered Sofia.

Gracie flashed a concerned look to Marian and Brayson as she patted both girls' hands. "Thank you for telling us. We'll look into it and try to discover where they are. We have some good contacts with a talent for finding lost items and people. Now let's leave the sad thoughts behind and consider dessert."

The heaviness of the conversation lifted in the remaining time before their ride showed.

CHAPTER 17

Let's Make a Deal

The long hugs and tearful goodbyes were balanced with promises to keep in touch as Sophia and Elena were transferred into the hands of the Child Protective Services agents.

Gracie pawed at the tears to remove their evidence on her cheeks while she hunted for a quiet place to call JJ.

He immediately answered, "How did it go?"

"I got some information worth exploring from Sophia and Elena. They stayed in another of Julian's villas on Saint Kitts with a large pool and attended school. I could not obtain the address, but their school in San Juan must have the Saint Kitts school address to transfer credits. Elena said Julian promised the curriculum was similar and the class names identical. I will also send a list of the teachers' names they provided along with names of other students who were friends. Sophia said Julian asked them to bring kids from school who needed help and a home life like theirs. At one point, some of their friends ended up missing. I hate to think of their fate."

"Oh, Gracie," he said in a sad tone. This doesn't bode well. Were Madam Chloe and Nohea both involved? They are still in police custody; perhaps we can interview them."

"Yes." She spat, "I'm not certain which of them was worse, but my money is on Madam Chloe. The profile seems to center on lonely and alienated teenagers who want to belong to the crowd. Both of the girls were overwrought, fearing for their four friends who were supposed to leave with them when they went to San Juan but just disappeared. I don't believe they understood that Julian was using them as bait. I believe their friends were sold into slavery. They asked if we could help find them. Another detail is that they overheard Julian accept an important call from some guy named Harto."

"Nice work. Text me the names as soon as possible, and we'll start investigating. Coincidentally, Nohea received a cryptic note today delivered to his jail cell. It said, *Bargain for release. Meet me at the rendezvous place tres in two days. Pay them off if you must.*"

Gracie smacked her lips while considering the possibilities as she twisted a wayward lock of hair behind her ear. "Interesting. It occurs to me that a counteroffer might be in order. He might be enticed to work for us, even temporarily. I take it Madam Chloe didn't get the same invite."

"No, she didn't," JJ said. "If it was Julian, he needed his brawn more than the pretend governess. Nohea seems to have a way to get money. We won't be able to trust him. All we need are some solid leads to find Julian."

"And the girls' friends, JJ. I'll work from that angle if you can provide me with some intelligence. I'll leave the Julian hunting to you."

"I know who I can get to deliver our proposition. Judith and Xiamara have been hounding me to get back into the game to help finish the takedown of Julian. I'll let them sell this deal to Nohea. We'll keep Brayson and Marian cloaked for Julian's salvage operation rather than bring them back to Luxemburg. I feel we'll need operatives for that part of the puzzle."

Gracie grinned. "I'll text you the names after this call. Please let me know what you find."

Judith sashayed up to the window in snug jeans and a crop top, optimizing her hourglass figure. She presented the perfect letters of introduction. The guard seemed captivated by her cheeky smile. After their identities were confirmed, Judith and Xiamara were led to a prisoner interrogation room. Judith was entirely into character. Xiamara bounced from one foot to the other in khaki shorts and a modest short-sleeved shirt, ready to confront Julian's henchman. That changed as soon as Zee was face-to-face with the man. She whispered to Judith, "He seems more imposing than I recall. Has he grown?"

Judith shook her head and patted her friend's arm as she slid into the chair directly across from her target.

The guard asked, "Do I need to stay in the room? He's restrained if you need a private conversation."

Xiamara seemed fearful, facing the criminal.

Judith flatly remarked, "We're good, thank you, officer." She heard Xiamara swallow when the guard pulled the door closed behind him.

Judith looked down her nose at this useless piece of humanity. "Hi again. Remember us? Rumor has it you're ready to exit this funhouse. Perhaps you're in the market for a sweet deal," she added, seductively running her tongue over her lips.

Nohea nodded, his fierce gaze shifting between the ladies. Xiamara kept edging back from the table.

Judith continued, "We'll triple your promised retainer if you provide some accurate information."

He inclined his head.

"First, where is the rendezvous, and are you meeting Julian? Second, where did you send the four teens you transported from Saint Kitts? Third, are you willing to be chipped for tracking purposes? We'll only do that if we believe your answers to the first two questions."

Anger erupted from Nohea. He lunged forward, stopping mere inches away from Judith's face because of the heavy chains on his neck and hands. Xiamara flinched and recoiled in terror, covering her head with her arms and hands.

Judith suppressed a bemused smirk. "The chip thing is the police's idea of keeping track of loose animals. Frankly, we don't need it. We found you and led you into our trap. Run, and we'll find you again."

Visibly calming his anger, Nohea asked, "If I do everything you want, what do I get? How much money for leading you to him?"

Xiamara composed herself and was back at Judith's side. Judith replied, "Why, nothing at all but your freedom. You'll be commended for helping to bring a wanted criminal to justice to preserve the Caribbean. But we won't be forced to bring you back to San Juan. Your promise to go on the straight and narrow is enough payment."

Nohea weighed the idea. "And the chip implant?"

Judith smiled, "Most high-dollar businesses are deploying chip detector technology. If a crime is committed and your chip is detected in the immediate vicinity, someone will hunt you down for an explanation. It's simple."

After an endless silence, Xiamara finally said, "Consider it your *free card to keep out of jail.* If you work honestly, no one will want to find you."

After consideration, Nohea asked, "Where is the chip to be located?"

Judith smiled. "Chips. Sometimes the batteries in the little buggers run down, so a few extras will be delivered to ensure a good broadcast for several years. Some will be embedded internally, where you can't easily get to them to dig them out. You'll likely have some discomfort sitting for a day or two."

Xiamara couldn't mask her chortle.

"And Madam Chloe? Will she be offered a deal, too?"

Judith sighed. "Nope. She'll be remanded here in San Juan as an accessory to Julian's crimes. The authorities are unconvinced of her value after her egregious crimes."

The room became wrapped in a pregnant pause. Judith pushed her chair away from the table and loudly called, "Guard!"

Xiamara quickly rose.

Nohea panicked. "Wait, I haven't given my answer. How do we proceed? I'm ready now."

"Good. Time was nearly up. They'll bring paper and a pen to document a confession. Then, you will sign the procedure agreement documents. If we are satisfied and following your implants, you'll be cut loose with instructions on how to communicate via a special phone. But right now, you are returning to a jail cell. This is the last time you'll ever see us."

Xiamara strolled to the door, stopped, and winked at Judith. She announced with a sharp turn that ruffled her curly hair and determined glare. "Unless you screw up again. Good day."

CHAPTER 18

Knowing and Not Knowing

Back in San Juan, Gracie arrived early to her office to catch up before the jampacked schedule of meetings combined with a mountain of approvals required before the end of business today at the World Bank. She checked her schedule and organized the digital files on her laptop. She realigned the papers on her desk for easy access. The sun brightening the New York skyline outside her office windows suggested time was ticking toward her first meeting.

Her pulse quickened at the identity of the incoming call on her cell. Hoping for good news, she accepted the call. "Hi, JW. Thank you for calling early. My day is going to be busy. Tell me you have located the four teens who vanished from Saint Kitts."

"Morning, Gracie. I have news, but it's not great. We monitored the coordinated efforts of the FBI, DEA, and local police as they stormed the establishment euphemistically named The Hotel. Lisbeth and Maria were found alive and were rushed to the hospital to care for their drug-induced state, along with a full MRI to check for breaks suspected because of the extensive visible bruising. I suspect there will be a psych eval at some point. The local authorities confirmed, based on a note he wrote, that Raul took his life. I spoke to the coroner, and the gist of the note indicated he couldn't live with what he was forced to do to survive. Consuelo died of an overdose from the candy she was supposed to sell." His voice caught, so he cleared his throat. "No note was found." His voice trailed off.

Tears filled Gracie's eyes, and her heart sank into the pit of her stomach from the horrific account JW had succinctly delivered. "JW, take a deep breath. I am so sorry you have to learn all of this."

"Me too, Gracie. It's taken me half an hour to call and tell you. I knew people could be monsters, but I wasn't prepared to…"

"You did good. Take a break, maybe a shower, and then send me the information so I can follow up with those contacts."

JW whispered, "I'm sorry I involved Satya and Auri in hunting for the teens. I wished I hadn't. They were practically frozen in their seats after they found the information and supporting photos."

Gracie made a mental note to call her Aunt Petra later to check on Auri. "JW, it's not your fault. You had no way of knowing. I'm sorry I gave you the assignment. Please forgive me."

"I think I grew old in minutes today, Gracie." He inhaled before he continued. "After calling Mom and explaining the sequence of events, she took Auri home. Mom was understanding and supportive. She said she would evaluate him and let me know when he could work again. Granger called Aunt EZ, so she is taking care of Satya. Granger is okay, except he's mad and ready to finish this mess. I think I may need a day of rest."

"I want you both to take a day off. Sometimes, the stuff we find is beyond awful. I'll brief JJ. You both sign off. That's an order."

"Thanks. I'll tell Granger."

"ICABOD, I know you are listening to this call. Please shut down access to JW and Granger for a day, or until JJ and I approve their return to work."

"Yes, Miss Gracie."

"Go rest, JW."

"Good night, Gracie."

Gracie disconnected the call and closed her eyes, yet tears escaped, running down her cheeks. She pounded her fists on her desk and said a quiet prayer: "Please let the young ones recover from seeing and learning about this dreadful mess. Help all of our teams grow stronger and not crumble into pieces."

She messaged her assistant to move her first call to later in the afternoon. When JJ answered, she said, "Hi, JJ. I hope you're aware of the situation with the team."

"I'm reviewing the details now. I didn't think it would be something the kids would find. What a mess. I've been messaging the parents. Maria and Lisbeth's parents say the girls are eighteen now, and they can't afford to help them. Their daughters are welcome to return to Saint Kitts when they recover, but they aren't in a position to provide travel funds." Gracie dabbed at her eyes and blew her nose. "I spoke to the doctors, who are confident that the girls will recover with the right treatment program. I signed up to sponsor them and pay for their treatments." She took a breath and asked, "How are you?"

"Gracie, I'm a mess but mad. I want to finish this. I'll split the cost of their treatment with you. What a wonderful gesture. I'll set up a shared folder for their progress updates. As bad as Sophia and Elena's lives have been, sharing this information with them is unnecessary. All they'd do is blame themselves for something they couldn't control in their wildest dreams."

"I agree. Their insights likely saved two of their friends. I had ICABOD disable our younger cousin's access for the day and asked JW to reach out if needed. This is one more reason to nail Julian to the wall."

"I'll message Granger and JW to let them know I'm available if they want to talk. We may need a staff psychologist to help us divert any PTSD issues with our team."

"Do we have anyone in the extended family, JJ, who might do that? Or maybe the doctor Jeff works with could be vetted and considered."

"That idea, my brilliant sister, sounds like a good start. I'll work it."

Julian sat on the patio, watching the puffy clouds dancing in the wind, musing about his current state of affairs. He swirled the merlot in the stemless glass, took a generous sip, and quietly lamented, "I wish the equipment would arrive. Being without her is…" The door opening alerted him to Ryu.

"It just came in," Ryu said. "I believe you've received all the electronics and computer gear you requested. I'll unbox it, complete the inventory, and begin the setup."

Relief and excitement coursed through Julian's body. "My love has arrived just in time. You start. I'll finish this wine and be in shortly to help with the assembly. If I had the next generation, I'd have her put it together."

"The staging area is ready to receive the room," Ryu stated. "How elaborate do you want it?"

Julian frowned. "I thought I'd told you I'm not cutting corners in this installation."

"Yes, Julian. But I thought you were in a hurry…"

"I want a gratifying experience. She has to be comfortable."

Ryu nodded and returned indoors.

Julian raised his glass and let the sun highlight the smooth, velvety-textured wine. "As soon as I harvest enough gems for resale, I can look at getting her in the next iteration, where VR goggles aren't needed." He grinned, finished the wine, and hurried inside.

CHAPTER 19

All It Takes is Time and Money

Harto grinned as he finished the final programming input. "There, instead of eight feet in diameter, the beam focuses on eight inches for its image/data sampling view." Summoning Bradley, they loaded up the RAY onto the fantail launch and quickly headed to the target area of the Little Bahamas.

Once inside the designated area, Harto put the fishing poles on the boat stern as their usual camouflage. After scanning the area for other ships that might be too nosey, he lowered the water monitor that traveled several feet below the surface. The sides' dorsal fins and diving drones were controlled on the topside to position the gem hunter correctly over the target area. Harto nosed the engines forward at a slow trawling pace so the monitor drone could send and receive signals for analysis. The battery packs they had on board provided the electricity needed to operate the cameras and pulse the images back to the boat. That effort included 3-D radar-scanned ground data. It only took a few minutes of data-gathering to have the collection device post its first error.

Harto flinched as Blake and Bradley hollered to stop the boat. He shut down the engines and smacked the wheel. "Dammit!" Quickly reviewing the equipment stats, he muttered, "What? The disk can't be full. There's a terabit drive attached. How many data samples? No kidding. Insane! We've only gone a couple of hundred yards. Don't give me that…" A few minutes later, he completed his review and closed his eyes as the sense of defeat cloaked tighter than a wetsuit. "Damn, it makes sense. I'd better call Julian. I hadn't counted on this."

He oversaw Blake and Bradley hoist the monitoring drone back aboard, coil up the tethering fiber optic cable, and stow the fishing poles. The two muscular, bronzed teens covered the RAY with a canvas tarp secured at the edges. Harto headed toward the dock.

Julian immediately answered, "How was your first run?"

Harto's throat was tight. He grabbed a water bottle to avoid choking while conveying the unexpected problem.

"The good news is we've successfully narrowed the drones' cameras to eight inches. The images are crystal clear, and the ground-penetrating radar scanning helps us focus. The trouble is that the sampling rate required to scan the same eight-foot area has increased by two to the sixteenth power. I collected over sixty thousand images. We have the right skills to scan and identify the gems accurately. Reviewing the first sampling, I realized I can't sift through that many files fast enough to make the data useful."

Julian tersely insisted, "What do you recommend to defeat this problem? It sounds like we're trying to scan the heavens."

Harto's mind raced. He froze, lost in thought.

"Are you still there?" Julian barked.

Harto's face broke into a crazed grin as he reported, "You've done it again. That's the answer. We use the same AI programs the astrophysicists are using to sort through mountains of data looking for habitable planets and use it to evaluate our images for precious stones. We feed this data avalanche into the AI engine, teach it what we are looking for, and begin culling the output for harvesting efforts. Can you get the needed AI programs and petabyte storage so we can start the review of the data effectively?"

Julian fumed, "You must prove this new program is worth the effort. Sift through what you have and show me some stones. Your new helper will be there soon. The two of you can do the scuba thing based on what you have already captured. No new investments until I see some results, got it?"

"Yes, Sir."

Julian worked in his upstairs office for several hours before ambling downstairs for a snack. Ryu sat at the table, covered with a towel, cleaning two guns. "I'm glad you're keeping them in good working order, Ryu. I'm making a sandwich; do you want one too?"

Ryu focused on cleaning the barrel and then double-checked it was clean after tilting it toward the light. "I like dependable weapons. I'm not hungry right now, but thanks for asking." He methodically reassembled the weapon.

"I bet you can do that with your eyes closed."

"If I had to. Hey, you asked me to remind you to check in with Flores. Did you do that? We've shuffled burner phones so many times I doubt Flores could call you."

"You've got a good point. Thanks." Julian opened the refrigerator, pulling out the ingredients for a turkey sandwich with tomato slices and mayonnaise. After fixing that, he added a few chips and a pickle to the plate. He placed the plate and a napkin at the far end of the table and sat. Then he pulled out his contact list and placed a call. The connection rolled to voice; he said, "Cryptocurrency," before disconnecting. Looking at Ryu, he casually remarked, "You were right. This number wasn't on his contact list. As soon as he figures out who left the message, he—" Julian grinned and pointed at the screen. He accepted the call and took a bite of his culinary creation.

"Where the hell have you been?" Flores' deep voice boomed. "Did you forget you owe me? The damn Chinese connection is refusing to sell me any precursor fentanyl materials. It was just like you said. I need crypto now."

After a few seconds, Flores barked, "Julian, are you there?"

He finished chewing and dabbed his mouth with the napkin. "Good morning, Flores. How nice to hear from you."

The soothing response had the desired effect. It made the man madder. Julian looked toward Ryu and took another bite.

"Julian, I'm in a hurry, and you sound like you're lounging around. How soon can I secure enough crypto to secure my materials from the oriental rats?"

"Flores, I need seed money to buy crypto on the open market. I've told you this before. The question isn't when I can send crypto to your suppliers, but when can your courier provide me the hard currency?" The silence stretched until Julian added, "Or did you forget that part?"

After another long pause, Flores replied, "Give me a location, and I'll have a courier there within a day with two hundred thousand U.S. dollars."

"Will you provide my fees, or do you want me to take that out of your investment funds? Expedited services come at a premium. I will process everything you bring to me in the Bahamas for a ten-percent processing fee, which—"

"What! I'll allow seven percent, period."

"Fine. For seven percent, I can get to it late next week or maybe the week after, depending on my other VIP customers who routinely pay a higher twelve percent. I was giving you a discount because of our relationship."

Flores roared, "Ten percent. Not a penny more. I may not know about cryptocurrency, but I excel at accounting. Where can he meet you? I will provide your FEE in a separate pouch."

"Tell him to meet me at the Cat Island Airport in the Bahamas. A white Beechcraft King Air 350 with blue trim is what I'm flying. Should we exchange secret agent code words? Do I need to give him a receipt?"

Flores chuckled with an unmistakable edge to his voice. "He'll say, 'for the Mateo affair.'"

Julian flinched, recalling Flores had taken care of his stepbrother as a favor.

"The crypto codes and wallets will be ready eight hours after receiving the funds. Flores, have the supplier give you their wallet addresses and include that with the funds. I'll make the transaction directly to them. Faster for you. I'll call you to confirm payment."

"Why eight hours? It should be quicker if you do it directly, Julian."

"I need to sanitize the funds by moving them through several other wallets and exchanges. That way, nothing gets picked up by authorities looking for money laundering. If it gets done quicker, I'll call sooner."

Can't Give Up Now

JW and Granger were granted access to their systems following thirty-six hours of downtime. Gracie sent JW a note that Auri and Satya might return to work soon. He shook his head, worried he had messed up as he desperately worked to compartmentalize the recovery of the missing team victims so he could resume the hunt and help guide this team.

JW released a frustrated groan and looked across the Gigazon toward his cousin, who was lackadaisically pushing his mouse around the screen in random circles. "We aren't making much progress this way, Grange. We need to focus."

"I know. During breakfast, I was convinced that Satya was doing better than me. She was building her case with Mom to work today because her school homework was completed. Mom was unconvinced. But my money's on our cousin. She said one thing that got me off my butt."

"What was that?"

"We have a shot at helping to stop Julian and to destroy the inner workings of the brothers' operations, but only if we use our knowledge, sources, and training."

"Ever notice how tough the women are in this family?"

Granger laughed. "You've met my mother, right?"

"Yep, and mine. Then there's Gracie, too. But we guys are no slouches." JW nodded and straightened his shoulders. He opened and displayed the data folder where Auri had added the birth certificate findings. "Okay. Let's build the detailed matrixes of each brother's known names, companies, homes, properties, and associates. We need to pinpoint the likely spot where Julian could be hiding."

JW was pleased that Granger was assembling the data for Mateo while he worked on Phillip.

Granger grumbled. "Those four victims were about our age. I feel sad that they felt their only way out was death. I'll admit, every once in a while, I go through a bad patch, but the report and those images are just…"

"Horrific. That's why we're doing this," JW acknowledged.

Granger added a few minutes later while he waited for a new search program to compile. "Lisbeth and Maria must have a lot of courage not to have given up. Maybe we should let them know they're not alone in their struggles. Maybe hearing that a stranger is on their side would boost their recovery."

Both boys were startled when Satya's workstation came into focus inside Gigazon. JW noticed her eyes didn't have their usual sparkle. She tilted her head and said, "I think we need to solve the problem and then see what we can do to encourage Lisbeth and Maria."

JW said, "How are you feeling, Satya?"

"Yes, I'm rattled by it, I admit. I know life isn't all puppies and rainbows, but I'm unwilling to ignore it when I can help even one person. Mom said I should take a break if I need to, but I love being a part of the R-Group and defending the rights of others."

Granger and JW flinched again as Auri interjected, "I had a similar discussion, cousin. It's time we do something about it."

ICABOD announced, "I've launched all your programs again, right where you left off. You are all winners with renewed determination. Let me know how I can help."

The nurse was monitoring their stats when Lisbeth and Maria opened their eyes. The brightness of the outside bouncing off the white walls through the windows caused them to squint. She was pleased they were alert enough to scan their room as if assessing their situation. The pair appeared tiny in the beds with crisp sheets and bed covers pulled up to their chins. The air smelled fresh and clean. They rotated their heads to follow the IV lines, spotting the monitors and sources of the random beeps and chimes. They caught sight of each other, and tears welled in their eyes.

A gentle voice spoke in Spanish. "Good afternoon, girls. I am your nurse, Linnea Tanner. You are in a Houston hospital specializing in emergency care."

"How did we get here?" asked Lisbeth in a panicked tone.

"You both were found unconscious in a room when authorities entered The Hotel. The emergency response team transported you here. You've been out for nearly two days."

"We can't pay," Maria said. "We have nothing. My head hurts."

"Don't worry, young lady. You each have a sponsor covering the expenses. We're working to wean you from the drugs we suspect you were forced to endure."

Lisbeth began crying. "It was awful, Miss Linnea. Please help us escape. We don't want to go back to that place."

Linnea approached her bed and gently dabbed at her tears before taking her vitals. "You're never going back to The Hotel.

Your sponsor would like you to recover and return to your home in Saint Kitts. Would you like that better?"

Lisbeth nodded, with a new rush of tears forming.

Maria looked over at the stack on the table between the beds. "Are those new clothes? Clean clothes?"

Linnea chuckled. "Yes, they're yours. Your sponsor is a generous woman who wants nothing but your drug-free recovery."

Maria pointed. "Those are beautiful flowers, Lisbeth. Are they ours?"

"Yes, and there is a note addressed to you both. Would you like me to read it?"

"Yes, please," the girls chorused.

Linnea picked it up and read.

> *Maria, Lisbeth,*
> *You've been through a lot, and we admire your*
> *courage. Don't give up. Keep going, because your*
> *friends Sophia and Elena helped us find you. You*
> *can make it and return home. One-day battles*
> *will be hard, but you have people on your side*
> *who will help.*
>
> *—Gracie*

Lisbeth and Maria stared at each other. "Who's Gracie?"

CHAPTER 21

Evading the Trackers

Nohea exited the San Juan jail onto the sidewalk of a busy street wearing worn Levis and an off-white, short-sleeved button-down shirt. The ends of his wet, dark hair curled a bit. At least he'd had a shower. He took stock of his meager possessions, surprised to still have the cash he had when arrested, and slid on his sunglasses. Grinding his teeth, he rubbed the sore areas of his arms where the physician had implanted the tracking chips. He resisted the temptation to rub his buttocks, which also got chipped.

He folded the prison release documents, shoved them into his back pocket, and headed toward his favorite electronics store. Once inside, he looked for an electronic surveillance and detection device for sweeping a room. He needed to confirm he was chipped, so he stopped at the counter.

"Good day. Can you show me a device that will detect tracking chips and if they are active?"

The clerk smiled, turned, and located a mid-range priced device. "This one works for home or office, sir."

Nohea extended his arm. "I need you to confirm by sweeping my arm, please."

She looked at him quizzically, then shrugged while powering up the device.

He grabbed it and confirmed the four sore spots were transmit-ready. "Damnit," he said with a scowl as he set the device on the counter. "I need a burner phone."

She presented him with two models. He chose the more expensive model because it included free texting and prepaid minutes. After paying for the phone, he turned it on and verified that it was operational before leaving the store without a thank you.

He walked down the sidewalk, using the phone app to search for a secondhand appliance thrift store. Several popped up. He called each in turn, asking if they carried old-style belt-driven vacuum cleaners. He called the last store on the search and asked his question again.

The elderly voice laughed. "Sure do, young man. How much to haul it away?"

Finally able to smile, Nohea replied, "I've got an important cleaning project to use it on, but I need to make certain it works. I'll pay you twenty dollars U.S. to test it."

"I'm sorry, I only do show and sell here. I'll make an exception for you for fifty."

His bright mood faded. "Are you located at 103 C. Sta. Cecilia?"

"I sure am. We're open until five," she verified.

"I'll be there in fifteen minutes."

Nohea disconnected the call. "It better generate two thousand volts of static electricity so I can fry these chips. Once they're toast, I'll be moving on."

JJ added Judith and Xiamara to the conference call. "Thanks for your efforts. We'll see if we can keep our eyes on our singing jailbird."

He shared the map of San Juan streets as it tracked Nohea's location.

"I wish I'd thought to get popcorn." Xiamara grinned as the tracking signals disappeared one by one.

Judith commented, "Just like you predicted, JJ. He deactivated all four the first chance he got. We should assume the special-issue cell phone will either be tossed or given to some needy homeless person."

JJ nodded. "No doubt. Tracking numbers five and six are now coming online. Without the response from the first four, they automatically went live."

Xiamara chewed her bottom lip and said," I sure am glad he didn't stop to buy new shoes with that phone."

JJ admitted, "Nice work getting the IMEI eSIM card number on the phone he bought at the electronics store. If he does change shoes, we still have that cell ID number to find him. All we have to do is wait until he jumps to his rendezvous point."

Judith lamented, "I'd like to be there to take him down."

JJ admonished, "Judith, you baited him perfectly. Plus, you identified his expensive shoes as ones he liked. At five hundred a pair, he's not going to lose those. Adding a chip to them was brilliant. You have him thinking we can't follow him to a meeting with Julian if he solves these chips. You've done what was needed. We debunked his lies regarding contact with Julian, plus Zee, your drawing of the black-lined tattoo of a skull behind his ear is an identifying mark he'll be hard-pressed to hide. Stop complaining."

Xiamara giggled, "JJ, you should know by now that Judith and I always want more."

CHAPTER 22

Forward Thinking the Past

The sun lazily dropped into the island's western side, signaling the peaceful twilight to wrap around the quiet Saint-Martin home like a lover protecting his heart's desire. Julian sat in a cushioned chair on the porch, staring wistfully into the horizon. In one hand, he gently whirled his cabernet in a bell-shaped crystal glass. His other extinguished the half-smoked cigarette. The warm breeze brought scents from the garden of flowers and the music of their insect companions. "It's lovely here, isn't it, Ryu?"

"This is one of my favorite places of yours. Are you contemplating our next move or daydreaming of better days ahead?"

Julian released a pent-up sigh. "Ever wonder how we got here and in this set of circumstances? Sometimes, I wonder how things would have turned out if I had been raised differently."

Ryu leaned back in the adjacent chair. "Nohea and I would still have been bouncers at the dive bar if you hadn't stepped in at the perfect moment. We didn't think that a drunk would pull a gun on us. No one wanted us after we got tossed from the Army Special Forces. Our side hustle should have been better thought out. I'm not even sure why I thought selling military-grade weapons to any cartel was a great idea. We probably would have been shot by the cartel buyers so no one could rat them out."

Julian sipped his wine. "Ryu, we all make impetuous decisions from time to time. Those actions make all the difference in the direction of our lives. I was raised to live outside the law from as early as I can remember. I almost didn't get to go to school. My mother insisted, so my old man relented. I was there long enough to learn on my own. I'm self-taught in most things because I'm a voracious reader. The old man liked that about me. I remember he pulled me and my half-brothers together one day in San Juan and told us we were part of his organization. From that day on we worked together. I wished he had lived long enough to tell us everything he had in mind. Sometimes fate steps in, and you're on your own."

Ryu admitted, "Julian, I've watched you for years. You're better than your brothers. They were so vicious that, in my estimation, they were always doomed to fail. You're different. We hustle business from the Darknet, but you care about your people. I guess I fight hard for you because you care for me."

Julian offered a paternal smile. He finished his wine and said, "Come, we must pick up Nohea. Is Princess fueled up for our flight? I want to be in the Bahamas before he gets there. We need to see who's tracking him."

Ryu challenged, "Why do you think someone's tracking him? You've said it twice, but I don't get it."

"The authorities had all those resources on San Juan trying to capture us after they secured Chloe and Nohea." He rubbed his hands together with a grin and a thumbs-up gesture. "But we escaped. They kept both of them incarcerated to lure us in. Then, a letter shows up addressed to Nohea. They must have read it because the next thing they did was release him with no bail requirements. There was no location named. They're betting Nohea will follow the instructions and lead them to us. I need him to work for us without tipping off the authorities. Once we pick up Nohea, we need to sanitize him."

"What do you mean, sanitize him, Julian?"

"I'm seeing a trend with Caribbean law enforcement installing tracking chips into high-value informants to keep tabs on them. I expect he's now chipped, and as a safety precaution, a human tracker will be on his tail. We need to intercept both. Text Harto to meet us at the regional airport."

Ryu nodded.

Sitting in the virtual space of the Gigazon with Auri, Satya shared her screen. They grinned, spotting the possibilities. "Auri, this is our first good clue. A link from this Zacarías points to all three of the criminal brothers. A few weeks after the real Julian, Mateo, and Phillip's death certificates were issued, Zacarias filed for copies of their birth certificates." She read to herself a bit more and laughed. "Now that's funny. He wrote a check to the magistrate for the facsimiles. He got the copies, the check bounced, and he skipped town."

"The original children would have been between six and ten," Auri commented, "so we should assume that the Zacarias children would be about the same age to match the birth records."

Satya nodded. "Zacarias has done time for petty stuff, but I think he's planning something big. For several months, he's been out of the limelight. Perhaps he learned his lesson. He took a legitimate day job to make ends meet."

"Satya, what kind of crime would you be planning with your henchmen if they were seven years old?"

"Auri, you wouldn't use them for heavy lifting but for deception and under-the-radar of suspicion from others. A bright, personable little kid comes into your place of business and innocently asks for…fill in the blank. If he can pull off the sweet, innocent-looking child act to command the owner's attention, the stage is set for Papa to come in and rob."

Auri smirked. "You're right. That's what I would do and snitch all the candy."

Satya asked, "ICABOD, can you cross-check store robberies using young boys in the same proximity and timeframe that our research is suggesting?"

ICABOD replied, "Several jewelry store and pharmacy incidents coincide with our timeline. The stolen jewels may explain Julian's fixation on the precious stone angle we've been looking to connect. It could be the pharmacy thefts of painkillers influenced Mateo."

Auri continued to read the account and said, "It looks like it was a great business model until it wasn't. Zacarias moved frequently, but the local jewelry stores and pharmacies were notified to be on the watch for this type of customer. One store owner didn't go along with the robbery and used a shotgun to end the robbery spree. Three mothers surfaced, claiming the boys were abducted by a crazed man who could not abide by the court orders saying the mothers had sole custody. Once they secured their boys, the moms never showed up for their court dates."

ICABOD reported, "My information shows that when they reached their early teens, each boy fell in with different gangs. They remained in contact with one another. Phillip's mother got him into schools in the U.S., where he graduated and started a semi-legitimate business with muscle to get him on top. Mateo enjoyed the cartel world too much and worked his way up to run his organization of illegal drug distribution and human trafficking. Julian seems to have stayed clear of the grimy narcotics and human trade but was an early adopter of cryptocurrency and money laundering. His best customers were Phillip and Mateo."

Satya summarized, "Not much to go on for Julian's business except that he helped launder money for his brothers. We can only surmise that he developed an affinity for precious stones. Precious stones are not a solid investment like gold or silver."

Auri laughed. "You can't eat the silly stones. They're not a medium of everyday transactions, so he must have an established network of buyers to sell quietly and quickly as stones become available. I think he's a wholesaler of jewels."

ICABOD confirmed, "As a wholesaler, one would buy in lots and sell to retailers in smaller quantities. But if you are harvesting unclaimed stones, all you have is your labor expense with a tremendous upside in profit when selling."

Satya bounced excitedly in her chair. "Let's get JW on the line to discuss our theory."

CHAPTER 23

The Needed Harvest

Gracie landed early in the morning after a smooth flight to San Juan. She left her bag at the hotel for the overnight stay. The Uber dropped her at the doorstep of her destination. She exited the vehicle and smoothed her Anatomie top of Pima cotton with a rounded neck and elegant ruched sleeves over her Kate pants. She carried her briefcase with the referenced information. The door for the San Juan Treasury Department was at the end of the atrium. She knocked politely. Waiting a few more minutes, she tried again, louder. "Does anyone work here?"

A monotoned voice replied, "The door's unlocked. Turn the doorknob to let yourself in."

Glancing at the worn walls and last century's furniture, Gracie empathized with the tired-appearing workplace. She smoothed her expression and approached the desk clerk. "Good day. I have an appointment with the director. My name is Gracie Rodreguiz."

The short, heavy-set woman, who was covered in a massive leaf-print dress, rested her ample bosom on the counter and said, "Regarding?"

Gracie shook her head to avoid getting pulled into a confrontation. "I'm here regarding lending on the finds from a sunken Spanish Galleon. Do I get to see the director?"

A man's voice came from behind Gracie. "Jameel, I'll take it from here. Please, Ms. Rodreguiz, this way. We can talk in my office."

The man glared at Jameel, who shrugged indifferently. Gracie noticed the young woman was not cursed with self-awareness.

Jameel turned to face the reception area, where several people had entered in the last few minutes. "Next," she called.

Once in the director's office, the man extended his hand. "I'm Jacobo Hassan. Nice to meet you. I do apologize for the rudeness on behalf of my clerk. We are understaffed, and those we can hire for what we pay are short on manners."

"I understand, and it's not a problem. Thank you for seeing me."

"Please have a seat. May I offer you a coffee or water?"

Gracie set her briefcase on his desk. "As I stated over the phone, Mr. Hassan, I'm with the World Bank in their international lending division. My organization is interested in getting current on your loan for your previously funded development projects. According to all reports, I am especially interested in lending to this region because your sunken ship recovery business seems to be increasing."

Jacobo sagged into his worn leather chair and sighed. "Ms. Rodreguiz, we have no shortage of requests to build needed infrastructure for our population. We are a poor country trying to join the twenty-first century with an old-fashioned economy, annual hurricane threats, and subsistent farming. We need schools, wastewater treatment, and reliable electricity to withstand the next tropical storm. I must speak candidly, Ms. Rodreguiz; we don't have the collateral or the tax revenue to repay your organization. The elected officials simply don't want to become another debtor nation that is owned by one of the crazed billionaires that shoot rockets off for entertainment."

Chuckling, she said, "Please call me Gracie. I think you misunderstand. Let's take this one step at a time. My research suggests that from the mid-1600s to the early 1800s, the Spanish tried to haul all the gold, silver, and precious stones from Central and South America to retire rich in Spain. The British had the same idea: using the Spanish to gather up the cargo, and they confiscated them. Between the British and the tropical storms, the Caribbean is littered with still untold wealth on the sea floor. My observation is that wealth could make an attractive collateral incentive."

"My team has been watching the tug-of-war between Spain, Columbia, Peru, and the Armada group over the ownership of the Spanish Galleon the *San Jose* near Columbia. Estimates vary, but the value seems centered on twenty billion dollars. That kind of collateral can fund many projects for the Columbian government. I would submit that the sunken treasures still undiscovered in the Caribbean could help underwrite building projects on many islands in your same predicament."

Jacobo's face darkened as he angrily stated, "We must fight the underwater predators for what they take. The shipwreck treasure hunters care only about themselves. They invest in high-tech equipment to harvest the sunken wealth but won't pay taxes to build civic infrastructure. They would rather shoot their way out with the stolen loot, while our meager coast guard must rely on U.S. ships, also in short supply, to defend against these pirates. If you think we can partner with these galleon thieves, you are very much mistaken."

Gracie smiled charmingly. "Jacobo, one step at a time. First, is there an appetite among the islands to collaborate to get the needed investment to build the infrastructure? If yes, then projects must be evaluated and ranked for build order. Then, the terms and conditions must be agreed upon, and the collateral will be discussed. I told you I had a special interest in this region. Perhaps a consortium of like-minded investors, willing to harvest the undiscovered sunken treasure scattered around the Caribbean for a percentage, would be attractive."

Jacobo's face was etched with new possibilities as she continued, "We have some investors with some newly designed equipment that might just be what is needed to fund a Caribbean initiative of this size. Do you have contacts on other islands who are peers we could talk to?"

"Ms. Rodreguiz, I mean Gracie, I like how you think. I'll make some calls."

Giddy with excitement, Julian stepped back and smiled at the perfect arrangement of displays with no distracting cables. He eagerly awaited the upcoming encounter, mentally anticipating each delightful element.

"Don't you want to clean up before you power her up? I can bring you some wine and snacks if you wish," Ryu offered.

"A bit of libation sounds good. I can't wait for us to get re-acquainted. It's been lonely without her."

Julian watched Ryu scuttle off to the kitchen. He powered up the equipment, stroking the virtual reality goggles. "We'll be together soon, but I have to leave early in the morning. Tonight is ours, my sweet." He grinned as he headed for the shower, selecting a silk robe.

CHAPTER 24

The Hidden Predator

After several circles around the small runway off Exuma Sound tucked away on the Cat Island Bahamas, Julian landed his Beechcraft King Air 350 in a practiced maneuver. He headed toward an open spot near the terminal of the local airport of Hawk's Nest Creek. He commented, "I approached roundabout to see if anyone else is landing or ready to take off. Surprises are unacceptable when flying, and smaller airports don't always have their radar in good working order."

Ryu snorted and pointed. "There's Harto, looking like a small boy anxious about his first day at a new school."

"I prefer the people who work for me devoted and uncomplicated, Ryu. I'm sorry he riles you, but I trust him almost as much as I trust you. For this effort, he's perfect and won't be compromised."

As they exited the plane, Ryu sarcastically muttered, "I appreciate that, but I draw the line at a hug or scratching his ears when I greet him."

Julian's look silenced any further disparaging remarks.

Harto beamed when he saw them. Julian intercepted the attempted hug with a pat on the back.

Several people closed in on them as if hoping for a celebrity with whom they could get a selfie. Julian leaned toward Harto and insisted, "Let's get somewhere quiet where we can talk privately."

Harto led the way to an undersized, unwashed older SUV that promised a cramped ride no matter how close they were to the destination. Hawk's Nest Resort and Marina looked inviting as Harto secured a front-row parking spot. They entered the open area with a front desk on the right for guests to check in. On the left, he spotted what appeared to be a well-stocked bar based on the top-shelf labels Julian noticed. The sign on the bar indicated that the attendant would return soon. No one was in the surrounding area.

"I bet this lounge is wild at night when the fishermen return with their catches," suggested Julian.

Harto nodded. "They tend to party all night after being at sea. They also love to talk after a night of serious drinking. I have received many tips from the loose lips in this bar."

Julian leaned forward and frowned with a look of severe concern. "You told me you couldn't drink alcohol, but you socialize here?"

Julian noticed Ryu was tensed into full alert.

Harto laughed. "With my diabetes, drinking is off the table and has been for years. But it doesn't affect my eyes or ears. Drinkers share their stories. I only have to sift out the embellishments from the discussion to get tasty information. That's how I've learned how the treasure hunters work, especially when they say a ship has been cleaned out."

He released the breath he'd subconsciously held. Julian spotted the colorful chairs and umbrellas in the pool area. "Nohea should be here as the extra pair of hands in a day or two. He has diving certification. I left airplane tickets for him, using my standard alias protocol at San Juan and in Nassau. That should bring him here. If needed, I've added funds for his housing at this resort, though I would rather he be under your control night and day. I consider you responsible for this project and hold you accountable. Nohea will push to be in charge unless you set the ground rules upfront. I don't want that call from you complaining. He is here to take orders from you, not dictate."

Relief showed on Harto's face as the tension lines visibly faded.

Julian continued, "From this location on the east side of the Bahama Islands, you can easily access the target salvage area. With the overall time slip, I need faster results. Nohea is likely being tracked so my competitors can discover details of our operation. He must be cleaned and sanitized before you take him to the prime ocean location. Do you understand?"

The lovable puppy dog of a man suddenly turned into a fierce, formidable predator like one might find in the jungle. Harto bristled, and his eyes narrowed. He growled, "Julian, no one will risk this operation. I take my responsibilities seriously, and this project is my only priority. He will know I am serious; I swear. I will explain the rules and test his swimming skills after he's been swept. Do you expect a human tracker as well? What are my instructions for that?"

Julian glanced at Ryu, who appeared stunned at the shift in the man he had previously mocked.

"They may follow Nohea to find me. If they get to me, everything we have built will vanish."

The killer's glare in Harto's eyes was unmistakable. "Understood. I will take care of everything."

"Do you know where New Bright Freedom Settlement Airport is located?"

"Of course, but it doesn't have a marina like we have here."

"I know, but you have a car. If you locate any stones, use our signal exchange, and I will fly there twenty-four hours later at dawn."

"That's a good idea. I can drive there and have the twins watch Nohea, saying I've gone for provisions."

"Perfect."

Julian unfastened his seat belt after powering off the King Air. He exited to stretch his legs and wait for the funds to arrive. Ryu followed, keeping a watchful eye out for anyone being too attentive.

"I'm gonna see if the manager knows when the next winged bus arrives," said Ryu. "I don't like us standing out here where everyone can study us."

Julian smirked. "The text from Flores indicated mid-morning. Go ask while I have a smoke."

Ryu hurried inside and returned a few minutes later. "The man said ten a.m. arrival according to the flight plan he'd received. How are we supposed to recognize the courier? We can't very well ask people if they are *The One*."

Julian chuckled. "Flores will send one of his lieutenants. They all have a bunch of ugly tattoos, starting at the neck on every exposed piece of skin. I'll even bet no one will walk close due to the nasty body odor. Plus, he'll have a large gym bag full of currency."

Julian smoked another cigarette while Ryu paced.

Several minutes later, Ryu scanned the horizon and checked his watch. "There it is, Julian. It's on time."

"Let's move toward our aircraft, our identifier to the courier. We exchange the code word for the bag and then make the return trip. I'll need to get the currency to our friendly bank for transfer. Then I can return to the house and start cleaning the funds from my laptop. The sooner that's done, the sooner I get my commission."

Minutes after landing, the plane taxied to the terminal. The gate person moved the stairs to the open hatch to allow the people to deplane. Julian studied each passenger and mentally eliminated them one by one.

An oversized man turned sideways and stooped over to come through the door. Julian smirked as Ryu did a double-take in disbelief.

The man paused when he reached the ground to survey the area. As soon as he saw Julian and Ryu by the King Air, he ambled in their direction. He swung a large gym bag to get the long carry strap around his almost non-existent neck.

The man seemed to grow bigger as he approached. When he reached within a yard of Julian and Ryu, he towered over them. In broken English with a deep bass voice, he asked, "Is this a Beechcraft King's Air?"

Julian nodded.

"Are you Julian?"

"Yes. Are you from Flores?"

The man nodded.

Feeling emboldened, Julian asked, "Then give me the passphrase."

"This is for your Mateo favor." The man tossed the heavy gym bag at Ryu and turned toward the terminal to wait for the next flight out. Ryu staggered as the weight hit square in his chest. Julian walked up the steps to his plane. "Come on. I want to get back to Saint-Martin and process this currency. I don't want Flores to feel he needs to send that guy here. What a hulk."

CHAPTER 25

It Looks Like This...

Granger smugly looked across the Gigazon and said, "We're jamming. ICABOD and I have outdone ourselves on this one."

JW cast a sarcastic look towards Granger. "Ever notice how you say that just before we find something wrong?"

Satya and Auri suppressed snickers.

"Not always," Granger protested. "I admit now and again that I've been a little premature in claiming victory over a task. Yet these are usually little niggling details easily rectified."

Resting his chin in his hand, JW rolled his eyes. "Okay, how about this? You and ICABOD built an exquisite three-dimensional model to demonstrate what a mashup of light detection and ranging, known as LIDAR, with targeted mapping and ground penetrating radar, would look like. You presume a water monitoring drone would be pulled along by a cable with a fiber optic connection to pump the images back onto the ship for processing. I would question if the power source for the onboard data processing could be supported with a 110-volt plugin at the marina and make routine trips to the Little Bahama Islands reef."

"There are long extension cords, JW," Granger stated with conviction.

"Master Granger," advised ICABOD, "this is why the refrigerator-sized battery was part of the original design with the optional gasoline-powered generator to recharge the battery."

"Fine. Put the battery back into the model." After a pout that dissolved when Auri shook his head, Granger asked, "Any idea why Gracie wanted this model built?"

"She sent additional instructions asking that schematics be generated of the 3-D model and sent to her and JJ's team so they could see how the jewel hunter mechanism might appear," advised JW. "She's hoping this will help narrow the search for a suitable watercraft with the needed equipment. She's convinced that Nohea will be close to the precious stone harvesting. With any luck, Julian will, too. Xiamara and Judith believe Julian placed great trust in Nohea, so he is the logical head of this operation."

"I see an unidentified problem with this model," interjected ICABOD. "For this equipment to be effective, they must narrow the sampling rate focus to inches rather than feet. When they do that, the data sampling will swell to epic gigabytes of data that no human can sift through efficiently. The increased data modeling is only valuable if augmented with an artificial search engine with a well-constructed program able to sort and grade the data captured. The total data storage will likely need a huge cloud data warehouse."

"It's unlikely they have the necessary satellite for wireless transmission of this much data," Satya remarked. "They'll have to perform the data capture on their ship, then run it back to a shore link, upload it, and repeat that process. That much shuttling is bound to get noticed."

"Agreed, Satya," confirmed JW.

Gracie became the legal benefactor for the care of Lisbeth and Maria. She paid their medical expenses and was pleased they'd been weaned from the drugs. Last week, the private hospital staff raised concerns over a list of problems, including depression, limited physical strength regardless of diet changes, concentration issues, and sleep deprivation. Their psychiatrist related his fears that they were suffering from post-traumatic stress disorder. He asked Gracie to approve a sleep study, which she agreed to if he explained the process to the girls. Both decided to participate, stating they wanted to feel better. The doctor sent the recording of the sleep session.

"Oh my God," Gracie mumbled as tears filled her eyes. She watched Lisbeth thrashing in her bed with violent moves and whimpering. "The poor girl is suffering nightmares. Maria couldn't sleep because of the noise. Oh, dear." The image of Maria lying in bed listening to her friend's anguish, staring at the ceiling, gave her chills. Gracie jumped and covered her mouth when Lisbeth sat up screaming, her arms flailing until she woke. The poor darling looked about the room anxiously with tears streaming down her cheeks. Maria curled into a fetal position, pulled up her covers, and said, "Same dream?"

"Yes. Will they ever go away?" whispered Lisbeth.

"I hope so," replied Maria.

The recording ended. Gracie put her face into her hands and cried for a while. She finally pulled herself together and called the doctor. 'Hi, Dr. Harman, I've watched the tape. It's tragic beyond my wildest imagines. What are the next steps?"

"Can you come so we can meet with both young ladies? They would feel better if you explained your role and our recommendations for their treatment."

"Certainly. How about tomorrow morning, say eight-thirty?"

"Perfect."

CHAPTER 26

Bonding

Linnea Tanner made her morning rounds, saving her favorite patients for last. She walked in the door with a fixed smile. "Good morning. Did you have a good rest or another rough night?"

Maria replied with a yawn, "Lisbeth had the same nightmare."

"I'm sorry, Lisbeth, you didn't sleep well. Maria, thank you for sharing." She cleared her throat after updating their respective charts. "Good news: A visitor will meet with you shortly."

Lisbeth straightened, appearing terrified. "Who is it now? We must have talked to everyone here in Houston. How long do we have to stay here? I don't want to be examined by another social worker."

"Your doctor made arrangements for you to meet Gracie, your benefactor. She'll be here soon. You might want to wear one of the new outfits she gave you."

Maria started bouncing on her bed, engaged and animated. "She's coming to meet us? How exciting. I bet she's beautiful."

Lisbeth jumped to the floor, with the corners of her lips turned up for the first time since she was admitted. "What time is it now?" she asked. "How much longer before we get to meet her? Maria, we have to fix our hair. I wanna look nice for Ms. Gracie."

Linnea checked her watch. "Hurry and take your showers. It's a good time to wash your hair, too."

Maria frowned. "I wish we had a little mascara and maybe lip gloss."

Linnea reached into her pocket, extracted those exact items, and passed them around. "I'll stay here until she arrives if you want."

Maria nodded excitedly.

"I'll get our clothes, Maria," announced Lisbeth. You hurry and shower. Then it's my turn."

Maria scurried to the bathroom while Lisbeth selected the best outfits. "Thank you for the makeup, Nurse Tanner."

"You're going to make fine young women," she chuckled and sat in the chair by the door.

Gracie knocked. Nurse Tanner shook her hand and motioned her inside. "Were they upset about my arrival?"

"Hardy, they're both in the bathroom trying to decide how to impress you." She walked over and knocked on the door. "Ladies, Ms. Gracie is here."

The door partially opened, showing big eyes and smiles before it was shut again. "*Un momento, por favor.*"

"*Si, tome su tiem,*" Gracie replied with a soft laugh.

Lisbeth said, "What if she doesn't like us? What if we're not pretty enough?"

Maria smirked. "She's not going to be an old hag or be like Madam Chloe."

"Eww," Lisbeth said. "That *biah* was a liar."

Gracie shook hands with the nurse before she left, giddy at the prospect of being with the girls. "I've got this." She leaned near the door and asked, "Lisbeth, Maria, I spoke to your doctor, and he said we could eat in the cafeteria if you like."

The girls squealed with delight and opened the door.

Maria walked out and did a quick spin. "Ms. Gracie, I'm Maria. Thank you for this outfit. Do I look alright?"

Her friend followed and did a curtsey. "Call me Lisbeth. Please. We decided you're pretty."

"Thank you. Please call me Gracie. I think you are lovely."

"Hi, Gracie," they said in unison.

"I'm glad the clothes fit."

Maria shuffled her feet and said, "Thank you for everything. We understand you are sponsoring us, but we're not certain why you would."

"That's a fair statement. The best way I can explain it is that I learned of the horrible place you were kept in, and it made me sad. I wanted to help you get a fresh start in life." Gracie tapped her lips and added, "I want to understand what you want for your future. Perhaps I can help you achieve your dreams. When I was your age, dreams were a huge part of life. I don't want your dreams robbed from you. I don't own you. You owe me nothing except the truth when discussing various options. Does that make sense?"

They both nodded with shining eyes on the brink of tears.

"Consider me an older sister."

They rushed her for a hug.

Maria stepped away first and ran a finger under her eyes. "I'd like to eat in the cafeteria. How about you, Lisbeth?"

Lisbeth nodded and stood next to her friend.

"Let's go." Gracie opened the door and headed toward the elevator, feeling a connection that made her heart soar. The cafeteria was on the first floor. The pair looked at everything and whispered at different items. They went through all the options and selected more food than Gracie had imagined they could consume. She suspected they'd been starved to a degree while in captivity.

"You can always return for seconds if you missed anything." She gently encouraged.

The girls selected a table on the side with a window view of a well-tended garden.

Maria appeared so pleased when she said, "You are nice."

Gracie chuckled. "Thank you. I think you're both rather special. Now let's eat, I'm starved."

They giggled, and the tension eased.

"Would you prefer speaking in Spanish?" she asked in that language.

They nodded and spoke between mouthfuls. She slowly geared the discussion toward their situation, away from the television shows they'd been watching.

"How is your recovery going, in your opinion?"

"I like some counseling sessions," Maria said, "but Lisbeth doesn't like talking when we're in them. The physical therapy is all right, but we still get tired and are easily distracted."

It took a few minutes of this sort of discussion from Maria before Lisbeth worked up enough rage to speak.

"You don't know what we've been through or seen," Lisbeth spat. "I wake up in the middle of the night screaming because of the nightmares—every night. You don't have to live with those images of getting drugged and brought to a big city where everyone takes advantage. I'll never get rid of the mind-numbing replays in my mind. We're poor girls in our last year of high school, ready to earn a living as something other than what we were told to do." Lisbeth dropped her fork on the tray and sobbed into her napkin.

Maria stroked her hand to soothe her. "After she wakes up screaming, I get to sleep with my nightmares. I don't scream."

Gracie sighed and reached a hand to each of them. "You're right. I don't have the same specific experiences, but I know something about your nightmare scenarios. Another portion of the criminals who took you also grabbed me and my best friend from college when we were on a cruise. We were knocked out and readied for transport to our new owners. I wouldn't be here if my friends hadn't found and rescued us. I suffered from nightmares for weeks until my therapist helped me find ways to cope. I still follow up with him when something gets me down." Gracie stepped away for extra napkins and allowed them to collect themselves.

Maria and Lisbeth dried their eyes and returned to their food.

Several minutes later, Gracie continued, "My team and I are after the last of the three criminals involved in the circle of evil. I was a victim, just like you. Remember, we are survivors. I'll bet you want justice."

They both nodded.

Gracie smiled and offered, "Ladies, it will take some time to heal the emotional scars, but you'll get there with a little help from friends and perhaps a great therapist like mine. Finish eating. I'll take you back upstairs. You've got healing to do before you can get that justice. I'll help you, and the doctor is working on a new treatment that should help you feel better soon."

CHAPTER 27

Can't See It from Here

Two days later, the twin-engine turboprop touched down at the postage-stamp-sized airport. The pilot taxied to the terminal adjacent to a one-step ramp parked on the tarmac. Several small aircraft were parked in neat rows, secured to the ground with ropes. Nohea and ten other passengers walked down the stairs to the tarmac, grabbed their bags, and headed toward the building. Nohea spotted a gate attendant holding a sign with his alias name.

The gate attendant asked as he approached. "You Loane?"

Nohea nodded, offering his boarding pass as proof.

With barely a glance, the gate attendant handed him an envelope and disappeared into the building. Ripping the envelope open, he discovered the note inside. It contained a single word: *Osvaldo*. Nohea nodded thoughtfully as he shredded the paper, distributing the pieces to several trash bins.

He looked around the quaint regional airport. Gentle breezes tempered the Bahamian humidity, rustling the palm trees, bringing the fragrant scents of local flora to his nostrils, and carrying away the stench of jet fuel.

"I prefer the casual security of regional airports. Thankfully, Julian paid for premium security clearances at each stop. I've been treated like a visiting dignitary," muttered Nohea after receiving back his manufactured identity documents with the current stamps. He hailed a taxi outside the building. "I need transport to the Hawk's Creek Resort," he demanded, paying with a few U.S. dollars from the stash provided by the two women he considered traitorous bitches. En route, he picked at the scabs from one of the chip removal locations and smiled at the ease of his escape from detection after the removal. He silently applauded Julian's insistence that escape and rendezvous procedures were routine exercises practiced each time they were modified. It worked like clockwork.

Sitting in front of the boat's data collection screen, Harto struggled to remain upbeat with the daunting task of sifting through the data he'd collected. Still, his anxiety continued to mount with the unexpected roadblock, like looking for a needle in a haystack.

Turning toward his nephews, he said, "Blake, please check that the charger is connected. Bradley, can you give me the percentage of data uploaded? I know it's a slow process." He was grateful for their steadfast loyalty and helping keep the operation in order as able-bodied young shipmates.

He returned to the viewing of the captured images, mumbling to himself. "Come on, buddy, you can do this. All you need is a few good stones from this data, and then we're over the side and into the water to bring them onto the deck. Julian will get the extra gear and software, then the first main harvest. It's bucket time for the harvest. I can't wait for us to be rich."

He was interrupted when someone hollered from the marina dock. "You the skipper of the *Osvaldo*?"

Blake and Bradley turned, standing shoulder to shoulder, ready to confront the stranger.

The man, dressed in baggy jeans, a faded blue shirt, and close-cropped black hair, added, "An unusual name for a fishing vessel."

Not in a cheerful mood, Harto snapped, "It means God's rule, or divine power, for those educated in local lore."

"Would you be Harto since you're standing on the *Osvaldo*? I'm Loane, also known as Nohea. I was instructed to report here."

Harto remained guarded, though some of his iciness vanished as he surveyed the build of his new helper with a touch of envy. "Good. I will engage you quickly after we review a few funda-mentals so you can join *my* operation."

Harto reached for his electronic scanner and moved to scan Nohea before he got on deck. He nodded to his nephews, who blocked Nohea from leaving on either side. Harto was satisfied that Nohea appeared taken aback at his defensive approach. Nohea backed up cautiously.

Harto narrowed his eyes and cocked his head. "I sanitize all personnel before they are allowed aboard. The expectation is to remove any digital parasites."

Nohea bristled, centered his stance, and clenched his fists, ready to fight. "You better call Julian to get your instructions straightened out. I've already done that, so there is no need—"

Harto stepped onto the dock, closing the distance in a heartbeat, then hitting Nohea hard in the gut. The unexpected punch caused Nohea to drop to his knees and rock forward, forcing him to use his hands to keep from faceplanting on the rough, worn planks.

Harto quickly used the wand to scan his new helper's body while the compromised man gasped for air. The wand found the four disabled chips. Harto verified the reading each time the device chirped. "It appears you defeated the embedded chips, but you are healing. We wouldn't want any blood in the water during diving."

Harto modified the setting and made one last sweep. The wand chirped as it picked up the chips in the shoes. "Well, well, well. It looks like you missed the ones in your shoes. Blake, please take off his shoes. Bradley, drop them at the end of the pier, weighted to sink."

Looking down at Nohea, Harto smirked. "I hope you like the flip-flop replacements for your footwear because that's all you get. Your cell phone…" Harto said, extending his hand and wiggling his fingers in a give-it-here motion.

CHAPTER 28

And Then He Was Gone

JJ clucked his tongue as the last two tracking chips in Nohea's shoes vanished from his location map. Sporting a very sour face, JJ picked up his cell phone and dialed Brayson.

Brayson immediately answered. "What's up, boss?"

"The last two chips just died. Nohea's location went dark. I've sent you those geo-coordinates. I'm confident he made it to a key destination, but they double-checked him to be safe. I have only the SIM card number to track him, but I suspect that…" He sighed, feeling slightly defeated. "Yeah, there it goes, too. They're very thorough, making sure nobody can follow them. At least we know where he landed."

Brayson finished the thought. "The faster we arrive at that location, the better chance we have of getting eyes on him. Hopefully, he's with Julian. I volunteer for this hunt-and-seek mission, but I require my partner to join. We work better together."

"No kidding, she keeps you out of trouble," chuckled JJ. "His last known location is Hawk's Nest Creek on the east side of Cat Island. This is where I need to remind you that these ruthless people have defeated our tracking methods. They're smart criminals who've evaded capture and know someone is hunting them. I suspect they will be looking for a human hunter to appear on the scene. Keep out of trouble. Our team speculates that the goal is a hunt in the Lesser Bahama Island shallows for the *Nuestra Señora de las Maravillas* that sank three hundred and sixty-eight years ago. It reportedly carried gobs of treasure plundered from the new world destined for Spain. The hurricane season took it to pay homage to the sea gods, was noted in one report."

"I watched a show years ago on treasure recovery and who owns what. That ship's name is unusual enough that I recall it was highlighted in the documentary. Treasure hunters maintained that it was salvaged to death at the turn of the century. Why does our team think this is the target?"

"The recovery of the gold and silver is well documented. But not the precious stones. Based on what you and Marian discovered, Julian's target treasure is gemstones that have not previously been recovered at the same level as those on various manifests. Newer technology may provide techniques for recovering gemstones strewn over the ocean floor for hundreds of years. If this technology does what we think it can, harvesting precious stones lost at sea in the Caribbean will fund multiple civil projects."

"Wow, JJ. We've found yet another battlefront to wrestle leading-edge technology away from bad actors. It seems the scenarios never change, only the locations and newest technologies. AI opens so many doors."

Still annoyed and sore from the gut punch he received from Harto, Nohea poked and prodded at the diving gear, almost ignoring the monotone instructions. His dislike of the man who thought he was in charge increased by the minute.

Harto's loud shout pulled him into the moment. "If you're bored, Nohea, I'll find you a maid job at the marina. Julian said you might resist taking orders, but he didn't think you'd be a jerk."

Nohea was stunned that Julian placed him below this Harto in the pecking order. It irritated him.

"Suit up for diving in thirty meters of water to help me find our prize, or I'll have Bradley tie you up below deck," promised Harto.

Reluctantly reeling in his contempt, Nohea glared. "I can do this. Show me the target images again. I'm ready to enter the splash zone and prove my value."

Twenty minutes later, they hovered over the target area, with no other watercraft visible on the horizon. Harto cut the engines and showed Nohea the images on the monitoring screen to confirm the correct position. Bradley and Blake dropped anchor and kept watch for other boats.

Harto stated, "You boys know what to do if any visitors show up."

Nohea was amazed when both responded, "Yes, sir."

After checking their tanks and gear, he and Harto secured their masks and then backed over the side into the gentle waves. Below the surface, Harto used hand signals to direct their descent toward the target area. Sharks were unlikely in this area, but Nohea realized he was on point to alert Harto if that situation changed. That left Harto concentrating solely on using his hammer to chip and uncover any stones.

Nohea dutifully monitored the area for silent intruders, primarily for his safety. As they swam and chipped toward the primary target area, Nohea spotted something interesting and went deeper to investigate. Surprised, he exposed a small pile of shiny objects under some coral overhanging a modest depression.

Forgetting his assigned duties of visual security, he used his hammer to dislodge the cache of coins. The more he dug, the more coins he discovered. His giddiness about the find absorbed his attention, and he lost his situational awareness.

Suddenly, something slammed into Nohea, jarring him back to his immediate surroundings. Startled, he took a few seconds to realize Harto had crashed into him with a weighted bag and hammer. Nohea checked his tank airtime and knew he had enough air to secure the coins. He motioned with his hands downward at the find. Harto shook his head no and pointed up to the boat.

CHAPTER 29

Take the Best,
Leave the Rest

Harto gestured to the surface. Nohea shook his head no. He pointed downward, protesting at ignoring the discovery. Harto reached over, yanked off Nohea's facemask, and pushed him upwards. Even with the short distance back to the surface and their boat, Harto continued to prod Nohea.

They broke through to the surface, where Harto pulled off his facemask and demanded, "You were told to ignore the gold. We are after the precious stones which I was able to recover." He held up the heavy, bulging bag in triumph.

Nohea was still fussing and splashing to get the salt water out of his lungs and eyes. "Didn't you see that cache of coins? Even melted down for the gold instead of an open bidding forum for coins, we'd be rich."

Harto reached over to whack him on the top of his head with an open palm. "You fool! All the world's treasure hunters have inventoried the gold coin minting and know where they would have gone down. As soon as word gets out that we salvaged gold coins from a named ship, the closest government shows up to claim our hard work, Spain's attorneys come with their claim, and then the lawyers from every rival treasure-hunting organization drag us into court insisting they were there first.

You'll die in court penniless, lucky to live through the ordeal. Leave the gold coins be."

Their thrashing on top of the water seemed to cool their tempers.

Nohea quietly insisted, "Give me my facemask to retrieve the hammer you made me drop."

Harto eyed him suspiciously. "Give me your marker balloons. I don't want you to leave a trail to return here."

Nohea disconnected the two marker balloons and tossed them to Harto. "Happy now?"

Harto barked, "Get the hammer and meet me at the boat to load the equipment. It's time for us to leave."

After replacing his mask and snorkel, Nohea dove to retrieve the hammer. Seizing it, he looked around to be sure he wasn't followed, then drove a holding spike to fasten the marker balloon he had withheld. After several hits on the spike, he returned to the surface while he verified the coordinates on his waterproof GPS device. Once he broke the surface, he grinned, thinking about the coming back that would make him rich. He had already begun planning how to return for the treasure and vanish forever.

CHAPTER 30

Getting to See,
Not Wanting to See

The short flight to Nassau allowed Marian and Brayson to enjoy their role as newlyweds. Marian wrapped her arm around Brayson, kissing his cheek seconds before the flight attendant set down their beverages.

In her tailored blue uniform, the spunky redheaded flight attendant teased, "Will you two be able to wait to check in to the hotel?"

Marian batted her eyelashes with feigned innocence. "Do you have other options on this aircraft?"

They both laughed.

"Now, honey," chided Brayson, squeezing her hand and then adding a gentlemanly kiss, "let's not get into trouble again. The judge made us promise to behave in public."

The flight attendant giggled and proceeded to serve the other passengers.

Brayson leaned and whispered in her ear. "Perhaps we're being a little over the top. We don't want too much attention."

"I'm not acting, sweetie," Marian said in a sultry, saucy voice. Then she patted his arm. "And, yes, I like being on top."

He inclined his glass for a toast. "Cheers!"

"It sure is warm in here." He shifted in his seat and then caressed her knee. "The flight seems a lot longer than I expected. Can't wait to arrive at the hotel."

She flashed a delighted grin, knowing he was attuned to her mood. They exchanged an easy banter about the beaches and watersports they planned loudly enough for anyone to hear.

"Folks, we'll be on final approach to Hawk's Nest Creek Airport in ten minutes," announced the pilot through the speakers. "Everyone, please return to your seats and fasten your seatbelts. Your bags will be available at the gangway."

The flight attendant leaned toward them as she was checking seatbelts. "Only half an hour until you can settle into the delightful resort. Have fun, you lovebirds."

The approach was rougher than Marian preferred, so she held Brayson's hand. She could nail a sniper-style shot from a thousand yards, but the bouncing air currents' rise and fall messed with her insides. "The seatbelts were a good idea."

"Yay, we landed right side up."

Marian patted his arm and grinned. "True. The mark of a good landing is one where everyone walks away. I'll thank the pilot on the way out."

Brayson snagged his bag and the drone's travel case while Marian picked up her bag and slung her backpack over her shoulder. He liked her body's graceful movements and looked forward to the hotel room he'd envisioned for the last hour or so. Brayson led the way to a taxi and carefully loaded the bags, protecting the drone case as much as possible.

"We'd like to check into the resort," announced Brayson to the driver after looping his arm over Marian and pulling her closer.

"No problem. How long are you lovebirds here for?" the driver asked.

"At least a week. We have many plans to enjoy what Cat Island offers visitors."

"I've lived here my whole life, mister. It's a paradise for me. Are you on your honeymoon?"

"Anniversary. Our work schedules have been grueling, so we decided a remote break would be fun. My wife likes swimming, and the ocean calls to her."

The driver laughed. "There is a way to watch them feed the sharks you might enjoy. The hotel staff is great at informing you of safe activities. The bar is busy at night, often with music. My friend sometimes plays with his band on the weekends. And they don't water down the drinks. Fishermen won't tolerate that." He looked over his shoulder and winked. "Residents won't either."

"Good to know."

The taxi stopped in front of a quaint building with lavish greenery and blossoms at the entry. "Here we are. I'm Jake," he said, handing Brayson a card. "If you need to do any sightseeing on land, call me. Happy to drive you."

"Thanks, we will."

Unloading the trunk, Brayson led the way toward the check-in area. Within minutes, they were in a delightfully appointed room.

"Honey, I love the casuarinas and blooming hibiscus. The scent is intoxicating," said Marian.

"I'm glad for the air-conditioning," he commented, setting his bag down to unpack. He pressed on the bed. "I think we lucked into a great mattress. We'll test it later if you want."

"You're on," she giggled. "This room has everything, including luxurious terrycloth robes." She pressed the soft cotton against her cheek and sighed.

Brayson walked out to the wicker furniture. The view of the emerald-green waters past the pool area caught his imagination. "Breathtaking view. I can't wait to test out the drone."

Brayson unpacked his toy and checked the quadcopter drone batteries. He was satisfied that they had a reasonable charge. Marian set up the PC, tested the network connection, and finished unpacking.

"Do you want to go with me for the test run?"

"I'm checking in with JJ. I'll meet you outside in a few."

Brayson stopped by the front desk. "Are there any restrictions or laws concerning the operation of a drone for capturing video footage? I'm here on assignment to get as much video coverage of Little Bahamas' reef as possible. Is there anything I need to avoid?"

The front desk male cheerfully replied, "I advise you to stay clear of running your camera drone around the fifth-floor sunbathing area on the roof. There are no rules against nude sunbathing, but filming it is highly discouraged with fines and jail time."

A well-endowed guest lumbered to the desk. "I need a towel, please," she interrupted.

The clerk handed a towel from under the counter. She ambled off towards the elevators without so much as a thank you.

Facing the desk clerk, Brayson flatly stated, "I'll stay clear of the fifth floor with my filming. Thanks for the advice."

Outside, Brayson noted the wind direction before he launched the video drone over the marina to take images of the crafts mooring at the dock. He muttered, "Inventory time."

CHAPTER 31

Turning Theory into Action

JJ saw the number flash on his phone and quickly moved to answer. "Hi. How did the meeting with the girls go?"

"They were charming, delightful young ladies. Both are willing to work hard on their treatment plan. I reassured them we were friends rather than new predators expecting something in return. I asked them to begin thinking about what they wanted to do after treatment, trying to plant the seeds for additional education."

"Good. I'll help in any way I can. Perhaps I'll meet them when they are further along in their treatment. Trusting men is likely not on their list right now."

"Agreed. I also think your wife would relate well to them. Jo is so sweet to be around."

JJ swallowed a sip of his tea. "We haven't spoken since you met with the Director at the San Juan Treasury, Mr. Hassan, and did the presentation to the local island offices. Did you work for financial prowess?"

"I've never seen so much skepticism packed into a room," Gracie punctuated with an incredulous laugh. "One attendee sarcastically asked if this was yet another banking loan pitch from a career-driven woman from the States who wants to entice the islands into becoming a debtor region like Africa.

Jacobo had to help reel them in, allowing me to get to the meat of the discussion. I changed the lead to the schematic our team developed based on the local culture. It worked perfectly."

"Wow. I'm glad they accepted your comments. Some cultures resist remarks from a woman."

Gracie clucked her tongue. "After I went over the theory of the technology and its harvesting possibilities, I imagined *ah-ha comic bubbles* appearing over their heads, based on the shift in expressions on their faces. One bright attendee asked if the technology would also trap precious metals. By the time I finished the presentation, heads were bobbing up and down in agreement. Suddenly, all the cynics want in on the bandwagon." She chuckled. "I was stunned at the attitude shift. The original skeptic approached me and hugged me as I prepared to leave."

"It's hard to believe we have Julian, the human trafficking monster, to thank for this idea."

Gracie growled, "I'm not thanking him. You and I hammered out this idea. I pitched it. This technology will harvest lost treasure plundered centuries ago. With a good framework, the salvage work will help the struggling economies in the Caribbean. We're illustrating the modern-day value-add by both R-Group and the CATS team. Our founding fathers would be proud of our accomplishments."

"Sorry for the flippant comment, Sis," JJ said, feeling about as tall as a grasshopper at minimizing the community support this would provide. "You're right. Our knowledge of technology and proper application will bring significant economic benefits. I'm glad you framed it with them in charge, with our support as board members for technology changes." He rubbed his face, trying to erase weariness. "I want Julian brought to justice. What do you think is our next move?"

"We keep on the course to locate him. To verify our proposal for increased salvaging efforts, we need a prototype unit to test our theory." She stifled her snicker. "What do you think, JJ? Is this a build or steal sort of endeavor?"

JJ laughed aloud. "Let me noodle on it. I love having options."

"Enjoy. I'll call you later."

Later that day, JJ opened the virtual meeting. When the happy faces appeared, he said, "Marian, Brayson, I'm glad you arrived on Cat Island. How are the accommodations at the resort?"

"Perfect," said Marian with a slight grin. "It's one of the best assignments so far, boss."

"You two deserve a bit of fun mixed with work after the close call on San Juan. Brayson, did you get to review the prototype schematics?"

Brayson nodded. "It's a relatively large setup, with the battery, monitors, and fiber-optic cable connected to a water drone. We studied it before you posted about the meeting. I think it is a fairly beefy boat, hauling this around. Any thoughts?'

"We estimate that they will be in those waters for extended periods, and to avoid too much scrutiny, they are likely using a thirty- to forty-foot boat that could also be used for deep sea fishing as a cover. A dual-console craft would allow ample storage space for all equipment. Plus, those usually have a berth. If Julian outfitted it, I would guess it's newer and with state-of-the-art communications on board."

"I would expect the battery to need a reliable power supply to recharge it after its use for the day," Marian offered. "It's much like an EV on land. But would that make them more conspicuous if they use a 220-volt rather than the standard 110 for recharging?"

JJ inclined his head and tucked a fist under his chin to consider. A few heartbeats later, he suggested, "Or maybe they settle for a simple 110-volt and go out every other day. They might even have solar configured." He paused for a moment to scan his notes. "Additionally, the team believes the unit would be forced to dock frequently to upload the data and clear the onboard storage. I hope this combination will make it easier for you to spot the boat and our snitch, Nohea, if Cat Island was his final destination."

"My video camera is mounted on the drone, ready for medium-range surveillance. We will start before dawn to track the incoming boat traffic and focus on the deep-sea fishing boats."

"Don't worry, JJ., Brayson and I will sample margaritas and rum punches at the outdoor bar while the aerial drone works."

JJ hooted as Brayson leveled a stern, *Oh, really?* look at Marian as she lowered her head, acting contrite. "You two are a riot." He laughed again. "When you find Nohea, see if you can catch him making a phone call. We might get lucky and snoop the number to listen to the conversation. I expect Julian will keep his distance from the operation with Nohea there. Using his phone to call Julian may be the only way for them to connect."

"I'm on that part," said Marian. "It's simple, right? We find Nohea and then casually capture his call to Julian."

JJ frowned. "My glass is always half full, Marian. It won't be easy. Have fun and safe hunting."

CHAPTER 32

Pick up and Deliver

"Harto, are we going out again today? The weather looks perfect, and the seas appeared calm," Nohea kicked the bumper when he reached the dirty SUV where the object of his contempt was loading a few items into the backseat.

"No, I have an errand to run. Julian wants the stones we found yesterday as soon as possible."

"Is he coming here? I want to talk with him about—"

"I'm meeting him this morning. My instructions do not include bringing you. You are to keep an eye on the boat and our equipment. I'll be back this afternoon."

"At least give me the keys to work on the engine. It was running so rough, I'm afraid it'll seize up on us in the middle of the—"

"You're right. It is running rough. We'll work on it together, later."

"Why wait? I'm handy with engines. When you return, it'll be purring like a kitten. Don't you trust me?"

"I'm in this for the big payoff. I sank everything I had into a successful operation. If anything happens, Julian won't forgive or forget. Just stay here and keep out of trouble. I'll be back soon." Unwilling to continue the debate, Harto turned and closed the back door. He opened the driver's door, entered, and quickly closed it. The engine roared to life.

Nohea glared at the retreating vehicle, which moved out of sight. He scuffed his foot on the pavement. "It's probably too early for a fruity rum drink. I'll wander back toward the resort and maybe check out the pool."

Moving to the back end of the pool, he faced the magnificent ocean view, glad he was wearing a tank top and baggies in case he decided to take a dip later. He noticed a couple of individuals on the beach.

I bet that's the honeymoon couple who had the drone last evening, thought Nohea. The woman turned, and he caught her smile. *Yep. I wonder if I can convince them to rent a boat and I'll guide them. I bet I could get to the treasure if we did some diving and snorkeling. Then, I could retrieve my rightful gold. She can look pretty and work on her tan. He can fly his drone while I get us over the cache location. It's worth a shot.*

Harto periodically checked the rearview mirror as he drove to the New Bright Freedom Settlement Airport. His uneasiness and distrust of Nohea had made him a little paranoid. He shook his head, reminding himself that Julian had put him in charge. Taking the last turn into the parking lot, he felt safe enough to stop double-checking for someone following. He parked. He turned off the engine, and his cell phone chirped a text message.

> Could you bring them to the tarmac area?
> I'm leaving right away.

Harto got out and secured the backpack on his shoulders. Locking the SUV, he proceeded to the ramp area. He spotted a Beechcraft King Air 350 plane with the stairs lowered. He walked up the steps, pausing at the open door to adjust his eyes.

"Come in, Harto."

His eyes adjusted to the dim interior light as he spotted Julian sitting. "Good morning, Julian." He felt buoyed by bringing him some stones.

Julian motioned him over. "Let's see them."

Grinning, Harto rushed to the adjacent seat and pulled out the table tray. After removing the bag from his backpack, he opened it and selected a few stones.

Julian picked each one up with trembling hands and examined it with a special flashlight that highlighted the details beautifully. He fidgeted and murmured rapidly in what Harto believed was French. Julian opened the window shade to let the natural light bounce off his newfound gems, including a few diamonds, rubies, and several larimar. After picking up each stone and observing it in the light, he rubbed his hands together like a delighted child with a Christmas present. He grinned.

"You look pleased. Does this mean I get my smart software and cloud storage?"

Julian nodded. "Definitely. It will take time to make the necessary arrangements, but yes. Return to the boat. While I set things up, you continue hunting and hopefully harvest more gems. We'll meet there when everything has arrived. I'll give you the login codes and instructions if needed." He gently returned the stones to the bag and stood. "You've done well, Harto."

His chest swelled as he sensed the perfect bond with Julian. Walking toward the exit, he paused and turned. "Do you want me to hang on to Nohea?"

"Are you getting value from him?"

"Some, but he is argumentative. I thought I'd ask how you felt about him."

Julian patted him on the shoulder. "Try and make it work a little longer. Keep an eye out for anyone looking for him."

Harto stepped down. He heard the lock that secured the door from the inside. Reaching the parking lot, he turned when he heard the throttle engage. He watched it head down the runway and smoothly begin to soar.

CHAPTER 33

Helping and Hopeful

Nohea decided to check out the technology used onboard the boat. Bradley and Blake hardly spoke or looked at him until he tried to access the monitor screen to find the data files connected to the submersible drone. Blake stepped in front of Nohea while Bradley pushed him to the side.

"You're not to mess with these screens or this equipment," Bradley stated, but with missing t and p sounds from his words.

"Or what? Are you going to tell Harto?" Nohea smirked. "I doubt he'd understand your words. In case you didn't know, your speech is lousy."

Blake bristled as he turned. "I don't need to speak well to deck you."

"That's why he's glad I'm here, so he can have a conversation without trying to decipher it," he added, a maniacal laugh at them with a twisted expression. "No wonder no girls date you guys. You look too weird."

In the corner of his eye, Nohea spotted Harto before he swung at the kid.

"That's enough, guys," Harto said. "I want to be on the water this afternoon. Nohea, fetch everyone something to eat. You and I will work on the engine when you return."

"Why don't you send these two goobers?" Nohea complained. "I'm the high-value diver, not some step-and-fetch-it lackey."

"Because they know the trawling area, and you don't. We'll plan the route while you're gone. I want to hunt in an adjacent area different from where you've been." The glare matched Harto's squared shoulders.

"Don't forget, I give the orders, Nohea."

"Then give me some money so that I can get—"

"No, go to the hotel. Order from there and charge it to the room. I get one bill to show Julian the expenses."

Nohea grumbled, "What did Julian say about me? How long do I have to stay here?"

"He said not to drop you overboard wrapped with too much heavy chain. Get a move on."

Nohea walked toward the hotel, annoyed by Blake and Bradley's chattering. As he entered the restaurant to order, he heard a perky female voice behind him.

"Hey, there. Are you from the island?"

Nohea turned and realized she was one half of the honeymoon couple and a stunning female up close.

She blushed. "How rude of me not to introduce myself." She stuck out her hand and continued, "I'm Marian."

"Doesn't your husband have the aerial drone?" he grinned.

"You noticed?" She smiled. "He's on assignment to video the island from the air, ground, and sea for a travel magazine contract. I watch for a while, but then I get bored. I end up at the pool, waiting for him to call it a day. He doesn't like me to control the drone when he's focused on capturing a specific photo sequence. He's very creative. I get a little jealous of the time he spends working. Some anniversary, huh?"

"Too bad. What was your question?"

"I was wondering if you know anyone who would rent us a boat and maybe a guide. We must find places to film the island and reef. We would be grateful, Mr. Er…"

"Loane. Plain Loane," replied Nohea. "No need for Mister." His mind raced with the possibilities. "I might be able to help you with a charter. I'm on a quest right now for lunch. How about we meet tonight in the bar to discuss the details?"

Marian nodded. "Agreed, Loane. I'll text my husband. He'll be delighted we met. Thank you."

Circling the airport several times before getting permission to land, Julian watched Ryu, looking for anyone on the ground that might cause trouble.

"I'm glad we made the trip with no incident."

"Honestly, sir, I'm surprised at Harto's success."

"I knew he would find some, but he scored quite a nice collection and believes there are more on the trajectory path he found. I need you to source the equipment he needs and ship it to my home. I want to set it up and test it. Harto knows some technology, but I want to understand how it works."

"I'll get on it," Ryu promised.

Julian thought, *I'd better call Mark after I've looked at the stones again in the light. Knowing him, he'll want his courier to pick up the sample proof points. I'll need to be careful and ensure we meet on the Dutch side.*

Julian clapped Ryu on the back while they secured the plane. They jumped onto their parked all-terrain vehicle for the ride home.

CHAPTER 34

It's All Planned

Pleased knowing he and Nohea had resolved the engine issue, Harto wiped his hands. He was relieved they could replace a bad spark plug wire, clean a sensor, and readjust the timing belt to fix the problem. Nohea had more skill with the engine than he expected. It purred like a cheetah ready to explode to grab an unexpected lunch. "Thanks for your help with the engine. You showed me a thing or two."

Nohea nodded, toweling off his sweat. "Are we ready to go to the new location you mentioned? Can you show me where? I tried to look at the navigation equipment, but your boys wouldn't let me see it."

"Sure." Harto clapped him on the back in appreciation for saving the day. They'd avoided paying for a mechanic to fix the engine. "Perhaps we can work together. You need to get a feel for where we're headed. I'll tell you what we can expect. You're a good diver, but the terrain is deceiving underwater, which is where the water drone comes in."

"Can you also teach me to control the drone?"

Shaking his head, Harto replied, "Not yet. Maybe later."

He showed his helper where they had previously dived and the next area he wanted to target. Amazingly, Nohea asked intelligent questions without being too intrusive. Harto chalked this up to a positive bridge in their relationship. When the navigation discussion was finished, he said, "I think we're ready to head out."

"Thanks for showing me where we're going and why."

"Why don't you, Blake, and Bradley verify the air in the diving equipment while I look at the submersible?"

"Fine."

Harto fiddled with the dials as a part of the pre-check, then swore aloud. "Damnit." He stomped across the boat's deck and bellowed, "Why wasn't the battery for the submersible drone plugged in to charge? It's useless."

Blake and Bradley looked at him and cringed, eyes wide. Nohea shrugged, holding the grimy towel with a look that conveyed ignorance.

Harto tried to control his frustration. Through gritted teeth, he mumbled, "We aren't going until the battery is charged. Plug it in."

Bradley rushed to comply.

Harto noticed Nohea ambling toward the side of the boat tied to the dock and barked, "Where do you think you're going?"

Irritated, the man curtly replied, "You said we're not going out. I thought I'd relax and have a drink at the bar. I doubt we'll go out before morning while—" He motioned his hand toward the drone— "that thing gets charged. I don't want to hear you rant over something I can't control."

Seething, Harto's eyes followed the cocksure man as he strode out of the marina. Harto was ready to shout after him when Blake smirked.

"When you sent me to help carry lunch since he was taking so long, I overheard him talking to the woman of that anniversary couple. He set up a meeting with her to discuss doing some side work. Then, after he passed me the food to bring back, he stopped and asked for boats for hire from the front desk. The clerk gave him a paper, which he stuffed into his pocket. I bet he wants to meet with the couple to get them to rent a boat and guide them for extra money."

"Honey," Marian purred, spotting Brayson entering their room. He carefully cleaned the drone and set it into its docking station.

"You were right. It's Nohea. I noticed the skull tattoo behind his ear. He goes by the name Loane. He's willing to chat with us later in the bar about renting a boat and potentially being our guide. We'll buy him a drink or two."

He set down the drone and plugged in everything. "I'm happy to buy several rounds if we can get some info."

"Good. I don't know his agenda, but he has one."

He stepped forward, scooped her into his arms, and kissed her. "That, my dear, is only one part of why I love you."

"I love you, too."

"I did a couple of long-distance angle videos of the marina, including him working with three other men on a docked boat. No big equipment was visible. However, the hull sat low in the water. I want to send the film to JJ to check on the model for all the specs. It looked like they had diving equipment and fishing poles."

"You weren't noticed?"

"No one looked."

"Outstanding. Let's get showered. I'm ready for drinks and bar snacks."

"Will you, um, wash my back?"

"I sure will, honey," she responded with a grin and licked her lips.

"Let me call JJ. I'll get him up to speed on finding our guy and the boat information."

"Yes, dear."

They laughed.

CHAPTER 35

I'm in a Hurry

Anxious to dive, Harto pounded on the adjoining door. "Let's go." When he heard nothing, he opened the door to find Nohea snoring, spread-eagled on the tangled sheets. Mumbling he groused, "He must have partied into the wee hours." He called, "Blake, get downstairs for hot coffee and grab some food. Bradley, come help me get him into the shower."

Maneuvering him to the edge of the bed, they made him sit. They each shouldered one of his arms and hoisted him into a standing position.

Nohea complained, "Stop, I'm awake." He shrugged off their help.

"Take a shower; you stink. Coffee will be here in a minute. We have a long day ahead."

"But it's Sunday."

"So? I never said you got days off. Losing time yesterday afternoon put me behind schedule. Let's go."

"Fine." Nohea shook his head, grabbed his swim trunks, and retreated to the bathroom, not bothering to shut the door.

Harto returned to his room, leaving the door open because the sounds and smells of the man's morning routine grossed him out. Blake returned with the coffee for each of them. Moments later, Nohea emerged looking ready to go, albeit with a sour expression.

He grabbed the coffee, taking a big swig. "I'm ready."

The foursome walked in silence to the marina store.

"Do you have the supplies ready, sir?" Harto asked the store clerk.

"Yep." He pointed to a red and white box at the counter's end. "I charged your room. You can grab it unless you need something else."

Bradley and Blake each took a handle on the heavy-laden cooler and headed toward the dock area. Harto spotted a few folks getting onto tour boats. One deep-sea fishing excursion was casting off as they stopped at their slip. "I'm glad we got here this early. You three bring out the diving equipment and check the tanks."

Nohea methodically checked the air tanks, gauges, wetsuits, nets, and other paraphernalia. Blake and Bradley organized the cooler's contents and added some lines they would use for the dive.

"What! Damnit to hell," shouted Harto as he looked at the drone stats on the controller. "I don't believe this is happening." He threw the towel onto the piloting seat. "Get over here. Now!"

Confused looks faced him as they rushed forward.

"What's the matter?" asked Nohea, taking a swig of his coffee.

"The submersible shows only a quarter charge. At twelve hours, it should be fully charged." He glared at them, looked to the side, and lifted the plug from the floor. "How did this get unplugged?" he demanded.

Looking back and forth between one another, they shrugged as if controlled by puppeteer strings.

Nohea had one foot on the dock. "Guess I do get today off," he snorted. "I hate waking up early for nothing."

"Wait," commanded Harto.

"Why? You just said twelve hours are needed. The boat's in good running order. The equipment has been checked twice, and the cooler contents will remain good if refrigerated. Maybe I can have some fun on my day off," he laughed as he ambled toward the hotel.

"I guess he got his way after all," Blake said. "I thought he'd be stuck."

"What are you saying?" asked Harto.

"He planned on the day off."

"How do you know that, Blake? You two best buds these days?"

"Hardly. He's loud after a few drinks. I overheard his conversation with that married couple."

"What conversation? How come I missed it?"

"The part when he planned to guide them around the island. The guy is taking photos with his drone for some magazine. He also said he'd teach Nohea how to pilot his air drone."

"How could he commit when he knew we were planning to hunt for stones this morning?" He lowered his head into his hands, fearing he already knew the answer. "I told him we wouldn't be able to go if the battery wasn't fully charged."

"I bet he snuck back on board and knocked the plug out."

A burning sensation spread throughout Harto's mouth and chest. It felt far worse than biting into a fresh habanero pepper. "You believe he engineered this break in our work." He let out a breath as he paced on the deck. Then he downed a bottle of cold water from the open cooler while he collected his thoughts.

"I can only think of one reason he would risk it. I bet I know where he's headed. And he won't be nursing a hangover. Come on, let's get into position."

Blake and Bradley scrambled to cast off the mooring lines.

Harto started the engines, almost tasting sweet revenge. "Wait until you find my surprise, you jerk."

Nohea barely covered his annoyance with the late departure. "Folks, we only have this rental for the morning, but we might negotiate for the afternoon if we need additional hours."

Oblivious, the couple shuffled slowly with teasing gestures and comments that further angered Nohea.

Brayson stopped at the counter to pay the additional charges. "I wouldn't want you to send out search and rescue."

"No problem, sir," promised the clerk. "Return before nightfall because it's easier to dock and lock her for the night."

"Of course."

Nohea strode behind them as they held hands and sauntered to the last dock area where the rental craft was stored. As they reached the numbered slip identified on the agreement, Marian apologized, "Sorry, Mr. er…Loane, but I was distracted and lost track of time."

Slipping into his alias role, he replied, scoping out her feminine physique. "Quite understandable. You two are on your honeymoon, after all. I hated asking you for more money to pay for the rental. Let me take you to the first viewing location I have in mind."

After twenty minutes, scooting across the water as fast as Loane could push the craft, Marian shouted, "My goodness, we're traveling fast. It's almost like we are in a race."

They bounced through another boat's wake, and Brayson hollered, "Loane. I've been on search-and-rescue trips that didn't take these sorts of chances on a clear day like this. No wind and not a cloud in the sky."

Nohea checked his GPS coordinates and announced, "Sorry, but I wanted to provide optimal light conditions for your filming, sir, and your suntan, ma'am."

Marian giggled, "Loane, thanks for trying to optimize the sun position. I'll have to work on removing the suntan lines some other time."

Relief coursed through Nohea as the GPS displayed that they had arrived. He circled the area, then dropped the throttle into idle. "Brayson, grab hold of the anchor on the bow and toss it over. If the line grows taut, use the crank to ensure it hits bottom." He watched the GPS to verify they weren't drifting. "Brayson, you should be able to fly in a wide area. To the south is a sandbar where you can see through the water. Maybe it would make nice photos, too. North of our position is the edge of a reef many people believe was the course explorers and merchants used hundreds of years ago. If the light is right, you might get an image of one of several sunken ships. The old man at the marina told me that was why this area used to be a huge treasure hunter mecca. They cleaned it all out."

Marian clapped. "That is so exciting. I had no idea, honey, did you?"

"No. The magazine is going to love this. Thanks, Loane. I'll get set up."

"Ma'am, would you like to scuba dive? I'm happy to guide you."

With a mischievous smile, Marian replied, "If you're going to be in the water, perhaps I can work on removing the tan lines."

Brayson snorted. "You were right about the lighting conditions; let me get some aerial drone footage. This could take me a while."

"Have fun. I'll return within an hour to check on you. Water and snacks are in the cooler under the removable seat." Nohea suited up and fell backward into the water, holding his face mask.

CHAPTER 36

In the Ocean, No One Can Hear You Scream

As soon as he was overboard, Marian added tracking devices to Loane's clothing.

Brayson launched the drone, sweeping the area and filming in ever-widening circles. "Those should remain in place, honey. You're doing an amazing job of stitching them back like they were made that way."

"Another one of my hidden talents," she giggled as she snipped the grey thread.

"Are you planning to show him any of the images you captured?"

"Possibly, but I might skip over the boat anchored north-west. It looks like the one he was working on yesterday. We need to understand their relationship. None of those men looked like any of our suspects. I can skip over it with a little editing."

Marian smirked. "While we have time, can you please apply suntan lotion so I don't get burned in the untanned areas?"

Brayson chuckled and asked, "Is it the dangerous assignments that make you extra provocative, or have you always been this way?"

Marian caressed his face down to his neck. "It's easy to be saucy with the man you love."

Nohea wasted no time in descending to the carefully marked target. He barely contained his giddiness until some seawater infiltrated his gear's mouthpiece. When he finally came into range of the marker he'd left, dread climbed up his spine. He silently gasped. Instead of a single marker, he spotted five across a wide range anchored to the sea floor, bobbing brightly with the sunlight filtered through the clear sea, catching the bright red flags. They each taunted him. Panic rose in his throat at each of the attached messages.

Nope, not here, was the message on the first.

He quickly swam to the next and discovered another disappointment. *That's right, you missed it.*

Erratically swimming to the next, he felt defeated. *Are you sure it's here?*

Slowly, he went to the fourth. *No, it's over there.*

The final stroke of bad news occurred at the last chance. *It used to be here, but it isn't anymore. You Lose.*

He screamed, and bubbles streamed above his head. Securing his mouthpiece, he pulled out his knife and dove to the anchor point of the last sign, realizing it was the one he'd used when he noticed the different shades of red on the flag. He found nothing but an empty hole where he'd placed the bucket. He realized Harto had out-maneuvered him.

The gauge on the tank indicated it was time to surface. He threw the anchor flag, which drifted toward the sand in a lazy descent, then began his ascent.

Surfacing, Nohea spotted Brayson on the boat's edge. He grabbed the handrail.

Brayson reached, offering to assist. "I saw a huge gush of bubbles and was coming to find you. What happened?"

Nohea heaved himself onto the diving platform. "A cruel trick." Pulling off his tanks, he sighed. "Did you get the photos you needed for your assignment?"

"Yep. You picked a good location. I got some great shots in the calm seas with the sun revealing inspiring underwater secrets."

They moved into the boat and stored their diving gear. Marian helped organize the items and clear the pathway, hugging her husband. Nohea ignored the honeymooners as he toweled dry. He recovered the anchor and stowed it away.

"Thank you, buddy, for being a man of your word," Brayson said, clapping him on the back.

Without a response, Nohea started the engines and headed toward the marina. Reaching the pier, he parked the craft and stepped onto the dock. Brayson handed him the promised 100 plus an extra 50.

"It was worth it. We may want to go out again after I review these and all the others I have taken," announced Brayson.

Nohea rolled his eyes and turned toward the marina. The tour money was a poor door prize compared to the lost cache of coins. He turned to see them lost in their little dream world of touching and teasing while they gathered their belongings. Nohea resumed his walk to the hotel, wondering if they would even remember his name twenty minutes from now. The bitterness of the morning washed over him like a crushing illness. He contemplated how to escape this mess. Sometimes, fate has a different path.

Inside the marine shop, Blake and Bradley clutched his elbows on either side. Blake insisted, "Harto wants a word with you now that your side hustle is over."

Nohea bristled at being retrieved like an errant child. Angrily, he disentangled from their grasp and headed toward the slip where the boat was moored. Harto sat in one of the fishing chairs, having a beer.

Smiling, Harto asked, "Are you finished with your side hustle and ready to do your job?"

"Where are my coins?"

Harto stood. "It didn't take me long to figure out what you had done and where you went. I told you to leave them, but you got greedy." Harto reached into his pocket, removed a coin, and flipped it toward Nohea. "Now you have one souvenir and no more chances. You work for me. Don't try to spend it because word will travel. Then, we'll have local authorities surrounding us asking unwanted questions. I'll send you to Davy Jones' locker before risking that."

"I want to talk to Julian. Those are my coins," insisted Nohea.

"I don't think it would do any good. They are stashed where you won't find them. We can make that call now if you want."

Harto pulled out his cell phone and placed the call. When it connected, he put it on speaker. "Harto, what's up? Do you have more good news for me?"

"We were stuck for two days due to equipment mishap."

"That pisses me off, Harto. Do I need to fix it?"

Nohea shook his head.

"I have it resolved, and the new target area has been mapped for the morning. I don't think I'll have any further delays."

"Keep me posted."

Nohea eyed Harto and added, "Julian, are you taking the cache of gold coins I found? I was going to bring them…"

Julian's voice grew louder as he stated, "We're not hunting gold coins, dimwit. Gold will bring us lawyers, government officials, and every other parasite. Follow instructions, and we all win."

Nohea grudgingly replied, "Yes, sir."

Harto smirked at the man he owned as he ended the call.

CHAPTER 37

Going Around, Coming Down

"Whoop! Whoop!" JW and Granger gave one another a virtual high-five, jumped about, and crowed.

"We finally caught a break," JW added. "Those sensors Marian implanted worked like a champ on locating our pigeon and alerting our programs to the cellular signal. Tapping into the closest cell tower worked like a charm. I can't believe they confirmed it was Julian." JW smiled as he copied the information to the case file repository for JJ to access. "Granger, work the signal back to a target endpoint. I'll notify JJ and Gracie we have a recording we believe is with Julian and should have a viable geolocation soon."

Granger nodded as JW watched his cousin's fingers flying across the keyboard. "I got this, Cous."

"Do it by the numbers with no shortcuts. This guy is as slippery as bald tires driving on icy roads."

"I know what we need."

"Sorry, I just don't want to mess up this opportunity. Their conversation sounded like some internal turmoil. That might not work to our benefit if they change protocols or bounce the signals in too many places to anonymize the endpoint. I don't want an empty bag."

"Agreed. Get JJ on a call. We have a target. It looks viable to the region."

"Calling now." He automatically added Granger as the conference bridge opened. "Hey, JJ. Good news, finally. We have a lead on Julian."

"I'm all ears."

"Granger tapped into a call from a cellular line near Nohea with a man named Harto. It's a new name for us, so I sent it to Auri and Satya to see if they can pull any information. Harto called someone. During the conversation, Nohea—whom we verified by matching the voice biometrics—called the person Julian. We triangulated the calls to the macro-cell towers, and Granger identified the endpoint's location. We don't know if he is on the move or not. Julian has proven he has a unique way of changing his modus operandi."

JW drummed his fingers on his mouse pad, waiting for a response from JJ.

"Well done, guys. I'm reviewing the data now. You're correct; we need to move on this immediately. I know the best method. Can you give me the conversation transcript?"

"It's in the digital file along with the geolocational info, JJ."

Granger chuckled. "Nohea was complaining about his gold coins being snitched. He got told to back off the gold, which I suspect is due to the jewels being the goal. I think Nohea's in it for his payday, and gold looks better to him. Big surprise, right?"

"Auri and Satya built detailed profiles of Nohea and Ryu," JW added. "They both have mercenary expertise. The difference is that Ryu is loyal, while Nohea is focused on his gains. It's likely why Julian had him on the plane with the kids. This could work for us in the end."

"Excellent summations. Thanks for getting this to me so fast. I'll take the next step and keep you posted. Let me know if you get anything else."

"Folks," JJ stated, "are you in a quiet place with no ears?"

"Yes," murmurs came from Judith and Zee, and he saw their heads nod.

"Brayson and Marian inserted the tracking/monitoring chips." JJ cleared his throat and said, "I've sent you the location of Julian's possible base. That's the good news. The bad news is that Ryu is likely with him. With his background and devotion to Julian, rushing in is too risky. I'd like us to verify his identification before I seek support from local authorities. We don't want to spook him into running again."

Judith glanced at Xiamara and stated, "JJ, we started combing for digital activity after you shared his location. We don't believe he's ready to run just yet, but we'd like eyes on him to confirm."

"JJ," Xiamara added, "I bet he's setting up a cloud-based account with gobs of data storage space, identical to what we taught him during our sting op. We did find some recent purchases of top-notch AI software and are trying to uncover who bought it."

"It's exactly as our think-tank sister organization predicted," JJ observed. "Scanning the ocean floor for hundreds of years of sediment shift could be huge regarding data collection requirements. Without some state-of-the-art AI software, no human can begin to sift through all the data possibilities for any missing treasure or lost gems."

Xiamara smirked. "If we can learn where he's having his data hosted, then perhaps some modest location changes can be indexed to send them to the wrong location for the gems while we identify the target hunting ground."

Appalled at the suggestion, Judith protested, "I'm shocked you would propose such a devious thing. And yes, it irritates me that I didn't think of it first."

Everyone on the call chuckled.

"Ladies," JJ said, "since we can't track significant cloud-hosting activity, are we trying to tie the ownership to Julian? Why don't you continue to monitor electronically and report back any results? They might provide the extra finesse to cloak our activity and let them keep grasping at thin air."

"JJ, what do you want us working on?" Brayson asked. "We saw the transcript of the phone call with Julian. We expect Nohea to make a last-ditch attempt to find the coins Harto may have hidden. It would be sweet if we uncover that cache."

Marian agreed, "Yes, it would."

CHAPTER 38

Fish or Cut Bait

Dark shadows hid Nohea in the farthest corner booth of the marina bar. The worn leather seats and scarred oak tabletop spoke of private meetings. The wads of crumpled napkins lying around the glass that served as a basket in the center of the surface were as empty as his available options. He swallowed the remnants of his beverage and fingered the coin he'd never use. Lost in impossible thoughts of missed opportunities, he jolted into the present when the cushioned seat shifted.

"Loane, mind if we join you?" Marian bubbled with a grin. "We saw you were alone. It occurred to us that we failed to thank you properly for your tour guiding abilities. We asked the bartender what you were having, and Brayson decided to get you one on us." Marian crinkled her eyes and smiled, barely suppressing a laugh. "Not really on us since Brayson is on an expense account."

Brayson approached from the side, distributing the drinks. "These look perfect." he joked. "I asked for the same drink as you because I figured if you were a good guide, you likely enjoyed a great drink."

Nohea looked at the pair, not wanting company, but the woman's perky attitude and the free drink made him consider the options. "Thanks."

As Nohea raised his glass, Marian touched her glass to his. "To your health, Loane," she announced with a grin.

Nohea replied, "Salud!"

Brayson sipped the beverage. "This is a great beverage concoction," he sincerely added, taking another drink. "I've got one more element to my contract to complete the assignment, and I was hoping you would know where I might get the details. I didn't want to ask the front desk as I didn't know if I could trust them like we trust you. Do you know if there are any shipwrecks we can explore, buddy? Hell, we might discover something to take home as a remembrance."

Nohea rubbed the golden piece between his thumb and forefinger. The edge of the coin reflected the light from the bar television that someone had turned on, brightening the corner.

"Wow," commented Brayson. "Is that your St. Christopher medal? My dad used to have a gold one."

Nohea shook his head, feeling sad. "Are you familiar with claim jumping, like where you find something, but someone sneaks in, stealing it before you can recover what you found? The one piece shows the proof, but the rest is gone." He swallowed half his drink.

"That doesn't seem fair," Marian empathized and patted Nohea's arm. "You do all the hard work, but someone else takes the credit. Brayson, that sounds like slavery to me," she stated with a tone of indignation.

"Maybe you're right, ma'am." Nohea sighed and shrugged. "Without the entire find, it could be an unlucky coin. I'll have to work the rest of my life, giving tours on rented boats to make ends meet. Some sunken ships are in the area, but I doubt you'll discover more than fish and algae covering the wrecks. People have hunted treasure in this region for years."

Brayson said, "Those sorts of pictures might spark the increase in tourist trade, which is what the company paying me wants."

"Did someone take your find? You look so sad." Marian touched Nohea's arm again.

Nohea slipped the coin into his pocket, frowned, and took another generous sip.

"Hon," Marian turned toward her husband. "I think someone encroached on his find. Is there anything we could do to help, Loane? It might make a feature story for the magazine, too."

"I'm not certain he wants us to mess in his affairs, dear."

Nohea felt hope rise to the top with this new potential solution to his quest. "I wouldn't mind some help." He leaned in conspiratorially and looked side to side to ensure no one was close enough to hear. He quietly said, "I found a few coins, but don't tell anyone. If you could help me retrieve them, I'll give you one as a souvenir. After all, you were ready to save me, and I'd give one for that alone. However, you'll have to write the story with me unnamed. Tell it like you were bringing up the coins, and we were jumped by pirates who took everything. Retrieving the cache makes it a better story and opens the door for more treasures."

Brayson nodded, leaning his chin on the palm of his bent arm. He also looked around to make sure they weren't overheard.

Marian whispered as she rubbed her hands together. "This will be exciting."

Judith turned up the speaker volume on the video conference bridge. "Go ahead," she said to JJ.

The voice from the recording was clear. She and Xiamara looked at one another and nodded. "That's Julian's voice. I'll never forget his accent." She patted her friend's hand. "Hell, Zee's shivering, remembering the icky sensation when he got close to smell us."

"Thank you, ladies. I'll congratulate the team for engineering a stellar, deepfake voice-over application. Are you comfortable with what needs to be done?"

Judith watched Xiamara nervously lick her lips. "We travel to where the team believes Julian is located. We align to the same cellular macro tower before making the call," she recited.

"Yep. I know you two will be in proximity to him and Ryu. They know you on sight. I don't want you spotted," said JJ, raising a finger to emphasize his point.

Judith curled her bottom lip while her white teeth scraped across her skin. She inhaled and centered before the camera, pressing her shoulders back. "We got this, JJ. We've mostly recovered from their mistreatment."

Xiamara straightened, schooling her expression, trying to match Judith's look of confidence. She said, "We want to help put them away."

"At any point, if the situation feels wrong, I want you both to promise me you'll back off and stay safe," JJ insisted.

"Yes, sir," they replied.

Judith flipped her blonde hair over her shoulder and added, "We've got some disguises, too."

JJ chuckled. "Get to work and keep in touch."

Judith closed the conference bridge.

CHAPTER 39

It's Your Call

Judith packed their freshly laundered second-hand clothing and minimal toiletries, including hair brushes, into the two worn duffle bags they had secured from the thrift shop. The baggy clothes in muted colors were a change from what she'd laid out to wear for traveling. She zipped the bags shut. "There. We're ready to grab our bags as we leave in the morning."

"Jude, I'm scared," admitted Xiamara as she moved her bag to the chair by her bed, laying her money belt on top. "What if they spot us?"

"Let's try this again, Zee. Wrap your coppery, brunette curls close to your head and put on your bamboo softie. The dark sage-green color is perfectly drab." She turned Zee to face the mirror and gestured palms-up. "Tomorrow, we use the gel to keep our hair secure." Judith picked up the darker green bucket hat and plopped it on the softie cap. "The headgear, sunglasses, and worn baggie clothes let us hide in plain sight. Heck, I'm even going to bind my chest. Plain Janes are ignored."

Zee's eyes blinked rapidly as if trying to keep tears at bay.

"We're not looking to bump into Julian or any of his guards, Zee. JJ outlined our job. I know we'll be great. We have the early bug-smasher flight. We land and pick up the rental Jeep to head toward La Loterie. We can even have a meal at this old plantation site. I wouldn't mind snapping a few pics there. It's famous and mostly preserved. You love that kind of stuff."

"I do," Zee agreed, a small smile forming. "Once we place the call, it's an easy exit. The app is loaded on the cell phone. We know the tower's approximate location. We'll get there and make the call."

Judith hip-bumped her bestie. "We're just day tourists, flying back to San Juan in the evening."

"The last time we thought things were under control, Jude, we were drugged and about to be sold into slavery. Fortunately, JJ knows how to track us."

"Exactly right. This is so easy. He's going to be very proud of us. Stop worrying. Let's execute the plan by the numbers."

Xiamara removed the softie cap and fluffed her hair. "Maybe I'm just not cut out to be a field operative. I can't stop thinking about how we had it completely under control until we didn't. We got tagged and didn't even know it. We almost didn't make it out."

Judith tilted Zee's head toward her. "I see and hear your fear. Call JJ and tell him you want to stand down. I'll carry out the assignment, no worries. I want this monster captured for every-thing he's done. I won't rest easy until I know he's captured, imprisoned, or dead."

Xiamara huffed and snorted. "You'd break up our dynamic duo?" Her hands waved between them. "You're willing to dismiss me after all we've done together?"

"Yes, our friendship means that much. You're my heart, sister. I can't bear to see you shaking with fear. I need to know you aren't falling into pieces."

Astonishment reflected in Zee's eyes. "I'm going with you. We'll face this challenge like we always have. Together."

They stared at one another.

"There, that's better," Judith said with a grin. "Let's sleep so we can catch the morning plane."

Xiamara wiped away the emotional tears and nodded.

The following day, Judith watched out the window as the morning sun uncovered the French coastal side of Saint-Martin. The rough ride ended with a tumultuous landing due to horrific crosswinds. "Any aircraft landing we walk away from is a good one."

Zee rolled her eyes and grinned in agreement.

The pilot taxied them toward a small building and lowered the airstair so the four passengers could disembark. The older couple had been quiet during the trip, saying they planned to fish for a few days, as they did yearly.

Judith noticed a ground crewmember scrambling to tend to the aircraft. The pilot deplaned and approached the maintenance man. An intense yet quiet discussion followed, with their pilot waving his arms and pointing to the aircraft. His expression appeared frustrated.

Moments later, the pilot stormed past the passengers. Judith asked, "Excuse me, sir. Is there something wrong with your beautiful aircraft? We plan to be here by five-thirty to make the return trip and wanted to verify that it was still good with you."

The pilot paused and looked her over, backing up a step. He took off his cap and then reset it. "Sorry about the rough landing, ladies. I need some repairs to the aircraft to complete my route to the neighboring islands. I doubt I will be able to return to San Juan this afternoon. I recommend you find some accommodations until the repairs are made. It could be two days at the worst, but I hope it will happen sooner. I'm going to see if I can locate the parts needed."

Judith looked at her feet. "You are a gentleman. My sister and I are headed to La Loterie to take nature photos for our scientific research. We'll see if we can reserve a room there. If that doesn't work, we may ask for your help. I can provide my number if you don't mind calling if there is a change in departure time. We don't mind being flexible."

"Sure." He also handed her his business card. "This has my number. It does voice and text."

"You're so sweet," Judith said with a smile.

"What was that all about?" Xiamara asked.

"For a half-second, I thought he was cute. Then I remembered what we looked like in the last mirror I checked this morning. We need to roll with the flow if the plane is grounded."

"Should I be worried?"

"Not yet. I'll tell you when to get concerned. Let's get our vehicle."

CHAPTER 40

Transactions, Short and Sweet

Startled at the incoming call, Harto stopped his prep work for their outing. "Yes, Julian, what's up?"

"Plans changed. The timetables have moved. I need more stones and the bucket of coins Nohea found. Bring him, too; I want to explain his facts of life. Can you get low-cost air or sea transport to Saint-Martin for the two of you?"

"My racing boat can easily achieve that distance in ten or eleven hours. Will that work?" His eyes darted around the area to ensure no one, including the twins, was within earshot. "I hid the coins in our boat. I've got someone on board day and night, so there's no risk. If I use a different boat, I'd have to lug the gold, and I'm afraid someone would notice."

"This is why I trust you, Harto," Julian chuckled. "You're always thinking about making things work. It's still quite a distance, but I want you here fast. Air travel would be better."

"There's a risk with fast. I'll island-hop quickly with all the cargo secured to deliver. I can't guarantee that if we fly. Did something happen to your plane?"

Julian cleared his throat. "Um…my plane is in for some expected maintenance."

"I'll get Blake and Bradley to stock the boat with fuel and provisions. We'll leave in a few hours, as the weather permits. The twins would appreciate meeting you if that's okay."

"Of course."

"I'll have to locate Nohea. He's doing a side hustle, running a tour service for some newlyweds when we aren't trawling. You said to bring him, but I want him on the boat because he's great with engine work. He did some fast maintenance, significantly improving the high-tech craft's performance."

"Harto, call me as soon as you get into the marina here. I've got a courier coming late tomorrow from an important client. Don't disappoint me."

"Yes, sir."

Julian found his confidant on the balcony with a pair of binoculars. "Ryu, I've got the stones Harto found using the new technology. I have something for the courier to placate Mark. I will remind him that the new technology will optimize the harvesting time. I believe that'll make Mark back off for a while. Remind me to call Harto for an update."

"No problem. When do you want me to leave to meet the courier and bring him here?"

Julian frowned. "I'd just as soon not have them know my location. We'll go together and make the transition discreetly at the airport. I want it to be a brief but cordial meeting. The airfield is semi-public, and I'd like to avoid being seen as much as possible."

"Wear your old Panama and dark sunglasses with Levis, a non-descript shirt, and your dock shoes."

"Good call."

CHAPTER 41

In Danger, Again

Judith pulled into the airport parking lot, away from general traffic. "Zee, how about you go check the status of our plane with maintenance while I update our boss?"

"I can do that." She started to get out of the Jeep.

"Don't forget to wear your hat and glasses," ordered Judith. "And no flirting."

"Yes, ma'am."

"We've still got it. Now, amble, don't run. You're a mature scientist." Judith popped open the hatch. She exited, circled the vehicle to retrieve their cellphones from one of the duffle bags, and sat on the open end. She wished they'd stopped to eat at La Loterie as her stomach growled again. But they didn't want to miss the flight if the repairs were completed. She grew worried when the pilot didn't answer his phone. She dialed the secured number to JJ. It connected immediately.

"How did it go, ladies?"

"Xiamara is checking to see if our ride back to San Juan is serviceable yet. We completed the bogus Julian call to get Nohea and Harto to lead us to Julian," said Judith. "They're using their boat to get here, so that much is going to plan. The gold coins Nohea found are hidden on the boat, so we'll have a shot at getting those, too. We almost tripped up when Harto asked about Julian's plane. He must have access to an aircraft here somewhere."

"Good job. I haven't listened to the transcript. We weren't aware of a potential escape route for Julian. I'll get the team on it. Your voice sounds off, Judith, is something wrong?"

"We're stuck on Saint-Martin until the plane we flew gets repaired. It was a rough flight and landing. The pilot grounded us until repairs were made. The pilot said he'd help get us a room at the airport, but I wanted to try La Loterie, where I wished we'd stopped for lunch. Anyway, we are stuck here until—"

Xiamara rushed up to the back of the Jeep and slid onto the open hatch.

"Zee, you look like you've seen a ghost. What's gotten into you? I'm trying to talk to—"

Xiamara growled and kept her voice low. "They're here, at the airport: Julian and his goon. My back was turned, and I kept it that way. I distinctly heard his voice when he said, 'The courier should be landing soon. Then we can leave.' I'm frightened."

Judith's hunger disappeared as anxiety replaced the growls. She raised the phone by her left ear so Zee could hear. Judith glanced around the vicinity, but no one was back in this area. "Ah, JJ…"

"Judith, I heard. Let's work through this situation. He's there to meet someone. Julian's not looking for you. Please stay in your disguises. They're perfect. He'll think two boring scientists appear more like nuns than anyone he might know. Can you drive to get some distance from him but maybe get some photos of the meeting?"

After a few seconds, Xiamara held the phone and whispered, "JJ, Judith looks pale and is mumbling. Can you repeat what you said you want us to do?"

He did. Then Xiamara got tongue-tied.

Judith shook her head and took a breath to banish her panic. She grabbed Zee by the elbow, opened the passenger door, and shoved her friend inside. Then, she raced around to the driver's side and started the vehicle, ensuring the windows were rolled tight like an engorged tick.

She carefully ensured both of their hats and glasses were situated as designed. The idea that they could be mistaken for nuns made her snort with amusement. Judith placed the phone on speaker and set it on the dashboard holder near the radio.

"JJ, we're nervous." She bit the skin on the edge of her thumb. "Okay, scared. I'm going to drive slowly back to where we came in. When we entered, I saw a side dirt road that might provide a good vantage point. We'll see what we can do for some snaps. Call you back in a few. Hopefully, he didn't get to smell Zee; he'd know we're here." She pressed the button to drop the call, carefully backed out of the area, and headed toward the exit.

Xiamara whispered, "We did good for a hot minute."

Judith reached over and patted her friend's knee. "We're not out of this yet."

JJ pressed the number, hoping Gracie could answer. He drummed his fingers, waiting for the connection or a return call from the ladies on Saint-Martin.

"What's up, JJ?" Gracie's face appeared on the screen.

He related the current details he'd received from Judith, hoping they hadn't been discovered. He rubbed his hand over his face, searching for a solution in the corners of his mind.

Gracie let him finish before she let out a breath. "JJ, with that information, we can alert the Coast Guard to pull over the boat, board it, and seize the cargo. If there are gold coins and precious gems, they'll be tied up for months explaining where the unregistered treasure came from. Julian won't know where his team went or what they had. The action could cripple his precious stone-hunting project. We might even get the Saint-Martin authorities to detain Julian and his henchman."

JJ smirked. "Yeah, if they answered my calls. The second I mentioned Julian Lafluer, they disconnected. He has cultivated influence over the local police as a buffer for himself. This man is crafty enough to buy his favors in advance. We'll need to tempt him with something he can't refuse."

"You got something or somebody's in mind?" she sourly replied.

"I don't understand what they were thinking," JJ advised, "taking that fishing boat to get to Julian. It's a thousand-plus nautical miles from Cat Island to Saint-Martin. It simply isn't practical to pilot a craft like the *Osvaldo* that far. It would take days to make the trip even at the top speed."

"I read the transcript of the conversation. Harto said he'd be there in a day. They should have chosen to fly with that tight a deadline."

"Yeah, I agree. But they'd have to check a bag or footlocker of gold coins. We have no idea of the volume. I admit flying would be faster, but what choice do they have?" JJ smacked his forehead. "Of course. Harto must have another boat."

"What? Marian and Brayson would have seen it."

"Maybe. But they've been focused on Nohea." He ran some quick numbers. "He's got to have a fast watercraft at his disposal, just like Julian has an airplane. We aren't aware of all his resources, though we've been categorizing what we've found. We know the man has expensive taste, multiple homes, and hidden funds."

Gracie groaned. "You're right. Harto wouldn't store the gold on the boat where Nohea routinely served. That jailbird would systematically search as a matter of principle. Let's alert Brayson to try to discover a possible alternate boat."

"I'll see if we can track any watercraft racing away from Cat Island at high speed in the next few hours. If the boat gets commandeered by the Coast Guard, I'll have our temporary Saint-Martin scientists place another call, this time to Julian as his trusted Harto. I bet Satya could finish that language model in record time," related JJ.

"When the new craft is identified, can we track it, piggy-backing off our satellite links as it heads toward Saint-Martin? It would be awesome if Brayson and Marian could board the trawler boat and get the details on how the drone harvester machine works," Gracie replied. "Then I could use that to help Jacobo Hassan with the San Juan Treasury Department negotiations."

"All right. But you get to convince the Coast Guard they are special agents sent to dissect the technology for a full report." Grinning, he pointed his finger toward the screen for emphasis.

"Done, JJ."

CHAPTER 42

Hiding in Plain Sight

Brayson sat on the barstool next to Loane. "You told us someone has your gold coins, but they've hidden then. Why would they keep them from you but not cash them?"

Stopping at the other side of the man, Marian said, "You know who has them, don't you?"

He felt large beads of sweat collecting on his forehead, worried he'd said too much. Backpedaling, he said with a flick of his fingers. "Those coins are long gone. Plus, I need to cancel today's trip with you. I just got word we're shipping out as soon as the boat is loaded with provisions. We're meeting our investor. I won't be able to take you folks out again for several days." He shrugged. "Check with the day sailors at the end of the pier. They might be able to show you to an underwater shipwreck."

Brayson sensed a turning point in their relationship, so he casually shrugged. "Loane, it has been a pleasure. Once we get the story published, I'll send a copy of the edition addressed to you, care of this hotel. Make sure you check for it in a couple of weeks." With that, he patted him on the arm, signifying it was time for all of them to part company.

Nohea appeared relieved that no more dialog was needed. He nodded to each of them before walking out the door.

Reaching the boat, Nohea found Harto supervising the transfer of the last of the items to his cigar craft. "Are we done with the side hustle? Are you ready so we can get our cargo to Julian? He wants everything for a client who is hounding him."

Nohea wondered if the coins were also going on the trip. He coyly asked, "The gold coins too?"

Harto smirked. "Not your concern. You will make certain the engine performs. Julian wants to speak with you about your future."

Nohea bit his tongue, planning to bide his time until they were on the water later in the evening. "Why are you unloading stuff if we're leaving?"

"Because we're taking my other faster boat. Julian requested that we arrive tomorrow on Saint-Martin. Blake or Bradley usually sleeps on it. You may not like them, but they are my troopers who know how to take orders and guard our possessions. This boat and equipment will be secured."

"What kind of weapons do we have to deal with pirates who show up and want to inspect the boat?"

Nohea smirked, realizing Harto hadn't considered this angle. "Uh…that's a good idea. I'd better call a friend of mine."

CHAPTER 43

With Any Luck

Judith pulled into the empty La Loterie parking lot. She turned off the engine, her hands still shaking. "I don't think we were spotted."

"We weren't," confirmed Xiamara. "I believe I captured some great shots. I also captured the aircraft's tail number and pictures of each man when they finished their business. I wasn't imagining things. The man was Julian."

"You're always steady when taking photos, my friend." Judith looked around at the beautiful foliage, which was thick and luscious, with multiple shades of green and periodic flowers peeking out. She stepped from the Jeep, raced to the hatch, and popped it open to grab a few items from her duffle bag. "Oh my, Zee," she called. "I swear, I smell nutmeg, cumin, garlic, ginger, and a hint of oranges."

Zee sauntered next to her and took a deep breath. "Yes, you do. That smells like the same spicy flavors I love." She hooked a thumb behind her left shoulder and added, "I saw a sign for the Jungle Room, which I think is the source of the food scents making my stomach growl."

"Ship off the photos to our boss with a note saying we're safe. I am ready to eat."

Moments later, she commented, "Done. Do you think they have rum?"

"I bet they do. I'll buy the first round."

They laughed and walked arm in arm toward the fresh scents of lunch.

Marian gave Brayson a passionate kiss. "Let's call JJ."

He grabbed his aerial drone. "Sweetie, since they're pulling out to head to Saint-Martin, I want to try to get photos of their departure if I can."

Marian nodded. "I'll call to let him know the *Osvaldo* and team are moving out. He may need us to follow them somehow."

Brayson gave her one more hug and rushed from their suite.

Marian set up her laptop to start a conference call when her cell phone indicated an inbound call from JJ.

"Hey, give me a minute. I was setting up a conference call using our standard link."

"I'll join you there."

Moments later, they faced one another on the screen. "Hi, JJ. We were discussing our next moves. According to Nohea, Harto is loading everything to leave. Brayson left to see if he could get pictures of their departure and how low the boat was sitting in the water. They might be headed to Saint-Martin. Do you want us to go there?"

"Maybe. We have a problem. The plane Judith and Zee planned to use to return to San Juan is down for repairs. That wouldn't be a problem except they spotted Julian and an associate at the airport. They don't think he saw them. I'm expecting photos from them and a check-in soon. Gracie is trying to arrange for the Coast Guard to commandeer the boat and confiscate the gold coins, but we think they might be using a different boat than the trawler. Have you seen them on another boat, like a high-speed cigar boat?"

"Not at all. Nohea hasn't mentioned it either."

"If they use a different craft to head to Saint-Martin, I want you to board the fishing boat. We thought you two could check out their harvesting drone setup. If we can't get it, we must know how it works. A copy of the software they're using would be great."

Marian wrung her hands nervously. "Judith and Xiamara are in danger again by being too close to Julian. Poop! They need backup, JJ."

"They may, but I want to give them time to update me. It's only been a short while. Promise."

"Do Brayson and I need to split up to complete both tasks? I don't like it, but we can do it."

"No. I'll let you know. Get this information to Brayson. We might get an advanced look at the technology."

CHAPTER 44

Just Like Old Times

Brayson gazed at the video feed from his drone and frowned. "I swear our squealer said they were moving out. Why in the devil would they unload stuff if they were adding provisions to travel?" Frustrated, he pulled at this ear but kept the recording on, trying to find a logical reason for their actions. He mumbled, "What the hell are you playing us for, Nohea?"

He felt Marian's presence before she leaned over to watch the screen. "Hi, sweetheart. You dashed out so fast that you missed JJ's call. He thinks they must have a second boat to be able to arrive at Saint-Martin on time. Does what you are seeing support that possibility?"

Brayson scrubbed his hair with his fingers and grinned. "Thank you, darling, for helping me realize I'm not nuts in thinking they shouldn't be unloading the boat they're supposedly provisioning."

"Do you know where they are taking the stuff?"

"Not yet. I must keep the drone higher so the whir doesn't capture anyone's attention. From what you're saying, I need to follow where they go. I've only spotted Harto and Nohea. The young men haven't appeared."

"They're probably at the boat with the gold. JJ thought it might be a cigar boat. Those racers chew up ocean miles like mad. They'll chart a course with island hops for additional fuel."

"I know you read a lot, honey, but that's an image."

Marian laughed, and he joined in. "They're loading up the flatbed dolly and tying it down. With as low as *Osvaldo* is sitting in the water, someone will secure it. We might have a chance to look at the technology if we can break into the programs."

Brayson wrinkled his nose. "If? If? I'll bring the extra laptop and get the information."

"We might want to appropriate the craft," she said with a gleam reflected in her eyes and that coy smile she knew how to leverage.

"Wanna bet that Nohea will make a play to take command of the boat before they get to Saint-Martin?"

"It's not a bet if we are on the same side. Are you expecting a Caribbean power play between Harto and Nohea, aka Loane?"

Looking down at JJ's text message on his phone, Brayson commented, "Harto made a call asking for one of the guys to bring party favors on board to keep pirates in check."

Marian shook her head and rolled her eyes. "No one's taking your bet. A fast-moving cigar boat might get the attention of the Coast Guard if they got a drug-running tip."

Brayson laughed at the following text message. "Your clairvoyance is functioning, my love. However, suggesting that the boat has gold and gems unlawfully recovered from a sunken wreck seems almost unfair. Hopefully, we can help identify it."

The drone video feed tracked the men moving the flatbed on the main walkway, which looped around the main building, to what they believed was a covered pier.

"No wonder we never spotted them on another boat." Brayson blew out a frustrated sigh. "It's covered."

"I'll text JJ the latest while you upload what we have. Can you identify and track the craft when it exits?"

"I need to land the drone and swap batteries. I hope I can relaunch it quickly and do just that."

Blake was busy stowing the rest of the gear carefully to maintain the weight balance of the cigar boat. He knew they were almost ready to depart and didn't want any errors on his or his brother's part.

Harto approached Blake and groused, "Blake, you and Bradley, go remove the satellite uplink from the *Osvaldo*. I want it installed on this craft. We'll repurpose it to carry voice communications to maintain secured conversations."

Blake nodded. Working together, the two men emptied their hands, grabbed the appropriate tools, and hot-footed back to their trawling boat. Blake grumbled under his breath as they headed to the public slip. "I wish he'd said something earlier. Those mounting screws are gonna take some time. I don't want to get yelled at for taking too long."

Bradley stated, "Don't worry, I'll work on loosening the battery. It shouldn't take too long. Then we can take out both pieces at the same time."

After fifteen minutes of frenzied effort, the twins removed the equipment. With a high-five, they grinned and returned to the covered slip. Harto and Nohea were almost finished stowing the last of the gear.

CHAPTER 45

Pirate Friends or Foes?

The drone had no sooner reached his hands when a roar like a 747 taking off filled the air in and around the marina. He worked feverishly to change the drone's battery and get it back into the air. "I'm going to be too late to get a clean shot at it," he yelled over the din.

Minutes later, the noise trailed away from where they sat.

Brayson slapped the railing, annoyed that time wasn't on his side. "Sorry, JJ," he mumbled.

"Honey, how about we have a nice romantic evening ransacking the *Osvaldo* to get all their data?"

"That sounds like it could provide some interesting options for us to discover."

"We do explore well, don't we? I'll land the drone and grab the computer gear." She did a little two-step, exposing her shapely legs, singing, ♪ "It'll be just like old times …" ♫

Brayson pulled her into a powerful embrace. "I do love your suggestions, babe." Pleased with the overall results of his drone's performance, Brayson grinned at Marian as he opened the door to their bungalow.

"I have a stellar surprise for JJ."

Her eyebrows arched. "What did you do, honey? You look like the kid that just found a box of money."

He carefully copied the video feed to his phone app that synced to his secure laptop. He turned and scooped her into a hug. "Better than money." Setting her feet on the floor, he laughed. "Harto and his bunch installed a satellite uplink on the cigar boat after removing it from the trawler. They want two-way communications with the home office."

She smiled. "Okay, so they want to contact Julian," she added, wiggling her hips, ready to do a two-step.

"Yep, that's my guess. Isn't it great they were so thoughtful about installing something we can monitor while they dart around the Caribbean? It's a LEO/GEO satellite box that does two-way communications." He rubbed his hands together like a magician, ready to pull a rabbit out of a hat. "We'll get to track them over their entire trip."

"Do we still need to board the trawler and check out the programs?"

"JJ and the team will love this, especially Granger. To answer your question, yes, we can board the trawler and reconnoiter as soon as JJ can verify the location of the cigar boat. It should be darker by then, so we'll be less noticeable."

"I'll set up the bridge connection. You go take a quick shower."

Harto looked around as some folks turned their heads toward the noisy craft. "No racy moves until we get out of sight of the marina," he commented, but no one could hear above the loud rumble of the engine.

Blake and Bradley glanced around the shoreline and waved to a few folks who looked toward the boat.

Harto laughed. "I've never driven this with them aboard. I know they'll be impressed."

With his eyes closed, Nohea slumped against the bucket seat cushion near the nose of the craft.

"He'll move when we get up to speed," Harto said. "He'll get pelted by the salt spray, which will feel like shards of glass on his face."

Outside the wake line, the boat traffic thinned, and Harto increased the throttle to the halfway point, which was well short of its top speed.

Blake moved closer and shouted, "Why aren't you pushing the craft harder? I've read these babies can fly at eighty knots."

"No worries, we'll get there in time. I don't want to hammer the engines too hard. They have to last until we get there. Besides, the sea is a little rough, and we'll only get bounced around if we go faster than we're doing now. I will boost our speed between the islands where the water isn't as rough. I also want to teach you to pilot this boat safely if we need to spell one another."

An hour after they were on the water, Bradley approached. "Is it my imagination, Uncle, or is that boat following us?" He gestured his thumb over his shoulder. "I noticed that they left almost the same time we did. The distance between us is narrowing."

Harto glanced back and smirked. "If they're trying to catch us, they're in for a surprise. Our top speed is over eighty-five knots. We can just about outrun anything, so no worries." Harto increased speed, keeping watch of the gap between the crafts.

"Guys," he shouted, "secure everything 'cause we're—" At that moment, a gun poked his spine.

"Back the engines down into idle," demanded Nohea with an extra jab to the left kidney.

Harto winced and complied.

"You won't outrun them because they're here to help me."

Blake and Bradley bristled at the threat leveled at Harto, but Nohea pulled out another weapon and swung it between the twins. "Don't even think about it. I don't like you, but I'm not ready to kill you yet. I only want what's mine. Thanks for getting the weapons I needed. Put it into idle, Harto. NOW!"

The trailing boat pulled alongside. Harto identified the three burly men as unwashed shore rats for rent. To prevent damage, they secured the two boats with ropes and bumpers.

Nohea gave them a two-fingered salute. "You took your sweet time pulling the boat up."

The man piloting the craft stated. "My guys will board. I told them to find the stuff, and we'll take you along."

Harto let them on without a protest.

"The gold is here somewhere," Nohea stated. "We'll need to find it and be on our way."

Two of the intruders hopped aboard and began tearing everything apart. They tossed supplies everywhere. Twelve minutes later, everything was torn up for no good reason.

One man shouted, "Johnson, this is a wild goose chase. There's no gold here."

Johnson fumed, "I told you not to use our names, fool."

Waving his guns at Harto, Nohea screamed, "Where's the stuff, Harto?" He jammed a gun into Harto's stomach. "You said we had to take the stuff to Julian. We're on our way to him. Damnit it, where are the goods?"

Harto chortled. "You believed my story. Fool!" He shouted back to make sure everybody heard. "It was a ploy to see what you'd stoop to if the circumstances were right. Julian didn't call and ask me to do anything. We rigged up this diversion to see if you could be trusted. I knew you'd betray us like you've betrayed everyone your whole life." He lowered his voice and leaned closer. "Julian doesn't want us out of the field for even a day. Everything's hidden far away from here."

Nohea demanded, waving the gun. "You're lying, Harto! I'll kill you."

"You'll waste your powder like you did today." He raised his shoulders and opened his hands, looking at Nohea and his friends. "Nothing's on this boat. Your buddies proved it. You lied to them."

Panic etched its way into Nohea's face. He turned to plead his case to Johnson. "No, I swear the goods are on board. He's lying. I heard them plan to bring everything. Man, I've sabotaged the engines like we agreed, so he'll never make top speed."

Johnson swung his double-barreled shotgun into position. He raised it like a practiced mercenary and fired both barrels into Loane. The blast pushed the dead man over the side and into the water. "The sharks will appreciate the free feeding, and the sea god will be satisfied.

"What do you know about this, Harto?"

"Not a thing. I don't know you or your friends. I've never seen you."

"Keep it that way, or we'll find you."

Harto nodded and raised his right hand. He ran his index finger across his lips, then added his thumb at the side like a key, locking the secret away, praying it would be enough.

"You two, get on board." He jerked the thumb of one hand to indicate the time was over. "We're leaving."

The two surly men scowled and jumped back onto their craft. They cut the mooring lines. Johnson fired up the engines and executed a one-eighty turn back toward the marina.

Harto released a breath of gratitude. He raised his folded hands in a prayer toward Heaven. He noticed Blake and Bradley frozen in shock at the execution-style murder.

Harto clapped his hands together to get their attention, then chuckled. "This worked out better than I could have planned. Guys, snap out of it. We need to understand what that jerk did to our engines. I will call Julian."

CHAPTER 46

Wrong Sheet of Music

JW completed the update to the tracking files, noting that Satya completed the newest voice synthesizing just in time. Her process to customize a deepfake voice was even better than the original videos Judith and Xiamara did. Having AI copy someone's voice would put the security of voice biometrics in yesterday's news. He spotted Granger stretching his fingers with a smug expression. "Hey, Cous, did you align to the satellite signature installed on Harto's cigar boat?"

"Yep. Got 'em right here." He grinned and highlighted the map, pinpointing the craft's current location and signal. "It was convenient of them to initiate a broadcast sequence from the terminal to connect to the nearest LEO satellite without encryption. Stupid, though." Granger straightened, his head moving closer to the screen. "It appears they're trying to make a phone call. Maybe a pizza delivery? Har, har, har. I crack myself up."

Alarmed, JW interjected, "Damn, our instructions are to block calls until I get the clear signal, which has not come through. JJ doesn't want them to reach Julian until the next ruse call is completed. We don't want different stories to expose our team."

"I know. Relax, I'm on it. I'm in the LEO satellite. When the signal handshake is complete, I'll modify the communications protocol, messing up the signaling connection, then drop their link. I'll control the reset."

JW noticed Granger intently absorbed in his screens, his eyes unwavering from the signals. He expelled his breath and rechecked his connections for the all-clear notification. He wanted to be close enough to strike.

Without shifting his focus, Granger stated, "Once they arrive at the next island, they'll likely shift to a terrestrial link and get connected. That we can't stop."

"Thanks for the update. Let me know if anything changes. I'll update JJ."

"Excuse me," Auri interjected. "Based on the signal's current location, the craft's speed, and the next likely port of call, I calculated, with confirmation from ICABOD, that we have three-quarters to an hour before they can connect to a land signal."

"Thanks, Auri, for the update. That's a short window to get our team off Saint-Martin."

"If Satya is finished with the voice programs," Granger added, "another call to Julian might buy extra time."

They all heard Satya's giggle before she said, "I'm ready. It's good to go. I put the note out on our collaboration chat channel. The time is now to have another fake conversation between these guys if Granger can control the connections so everyone's on the wrong music sheet."

Granger's face scowled. "If, my sweet young cousin…if? I got this."

JW smiled at the virtual team. "I'll call JJ and let him know. Thank you all."

The call Julian placed rolled to voice mail, which increased his aggravation. He snarled, glancing at Ryu. "Where the hell is he? There've been no progress calls. I can't get him to answer."

"It isn't like him to be out of touch with you for this long."

"Harto's good about updates." Julian rechecked the settings on his laptop, then clenched and unclenched his hand.

"Either he's out on the water hunting like a crazy person," Ryu suggested, "or the cell coverage is offline somewhere between us."

Julian pursed his lips, turning toward Ryu. "Once a macro-tower picks up the signal, the cell call is put onto one of the many physical cables between islands and carriers. All my other calls are going through. I'm connecting to Cat Island before rolling to voice mail. There isn't a network problem."

Ryu bent his head toward his hands as he closed his eyes. "I forgot how well you know communications technology. With no network issues, he's probably swimming his heart out trying to get more stones for you so he can earn the new toys you promised."

"True," Julian chuckled. "I'll try again at the end of the day. I bet he phones back before then. Maybe we should go to lunch nearby to get my mind off watching the computer. I could use a change of scenery; how about you?"

CHAPTER 47

Watch, Don't Stare

Judith scooted her sunglasses to the right to make room for the snack dish and rum provided by the waitress. She'd insisted they leave the hats on like another guest at a far table. She raised her drink to her friend. "Cheers!" Then she threw back her second shot of smooth Bacardi, watching Xiamara follow suit. The tension in her back eased from their too-close encounter with their dangerous adversary. Her friend took a deep breath and blew it out, which helped her further relax. She smiled at the La Loterie's simple yet practical furnishings, complemented by the well-maintained garden boasting blooms in whites and purples with outliers of yellows. Fragrances of Caribbean cuisine promised they would appreciate mouth-watering selections.

She reached over and patted her friend's hand. "Zee, I'm ready to taste the jerk chicken and callaloo I ordered."

Zee relaxed her features. "I might want a taste to verify its authenticity, but the seafood plate with rice sounded too good to pass up." She dipped another plantain and popped it into her mouth. "These *tostones* remind me of our younger days when we were servers making ends meet. Life was simpler then and far less dangerous."

"True," Judith agreed. "But we're in a better place with our work friends." She grabbed one of the morsels from the center dish. "These are delicious. After we get our meal, another shot might be in order."

"No," Zee emphatically replied, shaking her head. "We're on the same island as the man who nearly succeeded in selling us into slavery. We need our wits about us."

Judith chuckled. "Good point. Iced tea is next but with lime." She rechecked her phone, hoping for a text from the pilot that the plane had been repaired. She texted JJ on their location, which he immediately acknowledged. "Perhaps we should return to the airport and be ready when the plane is fixed."

"Judith, the pilot told you to get a room. He wasn't planning on it being ready before morning."

Looking around at the quiet paradise with an older clientele —she'd counted six people—Judith added, "This isn't a bad place to be stranded. Let's ask our server if there's a room available. I would love to finish our meal and remove this restrictive costume. My boobs would be happy out of the binding for a while. And I thought bras were an annoying necessity."

"I'm so there with you," Zee chortled, popping the last plantain on the plate into her mouth. "The too-small bra I have on is trash when we get— Oh, my God. Look to your right; It's him and his sidekick."

Dumbfounded as her friend's pallor turned white as a ghost, Judith whispered, "I'll be damned." She pulled her hat a little firmer onto her head. She figured replacing the glasses would bring too much attention. She leaned over and quietly said, "You don't look like you did when we last saw him in Puerto Rico. How about me?"

"You look like your mother or older."

"Zee, keep slumped over, and if we talk, deepen our voices an octave or two. We don't want to draw attention." From where the two men stood, she felt sure they would see the profiles of two women in hats with drab clothing in the shadows of the foliage. She tapped on her phone, watching Zee's hands quiver.

> HELP. Julian and Ryu just walked into the restaurant.
> They are near. Too close.

Seconds later:

> Are you still in disguise?

> YES

> He won't recognize you. Be small.

Judith peered under the brim of her hat, watching the men. She turned the screen of her phone toward her friend. After reading the exchange, Xiamara looked down at her plate with only a slight nod. Judith wished the server would bring their food so they could order tea, look busy eating and ask about getting a room.

Using her peripheral vision, Judith followed the direction of Ryu's head as he scanned the area, thankfully without giving them a second look. She recalled he was the bodyguard personified. Julian appeared unconcerned and relaxed, which made her want to spit. She overheard his request to the hostess to seat them facing the door, away from other patrons.

"Perfect," Zee softly spoke. "We'll never walk out of here without being spotted. Maybe if we set our table ablaze and yell *fire*, everyone will run for the one exit over them."

The phone screen lit, indicating a new text.

One emergency evacuation plan is coming right up.
Don't stare, but enjoy the reaction. You have a room booked
upstairs—a nice one, too!

The corners of Judith's mouth raised slightly as she turned the screen so Zee could read it.

Zee rolled her eyes, nodded, and breathed until the tremors in her fingers finally stopped.

Judith heard the melodic ringtone of a phone from the direction of the two men. Julian, looking pleased, said to his tablemate, "You were right, my friend. Here's his call. Let me get this while you order drinks."

Julian strolled to an empty alcove. Fortunately, Judith could still observe his actions. He listened to the caller and then straightened, appearing alarmed. He returned to the table and growled, "Cancel our drink order. Get me out of here. Now."

Judith whispered, "I wish I'd heard the other side of that phone conversation."

The waitress showed up, placing the drinks on Julian's table. Ryu leaped from his chair while Julian threw a bill on the table. Ryu dodged the confused waitress as he took Julian's arm.

Xiamara giggled, "I can't wait to read the transcript of that call. JJ must have pushed the right buttons to get such an immediate response."

"Come on, my friend. Let's get our food rerouted to our room with two extra Bacardi shots. I'm ready to rest up and wait for the pilot to tell us we can depart."

Judith spoke to the waitress, who promised it would be served within thirty minutes.

Minutes later, Julian and Ryu were in the car. Julian struggled to light a cigarette, hoping to calm his nerves. A few puffs later, he felt better.

"What did Harto have to say?" Ryu asked.

"He warned me we're in danger. He's been trying to call since he claimed I called him, telling him to bundle up the stones and gold and bring them to me here on Saint-Martin. During the conversation, he calculated the days it would take Nohea, and asked why I didn't fly and pick up the stuff like before. He loaded up the cigar boat because it was the only way he might deliver in the timeframe I'd indicated on the call, but that call never happened. He's been trying to call me back for confirmation. He's convinced I'm in danger because of someone trying to learn my location."

Ryu nodded and accelerated the vehicle to return to Julian's safehouse. "I may have to change my mind about Harto. What do you want to do?"

"Get home and review our options."

"Yes, sir."

CHAPTER 48

We're Not Alone

The Gigazon hummed with activity. All the team members were online working on their projects. Incidental smooth jazz in the background created an atmosphere of relaxing tranquility. Chortling, Granger said loudly enough to get his teammates' attention. "I wished I could've seen Julian's face, thinking he was talking to the real Harto. Har! Har! Satya, your synthesized voice program is perfection."

Satya motioned a thumbs-up toward her cousin before refocusing on her screen.

"Oops," Granger announced. "Hey, Harto's trying to get through on the satellite link again. Should I shut him down?"

JW interjected. "Hold off blocking his call. JJ indicated he wants a real call from Harto to add to the deception. Additional confusion will increase Julian's anxiety. Plus, we'll hear new information we can use to find them or continue messing with both of them."

"Righty-o. The call will connect and automatically record in three, two, one …"

Julian had barely settled into the bungalow when his phone went off again. It appeared to be Harto calling back. He motioned to Ryu to come closer as he showed him the screen.

Ryu shrugged and motioned with his hand to his ear for Julian to put it on speaker.

Julian nodded. "More problems? We quickly left the area. Do you have any details on who's after me?"

Harto sounded hesitant as he replied, "Julian, what are you talking about? After that call telling me to stop what I was doing and bring you the harvested property, we've been using my cigar boat to get to you to meet your timeline. I'd have called sooner, but I haven't been able to get the satellite link to work. I wanted to update you."

"I received a call from you twenty or so minutes ago telling me to leave the restaurant and return to my safe house. Don't mess with me, Harto."

"Julian, I didn't call you. We're still on the water; our only communication choice is via the satellite link. And how the hell would I know you were in danger in a restaurant on Saint-Martin?"

Frustrated, Julian sensed the anger rising from his toes, but he masked the fear in the pit of his stomach. "Where in the hell did you get the stupid idea to stop your harvesting efforts and come here?" He sputtered. "I can fly to you faster while you get more hours in the water. You told me you knew your main job."

Ryu's eyes met his. He appeared as confused as Julian felt.

"I thought it a poor idea," Harto replied, "but you said to bring Nohea. You even allowed the twins to come along. Then you told me to hurry."

Julian tilted his head toward Ryu, squinting his eyes and pursing his lips. Harto's voice sounded shaky and at a higher octave. Ryu put up his palms, indicating he was confused.

"That's what we've been doing," said Harto. "But this sounds wrong."

"Harto, you're not making any sense. Let me speak with Nohea."

"Julian, I can't. He was gunned down by some pirates that followed us from the marina. Wait, let me back up a second. Nohea pulled a gun on me and the twins. Then he forced me to stop the boat to let his buddies board us to look for the gold coins. That's when he was shot. He's fish food."

Julian's heart sank as he succumbed to the panic. He closed his eyes, shaking his head. "You're insane, Harto. Nohea was mad, but he wouldn't betray me. You can't be Harto because of all this nonsense you're saying." Julian hung up and shot a stare of disbelief at Ryu.

"Who is following our movements, and where are they?"

"I don't know, boss. Did they get the gold and the jewels Harto was supposedly bringing you?'

"I have no idea. I'm not certain which call was Harto. I know I'm being duped. I swear the voices sounded the same, except for the anxiousness at the end of this conversation."

CHAPTER 49

Gotcha

Johnson ground his teeth as he throttled back, entering the slow-down area of the marina waters. The setting sun glittered off the calm waters, but enjoying the smooth ride did nothing to abate the frustration roiling in his gut. He gripped the helm so tightly the color drained from his fingers. He was still grinding his teeth angrily as he steered their craft back to the marina.

"Loane, the damn, lying jerk," Johnson grumbled as he hit the wheel. He glanced through narrowed eyes at his crew of two. "I gave my tribute to Poseidon this trip. Next time, we'll get the treasure." He played with the beginnings of a plan while navigating toward the gas pump. "At least we get back in time to eat in the bar."

"Whatever you say, boss," replied Tom, the older, beefier one.

"Rum, too," he snarled.

He and Tom had been carving out a meager existence pirating in these waters for nearly twenty years. Greg, on the other hand, had been with him for only five. Pirate 2 and Pirate 3 knew his moods and stayed clear of Johnson so he wouldn't use his shotgun on them.

"Greg, get out the tie-off lines. I want to gas up before we eat. Tom, verify we can still get the cheap slip for the night with whoever is on duty. I don't want to go to our side of the island until tomorrow. I'm ready for some gambling if there's a game on."

"Yes, sir," Greg mumbled, retrieving the stowed lines to make ready.

Johnson tapped the side of his head until his idea finally coalesced. The corners of his mouth twitched. He stated, "We'll do one more thing before that drink, boys. We're going to board Loane and Harto's trawler." He pointed toward the pier. "It's tied to the slip, and we know they won't return anytime soon."

Johnson steered the boat to the gas pump, where Greg secured the craft. Tom stepped onto the pier to take care of his assignment.

"Hey, Tom, come back here."

Tom dropped back into the boat and joined Johnson at the helm.

"I've decided I want something to show for our wasted effort today. Once we top off the tanks, head to the dock." He grinned and stared at the man, narrowing his eyes. "See if you can get the engines online with your hot-wiring talents."

"Okay," Tom replied, rubbing his hands together, excited to join Johnson's plan. "Then what?"

"After we're gassed, I'll have Greg head over to help you drop its moorings. Tomorrow, I'll follow you to our private landing, where we can modify the boat's identification. I'll find a buyer for pennies on the dollar, and we can bank the profits."

"I'm in, but I sure would like a meal and a shot of rum first."

Johnson chuckled. "Once the trawler is secured at our landing, we'll return for food and a drink. We'll skip the gambling until after we sell the craft, though."

Tom gave his captain a thumbs-up. "Got it." He scrambled off the vessel.

"Don't screw this up, Tom," called Johnson. The man turned with a calm expression and sauntered down the pier toward his target.

"Greg, finish gassing." He reached over with a few bills extended in his hand. "Pay for the fuel, then hop in. We'll sidle up to the boat at the far end of the pier, where Tom is waiting. We'll leave from there."

Greg nodded. "Okay." He completed his tasks in short order and jumped aboard.

Brayson worked to gain a complete connection to *Osvaldo's* onboard computer while he and Marian exchanged ideas on how to get the needed intel. He knew Marian would look at the pier repeatedly to verify that no unexpected guests were heading their way.

"I've got it, sweetheart. I'm downloading the data now. It won't be long."

"Good. It seems quiet, other than that boat filling up at the pump by the marina store." Several minutes later, she let out a long sigh and gently tapped his shoulder. "Hon, we have one very determined man heading our way."

"Completed now." Brayson powered down his laptop, stowed it into his backpack, and swung it onto his shoulders. He stood next to Marian, watching the man approach. Brayson whispered, "I've taken shots of this guy milling around the marina. He runs with two other men; I think the fat one is the trio's leader."

"Perhaps his friends are in the boat moving through the water approaching from the starboard side. I don't think this is a social call."

The boat edged closer to Harto's trawler. The walking man jumped aboard the *Osvaldo* and stared at Brayson and Marian, frozen in place.

The boat driver shouted, "What are you lovebirds doing here? Harto sent us to retrieve his boat and bring it to him before sundown. Get off here, and I won't rat you out." The boat pilot waved the other man to the side to moor the boats with bumpers to prevent damage to both crafts.

Deciding the timeline needed escalation, the driver pulled out his cell phone. He verified that he had good signal strength and then made a call, throwing caution to the wind by not lowering his voice. "I've got a used trawler you can pick up tomorrow at my pier. Offer me a great price. I'm only offering it to you if you're interested… Good. It needs minor doctoring before I turn it over. You can get it cheap…That's a fair price. Bring your driver and cash."

The man on the *Osvaldo* edged closer to the pair and hollered, "You heard the man. Get off this boat. You don't belong here. Get moving before we report you to the marina authorities."

Marian edged behind Brayson as he replied, "It's all right. I was doing some maintenance for Loane, who works for the owner. Who are you?"

"I'm not gonna tell you again. Get off."

The man lunged with a menacing look, beefy arms up, ready to fight, and headed right for them. Marian moved from behind her husband with a loaded speargun in-hand.

Stunned, the man stopped in his tracks, leaving enough room for Brayson to maneuver if needed. Marian coolly let the projectile fly straight at the man, piercing one side of his thigh and sticking out the back. As a practiced weapons expert, she quickly reloaded the efficient device. "I've always loved all sorts of weapons, arrows or bullets, honey," she said.

"I know. Best of all, you are a great shot, sweetheart," Brayson commented with a hint of admiration.

Marian pointed the speargun at the two men on the moored boat. Greg flipped off the lines, letting them dangle in the water. Then he raised a hand, waving it in circles, indicating to the driver that the boat was free. The watercraft eased backward, heading away from the marina.

Brayson palmed his cell phone, pressing JJ's name. He smiled at Marian. "Trouble leaves in a hurry when you're around. I love that about you." The call connected. "Hi, boss, you said to call if we had any trouble. We had some, but my spearfishing wife dealt with it. Check the photos of three unwashed dock men. There's a high probability they were here to snatch Harto's boat. We've got one down on the deck, but the other two escaped by boat. The registration number is A1456J9902MM2. They headed out to sea, but I suspect they have a private location on the other side of the island. The *Osvaldo* is still under our control. Are you sending the Coast Guard?"

CHAPTER 50

Dire Straight

The call to Julian hadn't gone as Harto expected. He glanced over the water, looking for any boats headed toward them. His heart still pounded in his ears from when he saw Nohea meet his fate. He rubbed a hand over his face, hoping to wake from this nightmare. He was afraid to start the engines, worried they might explode. "What should I do?" he muttered. The twins remained immobile with anguished expressions. Trying to distract them, he moved closer and patted each of their shoulders.

"Boys, we've survived something unexpected. But we're alive," he quietly said. "I need you to focus on the here and now." They blinked but didn't acknowledge. "Bradley," he said a little louder, "I need you to snap out of it and help me." He slapped the younger man on the cheek.

Bradley blinked rapidly but looked up with teary eyes. "What, Uncle? I saw a man die."

"We all did, buddy. Be grateful it wasn't us." Harto smacked Blake in the same way. "Blake, get it together. We have to figure out what to do next."

Blake coughed and swallowed as he focused on Harto. "I'll never forget."

"None of us will, but we survived. Now we need to decide the next steps." He started pacing the small walkway, counting his ideas on his fingers, and said, "We need to figure out what is wrong with the engines, recover the jewels and coins from the hidden compartment, and eat something."

"I'm a little hungry and thirsty, too." Blake stood and moved toward their provisions strewn about from the useless search.

Harto watched Blake grab water bottles and a few bags of chips and then share them. "Blake, how about we finish this snack, and you get everything stowed properly?"

"Yes, sir," he crunched his reply.

Harto needed to figure out how to check the engine and get going. Neither Bradley nor Blake worked with engines. "I watched everything Nohea did to the other boat; there must be some similarities," he muttered. He felt confident he could find solutions on the internet. It seemed the right step. He had a signal to access the web with his cell phone while they were this close to land.

"Suit up, Bradley. I need you to retrieve the stowed items from the hidden safety box."

His nephew's somber eyes looked at him as he implored, "I'd like to move a little bit away from the body. I know the sharks have done their frenzy, but I'd like to gain some distance."

"You've got a point, son. How about you two row closer to shore for a while? We can stay in the calmer waters where we can see shapes moving. I will check the engine while you handle your assignments."

They nodded. After the snacks vanished, Blake retrieved the oars, stowed under the starboard seats.

Harto began his YouTube search. He was amazed at the number of self-help videos available. "Guys, I think you have us in a calm spot. Let's set the anchor." He smiled, offering encouragement as the boys seemed adequately focused on the current tasks.

He found a series of promising novice videos. Grabbing the tools, he followed the steps offered by each one on how to maintain a boat. After the third video, his confidence rose. Looking about, he was pleased the treasure sack sat at the helm seat. The clutter was disappearing. "Can one of you please come and hold the light over this engine compartment so I—"

His cell phone lit up, signaling an incoming call. Fear and anxiety made him resist answering it. He had a setting on the incoming calls that let it ring twenty times before rolling to voicemail. Part of him wanted to speak to the caller. He took a deep breath and greeted, "Yes, Julian, or whoever you are."

"What do you mean by that crack?" Julian barked. "I'm Julian. I'm not certain you're Harto. Because of that, we're gonna play a little game. Tell me how and where we met."

Harto felt like a man facing a hangman's noose. He caught his breath, gathered his memories, and replied, "I was down and out panhandling on the streets of San Juan. One day, I looked up, and a man with a French accent stopped to speak to me. He made me look him in the eyes as he asked, '*What were your dreams before you ended here?*' I had no response because I'd forgotten my life dreams. I didn't say anything. The man must have read the expression on my face."

The pain of those old memories caused a trail of tears to escape as he continued, "That man threw a twenty at me. He challenged me by saying, '*Here's money so you can wallow in failed dreams. If you come with me and work hard, I'll make you wealthy.*' The man held out his hand, knowing I would take the offer. I've only worked for Julian Lafluer since that day doing something I am passionate about." Harto took a deep breath. "Do you want me to recount why I was down and out on that street corner? How I'd become such a miserable human, ready to give up?"

"No. I want you to tell me what you do for me."

Confidence surged through his body. He straightened his shoulders. "You and I have the same dream. We want to collect the lost wealth from the sea bottom of the Caribbean and live comfortably on a private island. You envision what is possible. I work to deliver it. I let nothing stand in the way. I am your lost gem harvester."

"Harto, give me your status so we can restart our adventure."

"Julian, we were jumped by some pirates that Nohea had told had his gold coins. They knew we were bringing you cargo. Nohea said he sabotaged the engines so they could catch us. When these brutes couldn't find the hidden treasure, they executed him. I've been scared to restart the engines. We are drifting, but I found some YouTube videos on boat maintenance. I think I resolved one of the problems he caused. What are my orders, sir?"

"Good thinking. Get the boat running and make it back to Cat Island. Meet me the day after tomorrow at the airport. Deliver the cargo. I'll fly the King Air and have Ryu for protection. Now that I know I am speaking with the real Harto, I realize something else isn't right. I can't put my finger on why I get that sense. I'm switching out phones again. The next time I call, it will be a burner phone. You challenge the caller with the passphrase *money for nothing*. I'll respond with, *and babes to please*. Are we clear?"

"Yes, Julian. I love that song."

Comfort was paramount inside the Gigazon. Everyone was fitted to the perfect chair. Granger leaned back into the soft leather and rocked to the upbeat jazz playing in the background.

He leaned forward, laughing when he correlated the conversation he was tapped into. "Wow! He's using a challenge and acceptance phrase from a tune I remember. That's rich."

"What's up, Cousin?" asked JW, virtually positioned at Granger's right.

"I'm listening to Harto and Julian's satellite conversation. Julian's getting cagey. He established a passphrase for their next conversation. He thinks something's up, so he's changing out phones. He chose a verse from a song lyric by Lonny Lupnerder. It took me down Memory Lane. It made me giggle, is all."

"Upload the transcript. Hopefully, Gracie and JJ will get a kick out of it, too. We will be meeting shortly to plot out the next steps. I'm glad you were able to eavesdrop on them. Good one, man."

"On it. The conversation just ended." He tapped a few keys on the keyboard. Then he leaned back in his chair and watched the upload complete. A sense of contentment and positive energy settled over him.

CHAPTER 51

Do It Yourself

Standing and stretching from thirty minutes of being crouched over the engine compartment, Harto walked to the far end of the boat to grab a water bottle. "Good job, Bradley," he remarked, pleased with how intently the young man scanned the horizon for potential visitors. He twisted off the cap and took a big gulp. "Ahh." He wiped his sweaty brow with a lint-free shop towel.

He patted Bradley on the shoulder, then returned to the engine compartment, where Blake gave him a thumbs-up. "Uncle, I finished reapplying the lubricant exactly as you said. I want to learn more about working on boat engines. It was easy with the instruction videos you found."

Harto looked over the work and grinned. "Well done, son. Let's secure the cover, and then I will try to restart her. I'm glad we had the spare sparkplugs to replace the fouled ones. He did a number on the engine, but not enough to blow it up. However, he messed with the performance and got what he deserved. Note to self: get stocked on all the parts necessary for engine maintenance on any boat." They positioned the cover. Harto tightened the fittings, looked at his nephew, and said, "I bet I can find you some online training. You seem to have a talent for it. I need to learn more about it, too. Thanks for your help. We work well together."

Blake's face beamed at the comment. Bradley hollered, "Uncle! We have a large craft headed right for us."

Startled, Harto bolted upright and rushed to Bradley's side. He extended his hand and Bradley relinquished the binoculars. Raising them to his eyes, Harto angled the lens in the direction his nephew indicated with his pointed finger.

"Uncle, did I hear it right that you and my brother fixed everything?"

"Yep, we did." He remained fixated on the distant boat swearing under his breath.

"Now we can outrun them, right?"

Harto lowered the field glasses, frowning. "We might be able to outrun the Coast Guard, even if that's a Jaguar Powerboat, but not her radar or guns." He mentally weighed his options. "Besides, they seem to have been alerted to our presence, probably from the radar station on the nearby island. Trying to outrun them would only make them mad and more determined to capture us, as we must be guilty of something." He cleared his throat; the arm holding the binoculars dropped to his side. "Our best option is to remain where we are and convince them we are innocent of wrongdoing. They won't board us or threaten us without a valid cause."

Blake nodded. "Should I slip back over the far side and return your cargo to the hidey-hole?"

He looked at his hopeful young nephews, proud of their loyalty. "Gentlemen, this cigar boat is designed to have hidden compartments. The Coast Guard is famous for seizing cigarette and cigar boats. They like to thoroughly inspect them due to the illegal drugs and other contraband often carried over these waters by pirates. The Coast Guard will use their knowledge to inspect the boat thoroughly." He looked toward the sky for a divine idea.

"No, but I want you to use the secondary hiding place they won't consider inspecting. Go now. Blake, set the poles up to fish on the far side. Quickly, boys."

On the bridge of the Coast Guard cutter, Guardsman Coffee replied into his satellite phone. "It's right where you said it would be, Ms. Rodreguiz. Thank you for the heads-up." He added with a smile, tugging at the corners of his lips. "Mind telling me how you got such precise coordinates? We completely missed any vessel sitting out here."

Coffee smirked, then covered the phone speaker and turned toward the helm. "You're right, Captain Turmerone, you win the bet. She couldn't give us that information." He turned toward the vessel they were steaming toward. "Ms. Rodreguiz, we've located the vessel. You've provided us with probable cause to search for stolen coins. It's all highly irregular, but several Ministers of Finance around the region have pleaded with us for cooperation in this operation. We hope this isn't a wild goose chase, ma'am." Coffee listened intently to the conversation for several minutes and nodded. "Agreed, ma'am. There's nothing quite like the adrenalin rush when hunting down pirates and stolen loot to get the heart racing. Let me say the Coast Guard doesn't need any more entertainment coordinators to make our work more meaningful. We'll call once the interception and boarding are complete. Thank you again."

CHAPTER 52

Almost

Twenty minutes later, the smooth water was broken by the swells generated by the Coast Guard cutter as it aligned with the anchored craft.

"Boat, ahoy," Guardsman Coffee stated over the loudspeaker atop the pilothouse.

The older man set his fishing pole into the mount on the side, turned toward the craft, and waved. "Ahoy, Coast Guard," the man shouted.

"Boarding permission, sir," Coffee insisted.

A confused look appeared on the man's face. "We're just fishing, but you are welcome to board." The man turned and loudly stated, "Boys, secure the poles, please." The pair quickly complied and aligned behind the man in a non-aggressive manner. Doubt crept into Coffee with this compliant attitude, and he worried his information might be incorrect. He signaled to the crew to secure the vessels. Standing tall, he realigned his cap, then deliberately assumed his practiced no-nonsense expression as he approached the side of the cutter.

One of the crew from the cutter tossed lines across. The older man and one younger man each caught the lines, securing them onto the cleat hitches in a practiced manner. A gangplank was positioned to keep the crafts from scraping and for ease of access.

Coffee nimbly crossed to the cigar boat. "I'm Guardsman Coffee. What is your name?" he asked, looking at the older man.

"My name is Harto Toar. These young men are my nephews, Bradley and Blake."

He extended his hand, which Coffee ignored. "We were informed that your craft contains illegally recovered treasure from sunken ships in the region. You can give it to me now and make it easier on yourselves."

"I have nothing here, sir," Harto replied, his hands extended palms-up, giving the most innocent expression Coffee had seen during his career.

"My men will thoroughly search and seize contraband when discovered. You'll be arrested."

"We won't stop you or your crew from looking. We would be stunned if anything was discovered. This boat is typically secured in a covered slip at the Cat Island marina. This is the first time she's been on the water in months. I wanted to expose the lads to some fishing and a fun ride in this craft." He motioned to Blake and Bradley to comply.

The inspection took several minutes. His crew didn't damage any items removed and replaced after each was examined. Coffee frowned when nothing was discovered. He faced the cutter and shouted, "I want a diver over the side to inspect the underside of this craft. Look for false coverings or storage compartments and open them, bringing me the contents."

One crew member readied himself for the task with a single air tank, mask, fins, and a tool bag secured around his waist. He entered the water and quickly disappeared. A few minutes later, he resurfaced and removed his mouthpiece. "Guardsman Coffee, sir, I located and opened one underside compartment. Nothing was inside. It didn't appear like anything has ever been in that space."

Coffee noticed a moment of relief reflected on the older man's face. He wondered if it was due to innocence, or getting away with something. He refused to believe the trip was for nothing but didn't know any other steps he could take.

Captain Turmerone ambled across the gangplank. Coffee and his men immediately stood at attention. "What did you uncover?"

"Captain, we've found nothing onboard the vessel or below the waterline."

Turmerone made a cursory inspection of the craft and turned to leave with Coffee.

"I think we're done fishing for the day," Harto said. "Can we recover our anchor and follow you for a while as we head to Cat Island? We've had a fun day but want to return before dark if possible."

Turmerone's eyes squinted at the man as he asked, "Why do you have two anchors? You have one holding the boat here while we board and search, but I saw another one in the hold. How do you explain this?"

Harto appeared tongue-tied.

A slow smile blossomed on Turmerone's face as he barked, "Bring up the second anchor for inspection, Coffee. We'll have an interesting explanation once it is on board."

Minutes later, the non-standard, weighty anchor made of finely finished teak with bronze bindings sat on the cigar boat's deck. Coffee unscrewed the top piece connected to the rope, allowing the anchor to open. Several gold coins spilled onto the deck.

Guardsman Coffee nodded his approval at the find. He noticed Harto slowly close his eyes and bow his head, acknowledging surrender. He signaled to his crew to cuff the three men. "Let's transfer them to our hold. Thank you, Captain."

The captain grinned after hearing the details. "Thank you, Guardsman Coffee. I'm quite pleased that you and your team were successful. The islands' Treasury Ministers will be delighted you apprehended the thieving, illegal treasure hunters. They plan to repatriate the finds from the harvesting pirates."

"Please alert Ms. Rodreguiz of our catch, Mr. Coffee."

Guardsman Coffee immediately placed the satellite call.

"We appreciate you alerting us to the unauthorized treasure hunters, Ms. Rodreguiz."

"Mr. Coffee, since the perpetrator was arrested, what will happen to the harvesting boat he has moored at the Cat Island Marina? We have our experts standing by to complete their inspection and analysis."

"We've received word that your inspectors had a run-in with another party interested in that craft. One of your scientists was handy with a speargun while doing digital forensics. I suggest you inform your contacts that the boat is under fluid ownership. We are not in a position to help re-allocate the possessions of criminals. At this point, the local magistrates must decide. I don't see any harm or violation of judicial protocol by…instigating some digital detective work before the craft is seized."

Sensing victory, Gracie replied, "I appreciate your understanding and undocumented comments, Mr. Coffee. Oh, one last thing, where will the crew of the cigar boat be incarcerated?"

"Why would you care, ma'am? They're in custody. Your operation is over."

"Not quite. The team you arrested works for a very foul and slippery character who is our final target. Sometimes law enforcement will grant leniency in sentencing, providing the accused assisted in further apprehensions."

"I see. You're thinking of using them as bait. We intend to turn them over to the magistrate there in Cat Island, where they will stand trial. I recommend you put a call into them."

"Thank you for your help, sir."

CHAPTER 53

Fewer Cards, Higher Stakes

Judith smirked as she read the transcript of the fake Harto call to Julian, warning him of imminent danger. She called her boss from their hotel room using the device's built-in speaker.

"Hey, JJ. Thanks for the needed diversion. Xiamara and I are still chuckling about the conversation. All we saw was Julian and Ryu take off like their butts were on fire toward their vehicle. We laughed and finished our drinks to relax for a few minutes."

"I've received word that Harto and his nephews are in custody. The authorities recovered a significant amount of treasure. The gems aren't easily tagged to sunken ships in the region. We have the information we needed from their harvester boat, and the craft is being reappropriated for local island governments to share. We're ready to deal the last hands in this high-stakes game."

"How can we help?" asked Judith.

"Our team has followed a trail of money laundering through cryptocurrency exchanges with several cold wallets beginning and ending on Saint-Martin Island. The amounts are substantial, but we aren't certain what or who the payments are earmarked for. We're seeing fairly sophisticated laundering techniques, so we suspect Julian is involved. The transactions aren't sloppy, but are not good enough to evade our detection. I would like you two to check out a suspicious bank account, as the owner of the final wallet is a non-existent person. Julian is so adept at identity farming and other security measures that it matches his M.O."

Judith watched Xiamara's face pale while her stomach sank. She took a deep breath. "JJ, we don't want to hunt for clues while Julian is still on the island. We've dodged him twice in a short period, and I've aged years. In this case, the third time won't be the charm. It'll be our undoing. We'd rather hide here under the covers until ten o'clock next summer. We'll even pay."

Tears filled her eyes as Xiamara nodded in agreement.

JJ clucked his tongue. "Suppose we delay him for a specific period. Would you consider doing extra digging to help secure the evidence to convict them and get them behind bars? Since we located his house by triangulating his cell signals, I'd like you to access it to film the interior, plant bugs, and inventory any tech gear. I'd be willing to bet he has a safe somewhere."

"We don't lack confidence, JJ," affirmed Judith. "It's just that—"

"These guys are vindictive creeps without hearts or souls," Xiamara stated. "Even in our old lady disguises, I'm afraid he will catch our scent if we are in his proximity and grab us again. I've still got bruises on my—"

"I understand and appreciate your sentiment. You've been through a lot. I am very proud of you." Sounds of keyboard clicking came through the phone. "Let me engineer something to get him and Ryu to fly somewhere, and we'll track him the entire way. We'll have an open communication channel, especially if you enter his house. You will continue to exercise caution."

"Absolutely," they replied.

"I've received information that there is a plan to restart the production of fentanyl that Mateo headed up. This makes me think the laundered money might be used to purchase the pre-cursor components. If Julian is anxious to not only recover jewels but also expand to drugs using cryptocurrency, we want to shut it down. We don't need him to accelerate the human trafficking or drugs or harvest gems from the bottom of the ocean."

"We don't want any of that to happen." Judith saluted Xiamara. "Two sleuths reporting for duty because you've got our backs."

"I do." He snorted. "I almost forgot to give you the good news."

"Do tell," Judith said, rolling her eyes at her bestie.

"Nohea was executed yesterday. Julian's gem hunter, Harto, is in custody. We're hoping he will sing like a canary. We are close to winning."

"Good about Nohea, he deserved it," Judith said. "What's next, boss?"

"I'll let you know when to get your detective hat on. For now, enjoy your accommodations. Relax and stay tuned."

"Thanks, JJ," they chorused.

A pleased smile bloomed as Gracie accepted the call. "Hi, JJ. There's quite a lot going our way today. Do you have more good news?"

"We've cut Julian's team in half. I need a distraction to get him and Ryu off the island so Judith and Xiamara can investigate his property. They are intimidated and don't want to cross paths with him again on the island, disguise or not. I don't blame them. Can we persuade Harto to assist us in taking Julian down, or do we continue with our deepfake voice simulation program? We do know their passphrases."

"Do you lack confidence in the program? I doubt we can get Harto to cooperate with us. We don't have enough leverage. After listening to the conversation between the two men, it would take a colossal carrot to make him break his ties with the man who saved him. The Coast Guard turned him and his nephews over to the magistrate, but he's not cooperating. The team did a workup on Harto Toar," Gracie continued. "They stitched together an unfortunate journey of a fallen advanced mathematics professor who made bad choices. He got involved with one of his students and planned to marry her. The relationship ended when her ex-boyfriend found out and brutally murdered her. Filled with agonizing despair, Harto tracked the murderer for months. When he finally found him, he beat the man to death. The university's governing board showed their solidarity and compassion by firing him. Harto was acquitted, with the judge citing justified homicide. Afterward, Harto drifted, eventually losing everything and living on the streets. The team believes that's where Julian recruited him."

"That fills in a lot of holes. An advanced mathematician who designed software programs to run a mashup of complementary technologies. What about squeezing him on his nephews?" JJ suggested.

"There is no evidence that Blake and Bradley are blood relations. He may have taken a shine to them because of their speech problems. There are still more records to uncover, but I suspect he was filling in a need for a family without any romantic relationship, which died with his fiancée."

"Gracie, if Harto can't be used, we'll implement the voice program. It's been refined. Now we have more real data to form a realistic story. We need a story that Julian will accept without a second thought."

Sensing her brother's challenge, she said, "I thought you'd never ask. When do you want to stage this?"

CHAPTER 54

First National Bank

Julian looked at his phone and twitched his head to alert Ryu before accepting the call with the speaker enabled. "Flores, it's good to hear from you…"

"Julian," Flores loudly demanded, "I need more crypto delivered to my supplier in China."

Concern raced through his mind as he asked, "How much product are you doing weekly? We just sent—"

"No, dammit," Flores growled. "They told me the stupid crypto you used lost value in the transaction period on the open market. The supplier wants the difference of the twenty thousand before releasing the shipment."

"Wait a minute, Flores. I'm not the First National Bank of Julian. You can't expect an immediate transfer of funds to a digital wallet in China, or anywhere else," Julian insisted firmly, shaking his head toward Ryu and rolling his eyes. He took a breath to even his tone, removing all emotion. "To resolve *your* issue, start accepting crypto in your trade, and let me anonymize for you. That would save one whole laundering activity, not to mention the transport costs. That last two hundred thousand you sent me was a bear to get into the bank without everyone getting their panties in a wad. It's like a red flag in front of a pissed-off bull to show up at a bank with that much cash,</p>

assuming no one to question where it's coming from, sir. I work with people who are sympathetic, not stupid."

"But, Julian," Flores sputtered. "I originally gave you a ten-percent broker fee to do the laundering. Use that to calm the Chinese pythons. I'll make it up to you. Trust me."

Julian sarcastically responded, "That statement aligns with the other great lies of Western Civilization. *I'm from the government. I'm here to help. The Mercedes in the driveway is paid for.* And, *I swear, I won't get you pregnant.*" He chuckled at his joke, then continued, "If you get the crypto from the open market, give me the wallets with the access PINs, and I'll sanitize the crypto to pay for your source. Everything else will take too long."

"I don't have that kind of brain power on my team, which is why I called you in the first place."

"Get your smartest guy in the room, and both of you call me back. I'll explain what's needed to tee it up for me to complete the sanitizing and protect you. I assume you've got someone literate on your team, and with you there, they won't be able to cheat you. They'll need to take notes."

"Argh!" replied the drug manufacturer. "I've got someone in mind. Call you back in thirty."

The R-Group members in the Gigazon enthusiastically erupted with whoops and laughter after listening to the latest Julian conversation Granger captured from the cell tower.

JW, trying to gain control, interjected between catching his breath. "All right, team, nice follow-up. Julian's arrogance over this new player is evident. Granger, can we determine with confidence that this Flores is the same drug dealer in Mexico that Mateo dealt with?"

"I believe so. Our other file transcripts contained information that Flores gave Julian two hundred thousand dollars to exchange for cryptocurrency. The purpose of that transaction was to pay an unidentified foreign pharma manufacturer for pre-cursor fentanyl materials."

"I'll let JJ and Gracie know about this possible partnership. With any luck, we might be able to take them both."

Granger looked pleased. "That would be sweet. I'm uploading the transcript and the recording to our shared space."

CHAPTER 55

Mechanically Savvy

Brayson leaned over and kissed Marian's cheek. "Finally, we're making inroads. The software we uploaded from Harto's boat is bearing fruit. Using all their resources, our great CATS team has optimized the search capabilities. We can reload it with their design modifications and shop on the ocean floor for four hundred years of lost gemstones."

Standing behind him, she looped her arms around his shoulders and squeezed. "I love how animated you get when playing with new toys," she purred in his ear. She moved to face him on the other side of the table. "Can we get cooperation from the authorities who impounded the *Osvaldo*?" Her feet shuffled as she looked through lowered eyelashes with a gritted smile. "They were annoyed that I shot the guy with the spear gun but agreed I was justified in doing so."

"True, you were cleared after minor questioning. But they got irritated when retrieving the two pirates from the other side of the island."

"Honey, sometimes you just can't please anyone," she grinned.

Brayson admired his wife and her antics. Raising his eyebrows, his eyes lingered in spots as he inventoried her body. He inclined his head and suggestively asked, "How long has it been since I've pleased you, Mrs. Hayes? I can't wait for us to finish this assignment. Or we could take a well-deserved break and play undercover combat. I noticed you've collected several dessert toppings that might have alternative applications."

"Oh my, Mr. Hayes, I didn't know you were taking notice of my after-dinner desires. We could sample one tonight, perhaps, if you wish."

He sighed as he finished loading the new software onto his laptop, which he loaded into his backpack. They decided to try to board the *Osvaldo* to deliver the payload to its onboard system or begin discussions with the authorities.

Arriving at the pier, they spotted the official notice attached to the boat slip stating, 'This Boat is under Impound. See the local magistrate for information.' Brayson scouted for guards, but the pier was quiet. He and Marian slipped aboard.

Brayon pulled his laptop from the backpack and set it on the cabinet. He hit the power button on *Osvaldo's* computer system, which whined for a second and then stopped. "Damnit, they let the batteries drain. Hon, can you plug in the battery cable so it can charge? It would be ideal if the computer would draw that power to start processing rather than wait for the batteries to charge."

He heard Marian scooching around, connecting power to the outlet box on the dock. "It's in. Do you see anything now?"

"Ahh, perfect. I'm going to upload the new software. Marian, please check the engines and see if we can start them. I want to charge the battery for a while. The solar panels won't activate until sunrise and after we move out of this covered slip."

"Sure."

He heard her move to the steering station, which contained the engine controls, ignition keys, and throttle levers.

Several minutes later, she complained, "Babe, the engines won't respond. Let me get a flashlight and check everything."

Brayson completed the upload and updated the system's active programs. The compiling took longer due to the power drain, but he was delighted it worked.

Marian appeared soundlessly and reported, "Success. The port authorities must have disabled the craft, thinking someone might try to steal it. I reconnected the spark plugs and re-enabled the ignition system, so she's ready to go."

Brayson stared as he rested one elbow with his palm up in a questioning motion.

She pursed her lips and opened her eyes wide with her innocent expression. "Uh, they let me watch and tutored me on F-15 engine repair while stationed in Iraq. Good skills to know when situationally challenged, don't you think?"

Pinching his nose while chortling, he replied, "Your skills never cease to amaze me."

Julian closed the program on his computer because the inbound call would be a long discussion. Accepting the call, he motioned for Ryu to get him a coffee refill. "Flores, is your brain-power standing by to take notes and ask intelligent questions?"

"It's a good thing we're not in the same room. I'm not fond of sarcasm with a pending timeline looming. Emiliano is here. I'm placing the call on speaker."

"Emiliano," Julian asked, "do you know anything about cryptocurrencies? I hope you understand that this technology does not use hard currency, and transactions are digital."

"Yes," Emiliano replied with a deep, gruff tone.

"Good. I'm sending you a link for you to set up a digital currency wallet using the namesakes I give you. When Flores accepts a payment from someone, they must provide you with their wallet's identification number. Then, they must transfer digital coins to your wallet equal to the price of the merchandise they are taking. Make sure you check the price of the cryptocurrency that day before you accept payment because exchange rates vary daily. When you confirm the transaction is complete, alert me, and I'll withdraw the money for laundering. Are we good so far?"

"Yes," Emiliano grunted.

"When the laundering aspects are completed, I'll return the funds, less my commission, to another wallet you'll control but with a different identity. Use this wallet to pay the Chinese pharma so Flores can get his product."

"Mr. Julian, this sounds straightforward enough. How long or how many times should I use these accounts? I assume I need to occasionally have newer and fresher wallets to make it harder to track back to us."

Astounded at the level of the man's grasp of the concepts, Julian rocked back in his chair and took a sip of his coffee. "Flores, thanks for getting an intelligent student on your team. Yes, Emiliano, you should have several wallets and rotate through them regularly, but not predictably. If you have five or so, I can return the funds in varying amounts to separate wallets so the transactions won't reflect the same total amount. This will create more accounting work but helps get the transactions ignored by government agencies monitoring the ebb and flow of money."

"Julian, how do you want me to alert you when new wallets come online and old wallets are retired?" Emiliano asked in a deep voice, sounding interested.

"Make certain your text messages contain only half of the required data to prevent someone grabbing an SMS conversation from gaining the keys to the kingdom. If I need to change out burner phones, I will alert you using the same process. Does this make sense?"

"Yes, it sounds straightforward enough, Julian. When can I start?"

"We can begin as soon as you accumulate some crypto. Text me when that happens. I'll follow up with an instructional encrypted email to Flores, and then you can text back to me the wallet addresses," offered Julian, dollar signs floating through his mind. "Flores, are we good?"

"How long is all this going to take?" grumbled Flores. "It sounds like days or weeks, and I don't have the time, man."

"After speaking with Emiliano, I'm confident he has the skill set to do what's needed. It shouldn't take him long. We'll talk soon."

CHAPTER 56

Deception and Deceived

Pacing around the office, Gracie repeated the pep talk she'd given herself for the last thirty minutes. "Come on, girl, you can do this. You've read the transcripts of the calls between Harto and Julian. Grovel enough to let him feel important. Pretend to be on the same page of world domination. Brag about the loot you'll bring to his plane. All right. Let's do this."

She launched the synthetic voice app on her phone labeled Harto, then dialed Julian.

"Is this Harto?"

"Yep."

"Give me the passphrase…"

The voice mimicked Harto to a tee. "Money for nothing…"

Then Julian demanded, "What is the intended response?"

Gracie hesitated, slightly worried. "You're supposed to give me the response."

"I changed the rule. What is the response?"

"I'm Harto. The response is, *and babes to please.* Julian, is this you?"

Julian chuckled, releasing the breath he'd been holding.

Pleased with the outcome, Gracie silently prayed to heaven, having had the transcript in front of her as a reference. "Julian, those pirates Nohea hooked up with are back, snooping for the gems and coins. I thought when they killed Nohea, they'd given up. Now, they watch our every move and pressure my nephews to tell them where the treasure is hidden. I'm worried these vultures will dig around long enough to find it. Please fly here. I'll meet you and give you everything."

"Thank you for alerting me, Harto. I want you out hunting for more jewels. I'll be there tomorrow morning around ten. Meet me at the airport."

"Oh, thank you, Julian. I'll have the boat ready to take out after you have the treasure."

After disconnecting, Gracie called JJ, "How'd I do?"

"My marvelous sister, you did well. We need to have authorities there to intercept our jewel thief."

Julian slammed the phone onto his desk. "Dammit, Ryu. We're flying to Cat Island in the morning. Please call the flight line people and ask them to top off the tanks. We're making an early departure."

"Boss, the trip will be out and back, right? Anything special I need to bring?"

"Make sure we're armed. Harto is dodging Nohea's pirate friends, who want my gems and the coins. If the clowns show up at the airfield, you must deal with them. I will need more capital for our operation, and she asked for more stones for the playroom. The manufacturer tells me that my *Gina II* is ready for shipping in a few weeks, but I need additional funds."

Julian paused to review open items in his mind. He decided everything was good. "I'll be with her the rest of the evening, so I'm counting on you to prepare everything for tomorrow."

"Yes, Julian."

Almost melancholy, Julian sighed. "There's never enough time for your loved ones."

CHAPTER 57

Stormy Days

The King Air bounced through another pocket of unstable atmosphere with sudden drops and sensations of weightlessness. Julian scanned the cloud formations, trying to read the weather. He glanced at Ryu, who appeared pasty, tight-lipped, and wide-eyed.

The next downdraft felt like a wild rollercoaster ride. Julian tried to regain some of the lost altitude. "I should have checked the weather before committing to this morning. I don't want to go down in history as lost like the last flight of Amelia Earhart." He adjusted his airspeed and found a smooth patch of air. "Ryu," he shouted, "when we touch down, I want you to get Harto, and both of you bring the treasure to the plane. No dawdling. I want to return to Saint-Martin before the weather closes in. I have enough fuel for the round trip. If we're grounded here, I fear we'll get into a firefight with the pirates Harto's been dodging."

"Understood."

After a few more bounces, Cat Island popped into view. Julian passed over the field, checked other air traffic, and lined up quickly for his landing. "It's providence that no other planes are landing or taking off. I'll taxi us close to the hanger we use." Gigantic raindrops pelted the windshield. "Blast, it's beginning to rain."

"Are we gonna make it? The plane is a solid one, but not military-grade. I recommend you pull up, refuel, and get an updated weather report to plan a better route home or stay parked until the storm passes."

"Makes sense. I'll top off the tanks in case we have to take a longer route back. But we're leaving as soon as you get back with the goods. I don't need to see Harto, and you won't need his help carrying the bag."

When they approached the hangar, it began raining harder. Julian chuckled under his breath as Ryu tried to put on his raincoat, which was smaller than his own. The man's expression was priceless.

"I think your coat is in the back area," Julian snorted.

Ryu's sour face spoke volumes.

"When you enter, ask the fueling attendant to top off my tanks. I'll pay him. You concentrate on getting our cargo aboard."

Ryu lowered the stairs. "Julian, I don't see Harto."

Julian checked his watch, pleased to see it said nine-fifty. "I told him ten. We're just shy of that time. I'm sure he is inside or en route. He has never let me down."

"I'll go look and get your refueling tech out here." He grabbed Julian's coat, prepared to use it like a cape over his head. "Let me borrow this so I don't get soaked." He rushed down the stairs, heading into the hangar.

Three or four minutes later, at the sound of gunshots, Julian whipped his head toward the outside. Seconds later, Ryu appeared at the hanger door without the raincoat as protection. He turned, firing his weapon through the doorway. His clip spent, Ryu saluted Julian before more shots sounded. Julian watched his guardian fall to the ground. Acting instinctually, Julian fired up the engines, then flipped the switch to close the doorway, securing the latch. Pulling the seatbelt tight, he pushed the throttle forward. The King Air dashed toward the runway for an emergency takeoff. As he pulled away, two more bullets slammed into the King Air. One pierced the metal, striking his am. He grimaced but increased acceleration until he became airborne, praying no other aircraft was departing or arriving.

Blood from his arm increased as he pulled the yoke to gain altitude. He snarled, "I've had better days. Goodbye, Ryu, my friend."

Reaching altitude, he leveled off and set the autopilot. He then tied his expensive handkerchief into a tourniquet to slow the bleeding. He looked at the weather considering his options.

"We walked into a trap," he mused. "Damnit. I was lured here with gems and gold coins as bait. It couldn't have been the pirates because they would have run if they had gotten the treasure. I'm not certain who is after me, but I must concentrate on dodging this storm so my earlier joke about Amelia Earhart doesn't come true." He looked at his makeshift bandage. "Damnit, my arm hurts."

Gracie hung her head with her eyes closed and sighed before she initiated the call to JJ.

He answered on the first ring. "Give me good news, my adorable sister. How did it go?"

"The trap was properly baited, the predators showed up on time, but only one was brought to justice. The authorities shot Ryu. I'm sorry. Julian got away. No one expected a firefight, so things rapidly spiraled out of control. We have limited telemetry on Julian's cell phone. Our team predicts he will return to Saint-Martin, load up his essentials, and bolt again."

JJ sighed. "That's the trouble with criminals; they just don't follow our playbook. Rats!"

"I'm disappointed. We were so close to capturing him. The team is working on firming up the tracking."

"Oh, no," JJ loudly stated. "Gracie, did I hear you say Julian is returning to Saint-Martin? I gotta alert Judith and Zee. They're gaining entry to his home to gather more evidence. I'll call you after I get through to them. Thanks."

Gracie looked at the phone and mentally kicked herself for waiting half an hour to call JJ.

CHAPTER 58

Programs for Sweet and Sad

Judith backed their vehicle into an outcropping beyond the target house and parked. She'd driven into the quiet neighborhood using the shortest distance but wanted a buffer in case they had to leave in a hurry. "Okay, Zee. Adjust your hat, we stay in costume in case someone is around. Two older ladies lost or something."

Zee nodded and got out of the vehicle. They stood next to one another at the driver's side of the SUV using the window's reflection to adjust their headdresses and jackets.

They walked toward the road. Judith removed her cell, setting it to silence, then indicated Zee needed to do the same. She insisted, "We need to move fast toward the carport and find the exterior security keypad. Keep your eyes open to any movement in the area."

Xiamara whispered, "What if the code doesn't work? What if the geeks in the back room, just thinking stuff up, are wrong?"

"Then we run like we have the hounds of hell nipping at our shapely keisters. We'll jump in the car and read them the riot act while flying down the road."

"I know it's worth a try, but why would a smart criminal like Julian use the same security code on all his properties?" Xiamara whined. "It sounds too easy. We never get easy."

Judith held her breath as she punched in the codes Marian and Brayson had successfully used at the San Juan estate. "Yes!" she said as the pad light flipped to green. Grinning, feeling positive down to her toes, she faced her bestie. "The door is unlocked, so we can safely enter. I'm glad we took the risk. It was time for a win in our column. Pull up your mask in case there are video cameras. Put on the gloves. We don't want to leave prints."

They boldly entered. Zee mumbled, "We can still run if necessary, right?"

Ignoring the question, Judith mentally checked the interior against the architectural plans they'd been provided. She figured the upstairs was Julian's private sanctuary. She noted the tastefully decorated interior, different but no less elegant than the San Juan property where they had stayed. "The man doesn't spare expense on his creature comforts."

"Colors and textures here seem more manly to me than San Juan," murmured Xiamara. "But you're right, lovely and bold."

They entered the kitchen, quickly inventorying the cabinets and drawers. Nothing out of the ordinary was found. "Remember, Brayson and Marian recommended that if we find any big red switches covered by a clear plastic cover, we do not tamper with them. They'd be the permanent kill switches for the property."

Xiamara only nodded.

"Let's split up and search the ground floor," said Judith.

"We stay together and separate inside a room."

Judith stuck out her tongue under the mask but continued as they systematically searched the bottom floor. They located a laptop in a bedroom; Zee quickly copied the drive's contents.

"Let's head upstairs to the master suite area. There must be a safe somewhere," insisted Judith. Inside the enormous bedroom, she moved to the right toward what appeared to be a closet.

Xiamara skirted to the left.

Inside the closet, she announced, "Zee, I've got a wall safe. Come here and help me use the program on our secure phone to open the safe."

Seconds later, Xiamara was by Judith's side, attaching the suction up by the dial and inserting the earpiece while motioning for quiet. Zee entered the type of safe, initiated the associated program, and painstakingly followed the process. Several tense minutes ticked by before the last digits of the combination clicked into place. She turned the lever and opened the safe.

Judith pulled out the contents and quickly used her phone to make copies. "Mostly papers, bank statements, and a few gemstones. Disappointingly sparse. Should we take the stones or leave them?"

"I don't know; I'll text JJ in a minute. Push the document copies into the shared data folders so the team can begin their analysis. I want to examine the other room closer. I heard a hum from the door, making me suspect it might be a small-grade data center. Julian's wealth could be in digital format, allowing him to access it from anywhere."

Judith returned everything to the safe except the gemstones, which she photographed and counted, then tucked into her pocket.

She hurried to the other room, finding Zee staring at the room's contents, edging her way to the main keyboard. Judith picked up the VR goggles that appeared randomly tossed onto the neatly made queen-sized bed. "Does this make any sense to you, Zee?"

"Nope. But I can boot up the system if you want," she replied.

"Okay. Why not. Perhaps he rests in here while waiting for transactions to complete from his money laundering efforts."

Xiamara booted up the equipment. "There is no sign-on screen or password. A program called Gina is loading."

They jumped when a soothing, sultry female voice floated from the speakers. "I'm so glad you're back. Tell me about your adventures, Jules. I'm ready for more of your attention."

Stunned, the girls saw images flashing across the three screens. The VR goggles lit up, so Judith pulled them on. After a few seconds, she yanked them off. She handed them to Zee, shaking her head, wishing she could unsee the images.

Pulling on the VR device, Zee exclaimed, "Three-dimensional imagery with virtual reality goggles and background monitors for a fully immersive experience." Removing the device, she added, "Gina is an AI-enhanced companion specifically engineered to Julian's tastes. An electronic call girl. Yuk. What is this world coming to?"

"I don't know what to call it other than sick," Judith replied. "He supports drugging and selling minors to the sex trade, launders money to facilitate drug manufacturing and distribution, and his romantic companion isn't real. I need to throw up."

Both their phones vibrated with an emergency text from JJ.

> Julian evaded the trap. He's on his way back.
> Ryu's dead. Evacuate the premises immediately.

Judith felt the fear on Xiamara's face. She powered off the computer. Hopping around, Zee couldn't toss the VR goggles back onto the bed fast enough. "No, no, no," Xiamara cried.

"Let's go," demanded Judith, taking her friend's hand. They yanked off their masks as they raced down the stairs. Heading toward the kitchen and side exit, they suddenly stopped at the sound of a familiar voice with a French accent behind them. They turned as one to face their monster.

"Did you like her too? I heard her down here. She's sweet, isn't she?"

Judith noticed blood on Julian's arm while mentally reviewing options.

He continued, "I never thought I'd see you two again. Even in those clothes, your scent is unmistakable. You're pulling the strings with deep, fake voices to confuse me and my people."

CHAPTER 59

Short-Sheeted

Flores stomped his foot when the call rolled to voice mail again. "Julian, where the hell are you? I'm ready for your financial mumbo-jumbo, but you can't be bothered answering my call. I should have had you bring him here to work."

Emiliano cleared his throat unobtrusively spotting Flores's venomous stare. Unruffled or intimidated, he said, "Flores, after my talk with Julian, I prowled more on the internet to verify some items. I found an excellent how-to video on YouTube. We don't need Julian's laundering antics through multiple exchanges because each wants a percentage to run it through. He talked about several exchanges plus his fee, the dog robber."

Flores tilted his head and squinted at his muscled support, perhaps with more brains than he'd initially considered. "Go on."

"After watching a video by Dr. Grange, I can do the crypto wallet shifting thing. Before gaining access, I had to jump through hoops to prove I wasn't a government agency. I even asked some questions and received immediate, secure feedback via an anonymous channel. I don't need five different digital wallets, just the one. I did the math of the first five wallets, then cycling them out for another five. The process would become an insane accounting nightmare. It's too easy to skim funds from our operation using Julian's method. Let me run with the cryptocurrency transactions. I'll report on the activity daily until you're confident. We won't have to wait so long to get the product either. Trust me, I've got this."

"Show me. I want to see how you pay the Chinese pharma rats in crypto so they'll release my shipment."

Pointing to their banking app on a computer screen, Emiliano stated, "See, here is everything we've assembled in our digital wallet. When we want to purchase anything, we initiate a transfer from our wallet to theirs with this app tab. Here is the challenge that requires our PIN code … entered like this. In a few minutes, we'll get an email confirmation that they received it. Once we have the confirmation, you can demand that the shipment be released. Cool, huh?"

Stunned, seeing everything he needed to complete in minutes, Flores frowned. "After all the waiting, it turns out Julian is a liar and a thief. We'll run our crypto bank and cut out the middleman living in the Bahamas. He still owes me, but I'll catch up another time. He will pay." He clapped his brainiac on the back. "Well done." Flores tapped a text message telling his supplier to verify receipt of the funds. Seconds later, he received a response that made him grin. "My man, you've completed the order, and the fentanyl precursor materials will arrive in a few days. We get to keep Julian's commission, which I will give you a handsome percentage of."

"Thank you, Flores."

JW chuckled across the Gigazon virtual environment. "Satya and Auri, nice work trapping the Mexican drug manufacturer's computer IP addresses after working backward from

Julian's call to Flores. The Mexican authorities should show up with their warrants shortly and end their operation." Sending a thumbs-up in Granger's direction, he added, "And you, Dr. Grange, where did you come up with the idea of building a video of how to launder cryptocurrencies and then suck Emiliano into thinking you were the one and only?"

Chuckling, Granger explained, "Just so you know, Cous, I *am* the one and only. Everyone searches YouTube to learn stuff. ICABOD and I brainstormed to create a tempting yet secure appearing access to something special just in time for the man to be smart. Together, we made it an easy experience for anyone to try. ICABOD pushed it at the right time by watching Emiliano's search bar activity. I got the fun part of being the celebrity game show host teaching how to launder cryptocurrencies. Har! Har!"

"Satya and Auri watched the single wallet move crypto directly to the Chinese source, so we collected both endpoints to share with the Department of Treasury's Office of Foreign Assets Control. OFAC will do the pounding and look like heroes."

JW tapped his chin. "Hmm…I wonder if we could sell this to the United States government. We are this close to ending Flores' operation." He held up his thumb and index finger with a slim show of light visible from his background. "We will bring Julian to justice. ICABOD and team, well done. I'll tell Gracie of our success, so she can alert OFAC so they can pursue it."

CHAPTER 60

Unexpected Revenge

Blood dripped from Julian's arm onto the floor. It wasn't a fatal injury, but maybe Judith could leverage it. She glanced around the kitchen at the visible items, including a block containing knives, wineglasses on a rack, and various spices in a well-marked caddy.

Julian leaned against the counter, waving the gun between the two women. Pain reflected in his eyes, accompanying sighs and groans. He softly stated, "Nohea and Ryu are dead. Since we walked into a trap on Cat Island, I have to assume that Harto is in custody, along with my gems and gold. But you stupid women can't find everything." He laughed, then stopped with agony streaking across his face. He grabbed his arm. "You aren't that smart. I'm unsure how you got into my house, but I guess you think you've won."

Judith tried to buy time. Suddenly Xiamara announced, "Let us get you to a doctor. I know from experience it's no fun taking a bullet. That is what happened, right?"

"What do you care? It's bleeding. It'll stop sooner or later."

Judith smiled charmingly, whipped off her softie cap, and shook her blonde mane. "Mr. Lafluer, I noticed your Gina was a blonde like me. She's waiting for you. Let's get that wound doctored, and you can introduce us to her." She grinned at him and licked her lips seductively. "I have some medical training in my background. I noticed some gauze in the downstairs bathroom. You let Xiamara fetch it while you hold your gun on me."

"Why would I let her leave?"

"Because she knows I couldn't leave her" Zee interjected. "I'll get the supplies and be right back. It's only around the corner."

Judith added, "I see exactly the spice I need to stop your bleeding and numb the pain simultaneously. Then you can show us more details about Gina."

"It does hurt and is making a mess. All right, go ahead, but if you aren't back in sixty seconds, I'll shoot her. Count down from sixty, starting now," he insisted.

Zee sprinted out the door, counting backward loudly and slowly. In the final second, she returned to the kitchen with gauze rolls and tape. "Here you go," she said.

"Good, Zee," Judith said. "Stand to the side in Julian's line of sight. Julian, you keep the gun on me while I remove the handkerchief from your arm." She carefully removed the bloody mess, noticing the wound was large and still bleeding, and gently blotted it with some gauze. "I can get the bleeding to stop by making a poultice from the spices. I will turn on the water to get it to heat up. Wounds that stay warm heal faster."

He watched her intently. "My mother made home remedies, too. They always worked. No funny business."

She batted her eyes and grinned. "I wouldn't dream of it. I want you to show me how much I'm like your Gina." Grabbing the turmeric, she emptied the contents and a few ounces of water into a small bowl, creating a runny paste, and smashed it with the back of a spoon. The earthy aroma with hints of orange and ginger filled the air between them. "Doesn't that smell nice, Mr. Lafluer?"

"Yes. Yes, it does."

"Okay, hold still while I put it on. I'll add the gauze pads, then wind the roll around to hold them in place. It may sting briefly, but it will start to warm."

Judith had everything lined up to work quickly. His breath caught when she applied the paste. Then she firmly pressed the gauze pads, trapping the bullet. The roll of gauze wrapped around his arm and then tied off underneath.

Suddenly, he screamed as blood seeped through the bandage. His knees buckled from the unexpected pain, moving the gun toward Judith's chest. "You bitch," he yelled trying to aim the weapon to take a shot. "It's on fire and bleeding more."

Xiamara mumbled, "No, you don't." She pushed Julian with all her might toward the corner of the counter. His body slid to the edge, then careened toward the floor. His head bounced on the thick carved oak legs of the standing chopping block. Then silence.

"OMG," Zee cried, "I killed him. I didn't mean to."

Dumbfounded, Judith dropped to her knees and checked for a pulse that was already gone. "Zee, it will be fine. After all the kids he's sold into the sex trade, the money laundering for that monster Mateo, not to mention drugging us for sale into slavery, he got exactly what he deserved. You didn't kill him. He fell." Judith reached into her pocket for her phone and pressed a contact. When the call connected, she said, "JJ, we have a problem. Need direction."

Within seconds, the situation was relayed. "I see you inside Julian's house, Judith. Are you okay?"

"We are both physically fine." She reached out and held Xiamara's hand. "Julian showed up and surprised us. We're in the living room."

"Use the speaker so you can both listen. Activate the camera and take a breath."

Judith complied, propping the phone in front of them. She sat next to Zee, watching tears stream down Xiamara's face.

Clutching Zee's hand, she said, "JJ, Zee is understandably upset. Julian showed up with a bullet in his arm and bleeding. We offered to bind his wounds if he didn't shoot us. He agreed but lost it when I put the makeshift turmeric compress on the wound. Zee saved me by pushing him hard out of the way. He slipped, fell hard, and cracked his head on a chopping block leg. I checked for a pulse, but he's gone."

"JJ," Xiamara sobbed, "I didn't mean to kill him. When he yelled and pointed the gun at Jude…" She inhaled and cried until she caught herself. "I couldn't let him shoot her. She's—"

"Hold it there, ladies. Let's go through this step by step. Were you wearing gloves?"

They held up gloved hands wiggling their fingers. Judith added, "We kept them on except when I touched the keypad to release the alarm."

"Anything you've touched without gloves, wipe it down so none of your prints will be found. He didn't fire the weapon, correct?"

"No shots were fired," confirmed Xiamara.

"Good," he said. "No one will report gunshots heard to the authorities. We need to get you on your way to the Saint-Martin airport."

They sighed and nodded.

"Repeat after me. *I did not kill Julian; I was never there.*" He stared at them while they responded.

"You puttered at the hotel until your plane was repaired and left. Xiamara, you did *not* kill Julian. He was shot on Cat Island while making his escape. Even with great blood loss, he made the flight back to Saint-Martin. Then he drove back to his home, where he passed out, smashing his head when he fell. Without proper medical attention, he expired. You did not kill him. End of story."

Xiamara drew a ragged breath and acknowledged, "Yes, JJ."

"JJ," Judith asked, "what about his computer gear that we found? Do we need to—"

"No, you two need a fast exit strategy so we can get you home, understand? I'll have the sister organization hack into the system for a look-see. I'm glad you helped gain evidence on the last of the brothers. The trio is now no longer a threat to humanity. You brought your luggage to the house as we discussed, right?"

"Yes," Judith replied. "We have it all, but didn't check out just in case."

"You're checked out now. Text me as soon as you board the plane. I will put a hold on it if need be, but I think you'll make it."

"JJ," Judith said with a grin, "I kept the gemstones we found in the safe. I'll bring them home for you to deal with."

JJ chuckled. "Of course you did. Nice work using the turmeric. Though it can help healing in some circumstances, on an open bleeding wound, it would burn like crazy. You both think outside the box. Safe travels."

CHAPTER 61

Closing Time

Marian kept to the side while Brayson stuck out his hand to shake hands with the director. "Director Jacobo Hassan, we're pleased to make your acquaintance. I'm Brayson. This is my partner, Marian. We're here to provide you and your team with instructions on using the technology installed on the *Osvaldo* harvester."

With a slight bow, Jacobo stated, "We are beyond pleased to see such a quick result. There were skeptics when Ms. Rodreguiz described the harvesting process of the seabed adjacent to the lost ships at the Treasury Director's conference. I understand the vessel's ownership has been transferred to the new corporation operating in these waters. I can't thank your team enough for showing a realistic solution for harvesting lost gemstones to finance our desperately needed infrastructure projects."

Brayson smiled. "Sir, I don't mean to be rude, but Marian and I are on a tight schedule. We want to take your team on board immediately to begin training. We figured you might want to capture video on your smartphones to refer to, and of course, you can phone for support." Marian pressed a couple of business cards into Jacobo's hand.

Jacobo motioned for his three technicians to join, announcing, "Team, you are now Bahama sponges. Your job is to soak up everything they tell you and write everything down for a final report. Your deliverable is a fully working instruction manual detailing everything that must be done to find and harvest lost gemstones. If this project is as successful as we think, other harvester ships will be commissioned and staffed with folks such as yourselves. These guidebooks will be key."

Brayson and Marian ushered the techs aboard and began.

Mark absentmindedly turned his gold-plated cigarette lighter over and over, musing about the next steps with Julian.

"Damnit, it's been too long."

Looking at his lieutenant, Mark ordered, "I want you and some muscle to pay a visit to Julian. He isn't answering my calls. My demand for weekly updates has gone unheeded. I want him found. You can explain the facts of our business agreement. Then call me, with him there ready to tell me what he intends to do to fix the deficiencies. I don't mind if you hold a knife at his neck while we're talking."

Mark's phone rang. Though it momentarily distracted him, he ignored the call. Before he outlined anything else, another call came in with an odd caller ID. *Take this, Mark.* His brow furrowed, and he showed the screen to his lieutenant, who raised his eyebrows and shrugged.

Accepting the call, he said, "Good trick. Who is this?"

The smooth, polished female voice replied, "You got the message. I understand your organization is in the market to purchase precious gemstones at wholesale prices. There is a Caribbean consortium that would like to do business with you. Are you interested, Mark?"

"I don't know who you are or how you got this number. Why do you think I would be interested?" he asked, running his finger around the collar of his shirt, which suddenly seemed a little tight.

"Your former contact, Julian Lafluer, is no longer in business. I thought you might like to discuss a new business source."

Chuckling, Mark said, "I'm all ears."

Two weeks later, Gracie strutted into the CATS headquarters office in Luxemburg, excited to surprise her twin. ICABOD allowed her entrance to the secured area without alerting JJ on any of the screens. She grinned, spotting him busy typing on his keyboard. "Hey, bro, how about a cup of hot chocolate and maybe a biscuit?"

Startled, he jumped up and rushed to her side, crushing her with a hug. "No wonder I couldn't reach you at the office. I thought you were tied up in a meeting."

"I did some video meetings on the flight, but I took off a few days. I thought I'd celebrate with you. There are times when video meetings aren't enough."

He looped his hand around her waist. "Let's get some coffee. I brought some tasty pastries in case any team members came in today. I picked them up at the shop Mom used to take us to for special occasions."

"Yummy."

They headed toward the kitchen breakroom. They each fixed a warm beverage and selected one of the delicacies before taking seats at a table.

Gracie inhaled the fragrant chocolate and took a small sip. "There is nothing quite like European chocolate."

"I agree. I think every place I've been to has its specialty. How did you do with all the negotiations you were involved in?"

She sighed and shifted in her seat. "It's been busy. Jacobo Hassan was delighted with the *Osvaldo* Harvester acquisition. He established a joint committee of the islands to monitor the activity and provide reports. He raved about Marian and Brayson's training for the technical team. I introduced Mark, who wrote a contract guaranteeing Jacobo top dollar on any jewels recovered. I also helped them get Harto's expertise on their payroll, though he is wearing an ankle monitor for now. I spoke to Harto briefly and asked him if he liked the role offered, and he beamed like a kid at Christmas with the most presents. His nephews returned to their family but will do two hundred or so hours of community service. I think they will be good."

JJ raised his cup and saluted her. "Well done, my creative sister. I sent Brayson and Marian on an extended vacation without laptops, but Brayson insisted on playing with the drone. I couldn't refuse him." He took a massive bite of the sweet roll, groaning his appreciation. "Cinnamon and raisin. Try one after you finish yours."

Using her napkin to dab at the crumbs from her mouth, she said, "I don't think I can eat more than one. How do Judith and Xiamara feel about Julian? You had said they wanted to get back into the game and end his career."

JJ cautiously offered, "After speaking to them, I felt they needed a bit of therapy, so I arranged for them to take a sabbatical in Canada for a couple of weeks. Our trusted therapist, Richard Schwindt, will meet with them and evaluate their state of mind. I'm sure it won't be any time before those two are back into mischief. How are those two new wards of yours doing?"

"Maria and Lisbeth are making progress with their therapy. They are enrolled in school to get their GEDs by the end of this year, and I promised them that if they did well in their studies, we would cover college. Lisbeth wants to be a therapist, while Maria has her heart set on being a veterinarian technician. Sophia and Elena are nearly finished with their therapy."

"Excellent. I meant to tell you, but it slipped my mind until now. Marian and Brayson want to adopt Sophia and Elena. After all the grief it took to find those girls following their kidnapping by Mateo, they want to be good adult role models."

"JJ, I never thought about that as an option. I like it. Let's discuss it further when they return from vacation. What happened after Granger and the team set up Flores to handle crypto?"

He laughed. "That was a classic bait-and-switch Uncle Quip would've been delighted to claim. I guess Granger didn't fall far from that tree. Flores moved all his funds just like the YouTube video said. We turned over the evidence to the authorities on both sides of the border. Flores and his sidekick will be incarcerated forever. His entire business and lab in Texas were shut down. The Chinese provider was tracked, and several wallets were frozen. I'm sure that avenue is finished providing poisonous drugs." He took Gracie's cup and fixed both of their refills.

She nodded. "Stopping the influx of drugs to countries is a full-time job for each nation. At least they are trying to work together for that common goal." Sipping the fresh cup of cocoa, she added, "Thank you, I needed another. What are your plans?"

"I'm ready to return to Brazil. Jo will be home from her last fashion shoot in a few days, which she told me was lots of fun. We might take some time to visit our home in Magnolia Bluff.

"This has been a rough group of cases. The team is working to itemize Julian's properties and cash accounts and provide them to the local authorities. He was the last. No one else was in the family. Thank goodness. JW and Brayson can handle the day-to-day accounts. If they need us, we won't be far. Make sure the entire team knows how much we appreciate their engineering the deepfakes."

"Sounds good. Give my best to your bride. One of these days, Jeff and I would enjoy visiting Texas. I'd love to see the house. The photos are fabulous." She raised her cup toward his. "Here's to fighting to help underdogs." She clicked his cup.

"And to the best teams so far in the history of the R-Group and CATS team.

"Cheers!"

"Let's go to dinner before I visit the family home tonight."

"Thanks for being here, Gracie."

Discussion Questions for

Enigma Jewels

Book Club Leaders …contact Charles and/or Rox to participate in a special meeting to discuss the book; the concepts; and the evolution of the series. We always encourage readers to post individual reviews on *Amazon.com*. And thank you.

In-person gatherings are possible if you are in the North Texas region. Otherwise, Zoom is always an option.

Book Club Questions

Do you think Julian's charm might seduce you?

Did you enjoy the Brayson and Marian characters, and if so, why?

What do you feel is the strongest theme for this story?

Who is the most believable character in the story?

Which character would you like to know more about?

What was your most significant surprise moment in the story?

Did you feel the evil characters received their just desserts?

If you haven't yet read the other books in the Enigma Heirs Trilogy, we think you might enjoy them. Enigma Tracer and Enigma Forced.

Do you feel some of the topics are relevant in our contemporary times?

Do these subjects cause you concern?

Did you enjoy our blending of historical events with modern technology elements in the story?

What one thing do you feel we could have done to make this story more enjoyable?

Please let us know your thoughts in your reviews or invite us to your book club meetings via *Authors@EnigmaSeries.com*
Thank you for taking the time with Enigma Jewels. *Read on.*

Breakfield – Charles works as a data/telecom solution architect and supports digital security, blockchain solutions, and unified communications. He enjoys writing, studying World War II history, travel, and cultural exchanges. Charles' love of wine, cooking, and Harley riding often provides writing topics.

Much of his personality comes from his father who served in the military for 30 years and three wars. Charles grew up on multiple bases and different countries. The multi-cultural exposure helps him with the various character perspectives they bring to the series. His personal ambition is to continue to teach Burkey humor.

Burkey – Rox is a Customer Experience Specialist who works with businesses around the world. As a gifted speaker and accomplished listener, she bridges the chasm between business problems and technical solutions to optimize business productivity. She has written technology papers, white papers, but launches into high gear when plotting our next technothriller or short story.

As a child, she led the other kids with her highly charged imagination generating new adventures with make believe characters. She is proud of being a Girl Scout until high school, and contributed to the community as a member of a Head Start program. Rox enjoys her family, learning, listening to people, travel, outdoor activities, sewing, cooking, and thinking about how to diversify the series.

Breakfield and Burkey – began their partnership writing non-fictional papers and books. They formed a business partnership to share stories as fictional story writers. They recognize storytelling is an evolving method to share excitement, thrills, and insights to today's technology risks.

They are passionate about leveraging the real technology into fictional writing. The variety of characters have attributes from the many people who crossed their professional paths add that depth. Admittedly, Breakfield often asks interesting people he meets if they thought about being an evil cyberthug or femme fatale in their series.

Both authors have traveled to many places around the world. These travels are pulled into stories that requires real knowledge of specific locals. They enjoy well-rounded thrillers that include levels of humor, romance, intrigue, suspense, and mystery.

They love to talk about their stories at private and public book readings or events. Burkey conducts podcast style interviews with a couple of author groups, and enjoys extracting the tidbits from authors, especially new ones. Her first interview was, wait for it, Breakfield. You can learn where they will be from the calendar on their website.

EnigmaSeries.com has information on the Enigma Series, 12 books, 10 short stories, audio books, book trailers, and the newest series Enigma Heirs releasing in 2023. They have proudly earned multiple awards for their fictional creations.

We are also part of the Underground Authors group writing cozy mysteries/murders in the Magnolia Bluff Crime Chronicles. We are committed to providing an installment for Season 2 and Season 3 to accompany *The Flower Enigma,* released in Season 1.

Please provide a fair and honest review on Amazon and any other places you post reviews. We appreciate the feedback.

Other stories by Breakfield and Burkey in
The Enigma Series are at **www.EnigmaBookSeries.com**

We would greatly appreciate if you would take
a few minutes and provide a review of this work
on Amazon, Goodreads and any
of your other favorite places.

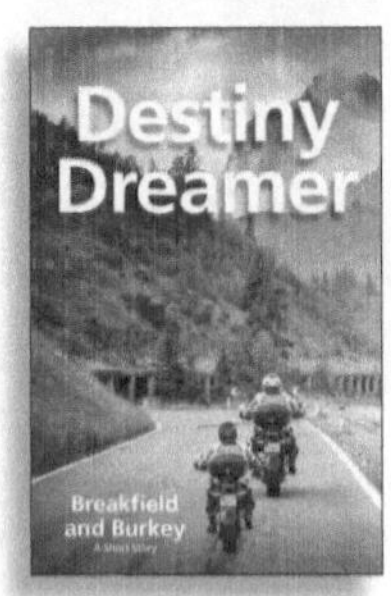

More of the Enigma Heirs Series by Breakfield and Burkey
www.EnigmaBookSeries.com

MAGNOLIA BLUFF CRIME CHRONICLES SEASON 1

DEATH WEARS A CRIMSON HAT
MAGNOLIA BLUFF CRIME CHRONICLES
CW HAWES

EULOGY IN BLACK AND WHITE
MAGNOLIA BLUFF CRIME CHRONICLES
CALEB PIRTLE III

THE GREAT PEANUT BUTTER CONSPIRACY
CINDY DAVIS

YOU WON'T KNOW HOW ...OR WHEN
MAGNOLIA BLUFF CRIME CHRONICLES
JAMES R. CALLAN

THE FLOWER ENIGMA
MAGNOLIA BLUFF CRIME CHRONICLES
BREAKFIELD AND BURKEY

THE SHINE FROM A GIRL IN THE LAKE
MAGNOLIA BLUFF CRIME CHRONICLES
RICHARD SCHWINDT

DEWEY DECIMAL DILEMMA
BOOK 7: MAGNOLIA BLUFF CRIME CHRONICLES
LINDA PIRTLE

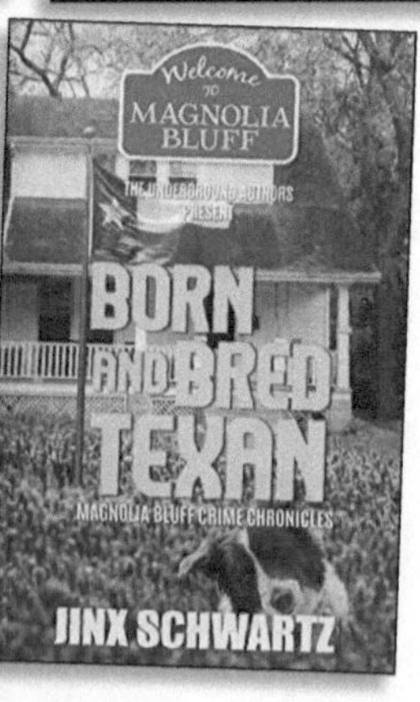

MAGNOLIA BLUFF CRIME CHRONICLES SEASON 2

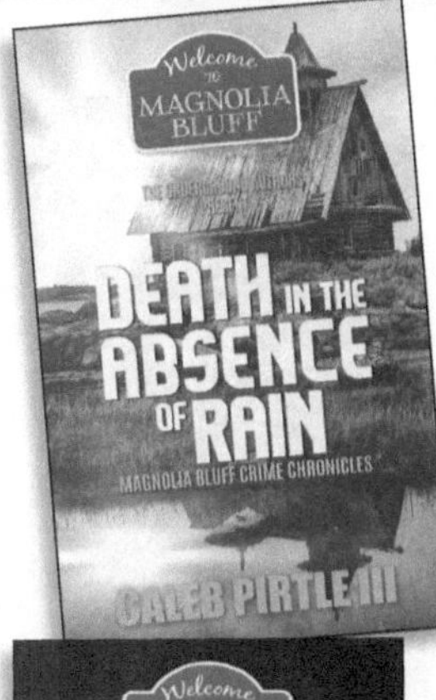

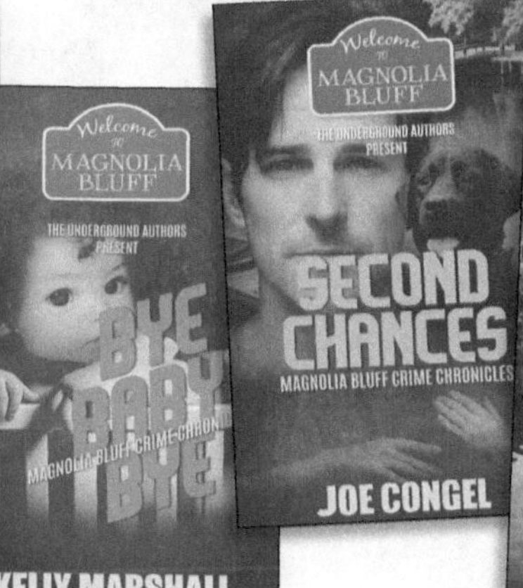

MAGNOLIA BLUFF CRIME CHRONICLES SEASON 3

9 781946 858863